THE LARK

BY KATE L. HART

Impact book with a message

The Lark

Library of Congress Control Number 2019920500

Cover design and drawing by Angel Leya

Chapter One

London, 1840

Alive to the terrifying movement of carriages coming upon me from every direction, I crossed Drury Lane. I stepped quickly, enamored with the pace and mass of people in London; it courted me, young and fresh with the anticipation of some new sight everywhere I looked.

My heightened sense of excitement kept my eyes scanning the huge theatre in front of me. Despite that I never yet walked through its doors – and no matter the trickery I would use – I had to go in. It was my home.

"Watch your step, Miss Eva," Miss Bolton, my lady's maid said, her vice-like grip on my arm yanking me toward her. "Oh dear," I said, maneuvering around a horse pile just in time. At Grey Manor, I would have smelled such a pile before I came to it, but every scent in London competed so powerfully I could not differentiate one stench from another.

"Come, we do not want to tarry on this main road," Miss Bolton said. She pulled me along while looking around uncomfortably, as if expecting us to be attacked at any moment.

"The hackney could have dropped us at the door," I said when we reached the other side safely.

"No member of the beau monde ton would deign arrive at the theater in a hackney. If you truly expect this little lark of yours to work, you must temper that

skip in your step," she said. "You do not look at all
like the quality." She tugged me forward while glaring
at a young peddler approaching us.

The lad turned instantly from us, looking for softer
pockets. At the corner of the building, a mother sat
with two small children, all three filthy, like I'd never
seen, nor smelled, before. It tore at my heart, and
though Aunt swore giving to every street urchin would
bankrupt me, I could not help it.

I slipped a few shillings into my glove before I left
the hackney, so I could provide dinner to at least a
few. I handed the coins to one of the young girls and
smiled. I was rewarded. The girl turned her blue-grey
eyes to me and smiled shyly back. I wished to smile
hopefully at the mother, but she did not look up and
coughed the cough of factories.

Miss Bolton pulled me forward, and we walked to
the side of the building under a colonnade. I shoved
my limp glove into my muff and reached out with my
bare hand to touch the cold stone columns as I passed
them.

The Theatre Royal – my dreams come true. As one
of the patent theaters fighting to keep exclusive rights
to perform spoken drama, they planned to immerse
theater-goers in Shakespeare this season. After a
preseason showing of Midsummer's Night Dream, the
Drury Lane Company would set up to perform the first
of many tragedies during the height of the time.

If I could see two, perhaps three of the Bard's
enactments, I would consider my time in London a
success.

Perhaps as successful as my cousin Julia would
consider her time if she could engage herself to a very
specific duke.

"Come, Eva," Miss Bolton encouraged. "Reviews
raved over Midsummer Night's Dream," I said more to

myself. "They could have been puff pieces," she answered. "I read three," I said.

"We will judge for ourselves," Miss Bolton said, but then stopped to read an advertisement for our play with instructions for our entrance. While she was distracted, I said: "Perhaps the stage somehow turned into
'a bank where the wild thyme blows/
Where oxlips and the nodding violet grows, '[1]

"Do you think it possible?" "Do you intend to dream in the frigid air, or take the few steps to see for yourself? We must enter from the front; the boxes are accessed from Brydges Street.

"I suggest you change your look from ecstatic to somber, or even put upon, or you will never pass for a servant," Miss Bolton said. She gave me a head nod to start moving again. We turned the corner and walked toward the front of the building, cozied beneath another line of columns.

"Is the façade styled Greek or Roman?" Miss Bolton asked, scurrying after me toward the entrance.

"The Athenian influence is present because of the Corinthian columns. But it is a modern work that does not respect Late Greek, nor Roman, " I said, curtsying as I would when I was a child. She caught the sarcasm of the action but smiled serenely because she forced me to focus when I wanted my mind to run.

We walked through the pillars into the grand entrance of the Theatre Royal. We stepped aside to a women's cloakroom. I handed the attendant my muff. I removed the hood of my paletot sac and unbuttoned the cloak-like coat.

Usually, Miss Bolton assisted me, but this time she undid her own cloak like we were equals.

Her fingers twitched while I slowly worked the ribbons on my bonnet, but she did not help.

"You're early. Your set don't usually come 'til interval; weren't there no tea to be invited to?" the attendant impertinently asked Miss Bolton. The attendant was outfitted almost the same as Miss Bolton usually was, a dark blue tunic, and skirts of the same color.

Miss Bolton looked very different this evening. So different, the attendant gave her preference as my superior, as anyone comparing the two of us would.

I did not correct her. This was part of our ruse.

"The rest of our party will not be here until the entr'acte, but I am really rather fond of this particular work," Miss Bolton said grandly, rebuffing the woman. Miss Bolton took her long evening gloves from her pocket. I tugged on her skirts to straighten her out, in the way she always did to me, but I could see by a look she wanted me to stop. Miss Bolton looked elegant. She wore an Aegean blue satin gown that matched her eyes. Her slightly plump waist cinched into a point with a black sash, and black lace trimmed the bottom of her many flounces. Miss Bolton, with light hair tinted in peaches, looked like Venus in any of Titian's works. An etched print of my father's favorite painting by the master, Sacred and Profane Love, hung in the gallery at Grey Manor.

When Miss Bolton first came to us, just after my mother died, I noticed to my father her similarity to Venus in the painting. It was one of the few times he ever grew angry with me. He said never to say such a thing.

I supposed it inappropriate because Venus was nude in most of Titian's paintings. I never said anything about the matter to Miss Bolton, but often wondered when she took so much time to perfect her appearance before going into public if she would find the comparison a compliment or insult.

I watched trying to hide my impatience as she patted her light hair in the mirror until she was satisfied. I did not bother to glance past her and take in my own image.

I could not look at myself in the awful cream-colored gown Aunt picked out. It drowned out my face and clashed miserably with my bright white gloves.

I was dressed elegantly enough to hold my head up at the theater, but not extravagantly as my cousin would be.

"We are in Lord Devon's box this evening," Miss Bolton said to the attendant. "Can you direct me to the private boxes?" "Stage right or left," she said, impressed.

Miss Bolton answered, listening to her instruction carefully tilting her head toward her. She nodded her thanks and we walked out of the room. We walked through the entrance hall toward the rotunda, and my heart started palpitating too quickly. "I see the dome," I whispered. Miss Bolton did not respond, but I could see her jaw set with determination.

We stepped into the main lobby, then to the stairs that moved into the sacred area where only the privileged were allowed.

With her head erect, and shoulders perfectly placed, Miss Bolton took the lead and walked by the attendant who was to guard the rotunda and the stairs to the boxes. I held my breath. She spared one pointed glance for him. She did not remove the ticket from her pocket, because she did not actually have one. I tried not to look nervous as I passed him but bit my lip, my most obvious tell. The attendant did nothing to stop us. Few people occupied the boxes before intermission, and he did not appear on high alert for anything underhanded. Miss Bolton assured me the man would see our finery and let us in, and as always, I should have trusted her implicitly.

Miss Bolton played the part of the highest-ranking duchess, better than I acted the daughter of a country baronet, a position I actually claimed. She only took on the ruse when we were, in fact, doing something underhanded and it was imperative that she maintain her act of calm nobility, verging on offended, if any slight snub be employed against us. My heart slowed when we entered the deserted corridor to the private boxes. Miss Bolton found Lord Devon's box with very little trouble. It was over the stage right pit.

We stepped into the well-lit theater box, hung in scarlet curtains. Gilded columns on both sides stood strong, yet somehow delicate and gorgeous. I covertly slid into a chair crammed against the side drape where I would not be noticed. Miss Bolton sat at the back of the box to listen as she pulled lace and a needle case out of her pocket.

Wrapped in the curtain as I was, the exclusive box shut me off from the rest of the seating. I felt intimate with the large forestage and giddy at being so close to Lysander as he performed. I always loved the character.

Even after he is afflicted with the fairy's curse, he never becomes cruel to Hermia.

After some pantomiming, the house curtain rose. I watched spellbound at Athens reborn on the extravagant stage.

The heat rose to my face – I was not expecting the men's bare legs and stuffed cod pieces to be so realistic in their period costumes. I barely heard the rustle of the curtain but felt eyes on the back of my head. My breath caught in my chest. I turned to find a finely dressed man in my space.

Miss Bolton stood and gave me a look of concern.

I stood with my back to the curtain so no one in the audience would see the two of us in a state of intimacy we did not share, nor would I like myself spoken of as if we did. Frightened that Miss Bolton had mistaken the box, I turned in confusion to look out at the stage. Seeing where I was situated, I felt she could not have.

The gentleman ducked out of the box to confirm his placing, and I waited to see if he would come back. This could not be Duke Garrett or any other from Lord Devon's party because the three generations of grandfather, mother, and son, whom we would meet at the interval, were at Tea with a friend.

Aunt tried very hard to get an invitation from Lady Garrett for Tea, but could not succeed because they were engaged.

I went to sit back down, but the man came back into the box. The gentleman pierced me with his most determined stare holding a moment, perhaps to draw some confession from me. I said nothing, trying to decide who he was.

He must have mistaken his box number. If he were uncertain, I could be haughty to him, and he may leave. He considered me with dark brown eyes that appeared intelligent and upset – a lethal combination that would not be convinced easily. The play progressed without me being seated.

"Are you here to be seen?" he asked, quietly stepping toward me, clenching his Grecian jaw in frustration.

I hissed back: "Yes, because hidden in the curtains at this most unfashionable hour is perhaps the best way to be noticed."

Miss Bolton flinched.

He squinted at me. He whispered waspishly: "Are you hoping to entrap me, because I assure you such tactics will not be tolerated!"

"Again, since there is no one from the gossip rags to witness this encounter, I would have set a fairly pathetic snare. Consider Sir, we have not been introduced and I am a little more discriminating about whom I weave my cunning web around," I answered. My voice dripped with disdain for this man interrupting my one opportunity to witness the Bard without having to explain to my cousin what was happening.

Miss Bolton cleared her throat, but I ignored her. I could not appear as if I brought my governess into public with me.

He stood dumbfounded, unsure what to do next, so I went on the offensive. "And you Sir, did you come to assault a lone female in a theater box, because my lady will witness to any injustice, and there is crowd sufficient to hear me scream," I said boldly.

"I am here to see the actress playing Hermia. She is said to be a rising star and I wish to see her dramatic début. I do not wish to be disturbed."

"Well, perhaps we will each of us take a curtain and pretend the other is not here."

"If anyone found us alone together – " "My aunt thinks I am at Tea with a friend; I assure you I will keep myself hidden at all costs."

"Very well," the gentleman said. He moved deeply into the drape on the other side of the box. Miss Bolton eyed me, clearly uncomfortable with the situation.

I shrugged, trying to ignore the empty pit in my stomach. The man did not seem to mind hiding. He would notice his mistake and all would be righted at the interval. I hoped he belonged in the box across from us, so I could wave at him after he realized he interloped in Lord Devon's box.

Determined to see the play, I resumed my seat, adjusting the drape to be sure no one could see me. The man glanced at me to be sure I was hidden and then became engrossed in the stage.

If we were discovered, I would play the innocent countrified maiden unaware of my mistake. Aunt would believe it easily enough. We sat in silence the first half of the play. The only sound I heard from his side of the box were amused chuckles at just the right moments. I liked my interloper better for his ability to detect the funniest quips.

As the curtain closed at the interval, I stood, meaning to slip out, and found the interloper blocking my access to the exit. "Pardon," he said, stepping back.

"She was very good," I said with a slight curtsy.

"I wasn't disappointed," he answered with a polite bow. I left, and Miss Bolton slid out just after me, so the man did not get close. She looked around cautiously to be sure we had not been seen. Once in the corridor, she took up her position in front of me as if she were the nobility, knowing it would be safer for me to be subservient. I did not wrestle with her for position as I had in the box.

"I think we will leave our outer things, and circle around the building to put just a touch of the chill in the air upon us," she said.

"Are you certain we must go into the cold?" I asked.

"You look rosy, almost as if you sat in the heat of the theater for the last two hours with a man you do not know," she said playing her I-tolerated-your-whim-so-you-must-tolerate-mine card.

"Very well," I said. We climbed the stairs to the upper level of the rotunda. The circular balcony looked down on the statue below, so the commoners could look upon the quality with envy. The saloon was on this level and when I paused to examine a beautiful statue of a woman standing in a niche, Miss Bolton pulled me away, though it was early for riotous theatergoers. We walked down the stairs to the Russell Street entrance and stepped outside into the colonnade where we started our evening. "Thank you, Myra," I said taking her arm for just a moment betraying the intimacy that existed between us.

"Did you enjoy it entirely?"

"Even more," I said, sighing. Suddenly she pulled my arm and shoved me. I turned to glance up just in time to see my Aunt Claremont Hull alight from her carriage. I moved behind a pillar. "Do not dawdle, Julia," Aunt snapped. I looked in terror at Miss Bolton. She put a finger to her lips indicating I should be quiet. "She must enter from Brydges Street," she assured in a whisper.

A number of theatergoers climbed out of an omnibus and started into the colonnade from Drury Lane. This caught Aunt's attention, and I moved further behind the column while Miss Bolton analyzed the crowd coming toward us. My heart palpitated heavily when she looked suspiciously at the mass of people.

"Watch your pockets or confront your aunt," Miss Bolton said giving me my options. I could think of no excuse for being outside the theater without my outer clothes. Aunt would be livid if she found out we snuck into Lord Devon's box. Yet, I did not wish to challenge the throng.

I held my breath hoping not to be detected and waved Miss Bolton forward. We moved cautiously up a few pillars, toward my Aunt and away from the crowd. A stagehand walked by us gawking but said nothing. He seemed in a hurry as he navigated through the crowd of people turning into the Russel Street Entrance of the building before they reached us.

Miss Bolton was right, of course. We listened as my aunt walked toward the front entrance, speaking too loudly that she hoped the duke had not yet arrived. We adjusted ourselves when she entered the columns, but she did not look in our direction. She even said something about me – the colonnade echoed that Aunt would consider me an ingrate if I was not waiting for them in the entrance hall. I chanced a glance. Aunt Claremont Hull's perfectly kept figure swayed quickly away. Her thick chestnut hair, the same color as mine, was twisted elegantly on the top of her head under her bonnet, while ringlets grazed my neck. Aunt wore a warm dress with enormous puffy sleeves attached to a boisterous collar that covered her entire shoulders. She did not wear a cloak over her sleeves, sacrificing comfort for the latest fashion, and would only deposit her bonnet and muff in the cloakroom.

"Should we go back in the side door?" I asked when we could no longer hear them.

"We cannot be caught sneaking into the boxes; they will be monitored much more carefully now, especially from the direction of the saloon," she said.

"Let us be patient and quiet. We will slip in the front way without being noticed." We moved away from the crowd steadily pushing their way into the theater. We waited near the corner of the building. In the time it took my aunt and cousin to leave the cloakroom, we grew excessively chilly in the late February evening. Finally, we turned the corner to the front of the theater. A long line of carriages waited, which explained why my aunt, determined to beat the duke into the theater, chose to be let off on a side street. "Here's to the second half," Miss Bolton said as we quietly walked into the entrance hall – this time she was the subservient one. We quickly passed the cloakroom as if we had just come from there.

The attendant who guarded the entrance to the rotunda glanced at us. He looked from Miss Bolton standing just behind me, to me, neither of us wearing our outer clothes. I smiled and shrugged just a little. He looked a bit perplexed but said nothing as we passed by him. He watched us walk all the way to my aunt, who had our ticket.

Chapter Two

"The halls are domed, lending it a Roman accent, but the gaslighting is a new age wonder," I whispered.

I couldn't help gawking at the glowing crystal chandelier in the upper rotunda. Miss Bolton smiled demurely.

We moved into the circular room that would soon be thronged with the top tier of fashionable theatergoers, now stuck in their carriages.

Julia spotted me first and waved me toward her. Her coral gown with golden trim swung with the action.

She looked the epitome of fashion, her tight dress flouncing from the waist, showed off her long torso. The motion she made to beckon me added to the picture she created, like she danced instead of insisting I join them. The coloring of the gown made her light skin whiter and the golden veins of her hair stand out against the buttermilk.

She looked every part the Earl's daughter. I walked over to them with my most somber expression, which neither lady took seriously.

"That will do; if you can manage to look unimpressed throughout the play, I will not be sorry I agreed to bring you," Aunt said, by way of hello.

She examined Miss Bolton's beautiful dress and gritted her teeth.

"Miss Bolton, my carriage is to the side of the building," Aunt said, while pointing the direction and dismissing her.

"It is freezing out there," I said.

"It is no matter," Miss Bolton said. Aunt was very vocal that Miss Bolton did not know her place. This

1

came after one of the dressmakers kept addressing Miss Bolton as if she were my guardian.

I shifted to brush hands with Miss Bolton, meaning to hand her five shillings I dug out of my pocket. "You will be able to see better in the dress circle anyway," I whispered, "I will linger to give you time to get back in the carriage."

She did not take my money.

"I am not one of your charity cases on the corner," she whispered cuffing me under the chin.

Sardonically and louder so Aunt heard, she said, "I am perfectly capable of paying my own way into the show; the theater is not exclusive to the upper classes anymore. I will find a seat among my equals."

Miss Bolton glanced at Aunt like she'd just told her something moderately clever. Aunt's mouth opened, but nothing came out of it.

Julia, to smooth her mother's creased brow, said: "Of course, she should get a seat. Oh, mother, you know tonight's performance cannot be missed. It will be the most attended of the season.

"Duke Garrett has returned from the country, and promised to be here."

"I suppose everyone, even the servants, want a glimpse at the newly titled duke," Aunt Claremont Hull said toward Miss Bolton who did not respond.

I did not roll my eyes. I kept my face somber and tried not to notice the rustling of dresses of the women who had stepped closer to listen to my relations' conversation, spoken too loudly and with such obvious boasting not to be overheard.

To keep their attention, Julia quickly said: "It is a delight to be in his Grandfather's box. We could not miss the revival of one of the lesser performed works of Shakespeare."

"It is spectacular, the costumes alone are…" I started. Miss Bolton tugged on my skirt with huge eyes as a reminder that I should have no idea what the costumes were like. My aunt and cousin continued the conversation for the benefit of those around us and did not notice anything I said.

"Goodbye Miss Eva," Miss Bolton said, as she straightened the rest of me, so her tug did not look peculiar. She tried to smooth the dress flounces to give me a figure, but the dress Aunt picked out hid me from neck to slippers like a ruffled bed sheet. Giving up, Miss Bolton turned and left me with big eyes as a reminder to hold my tongue. Aunt glared at the back of Miss Bolton, who made a very pretty silhouette as she headed toward the stairs to the Dress Gallery.

"Eva, won't you be glad to see your grandfather's old friend?" Julia asked.

"Yes, Lord Devon would invite us, as such close friends of your grandfather's Eva, of course, he'd invite us," Aunt said absentmindedly. She still watched the back of Miss Bolton.

Aunt, using my connection to Lord Devon as an introduction, called on his daughter, the Baroness of Farnborough, the Lady Theresa Garrett. The Earl of Berkshire, Lord Devon, my grandfather's oldest friend, was not available.

The two ladies strained my relationship with him to include Lady Theresa; we had heard each other spoken of so many times. They then proceeded to trade invitations. Lady Theresa offered us a night at the theater in her father's box, assuring us her son, the young duke, would attend. Aunt graciously offered my Uncle Claremont Hull's services to sponsor them to attend a ball at the Marquess Holland's home the next evening.

"Is Uncle coming?" I asked.

"No, he is indisposed," Aunt stopped looking almost confused. "Neither he nor Edmund could make it this evening."

My cousin Edmund had not been invited, but for Uncle to stay away when such an important new acquaintance was being made bordered on iimpropriety.

"My father did not wish to meet the Duke of Surry," Julia confided in the quiet undertone she used when her father failed to show interest in her pursuits.

She believed her position as the daughter of an Earl, and her unequaled beauty, gave her every right to marry His Grace, yet her father did not even bother to be introduced. Despite that Julia's looks favored the Earl's side of the family, he did not seem inclined to notice her.

I looked very much like my mother and Aunt, the sisters similar in appearance. To the Earl's credit, he did not appear influenced by his wife's looks either. He overlooked me as well. Because Julia could not look downcast when on the hunt I whispered:

"Likely Uncle did not wish to witness my disgraceful enthusiasm for the play, Julia."

She scrutinized me.

"The box will be crowded with six, and he does not care for fiction," I reminded.

"That is true," she said, letting this satisfy her.

The crowd grew with alarming speed. Being surrounded by so many people felt a little like being submerged unwillingly in water. My discomfort must have shown.

"You will become accustomed to the crush," Julia assured, moving in closer to me.

"Should we perhaps take our places in the box before the interval is over?" I asked.

"Nonsense, we will wait for our host," Aunt Claremont Hull said quietly eyeing me, unconcerned with the throng surrounding her.

"Here they are," Julia said. A woman in her mid-forties entered the rotunda on the arm of a man in his early seventies. I recognized my grandfather's old friend immediately though he had changed dramatically since we last parted. I had not seen the older gentleman for six years, not since I was fourteen. I wondered what happened to the spry man who had been old but never seemed so.

He walked without the aid of a cane, but needed one, and leaned heavily upon his daughter's arm. A group of younger men poured into the rotunda, most politely trying to maneuver around the older gentleman and his daughter.

I assumed one of these was Duke Garrett, but couldn't be sure which one. I'd never been in the company of so many men my own age and couldn't help looking down instead of boldly scanning them as my cousin did. My Aunt stepped forward when Lord Devon finally hobbled near us. He squinted with hazel eyes and took a step back like she surprised him.

"Thank you, Lord Devon, for allowing us to share your box this evening," Aunt said, unable to hide the panic in her voice at his confusion.

"Ah, father. May I introduce the Countess of Somerset, Lady Peter Claremont Hull," Lady Theresa said. "Oh, yes, of course," he said. A look of contempt crossed his features as if he did not like her, but considering they did not know each other, I supposed he did not like sharing his box with her.

"This is my daughter Lady Julia Claremont Hull," Aunt spoke overly loud to the older gentleman in case he had hearing problems,

5

"And of course, you've met my niece, Miss Eva Grey."

Lord Devon's head snapped up. "Miss Grey? I did not realize you would be of the party. I have not seen you since you were a very young lady."

I bowed my head and took the hand he offered me. "You look very much like your mother," he said glancing at Aunt again, slightly unnerved.

Did he see my mother when he looked at her?

"It has been some time, Sir," I said with a curtsy.

"Your grandfather and I were the best of college chums. I was sorry to hear of his passing last June," he said. I nodded, knowing this was the only reason I'd been invited to share Julia's season in town with her.

The man examined me, showing little interest in Julia or Aunt. "You are all grown up, and I am glad you are the very image of your mother," he said taking my hand. He examined me with a pleasant smile while he patted my hand. I bowed, and in the action, he and I formed our own group away from the other ladies.

Lady Garrett explained to Aunt and Julia her son would be along soon. Aunt used her bright, looking-for-approval voice, but her words blended as chirps among the conversations erupting around us. Her stream of nonsense drowned out under the strong tones of a woman who talked through her nose loudly, and a man, out of breath speaking to someone I couldn't see. It distracted me to rudeness as I took in everything around me.

I fought to concentrate when Lord Devon said: "I am surprised your father let you come to town. Is he not with you?"

"No Sir. Miss Bolton is with me," I said.

"Yes, your father is very fortunate in her service to your family. I do not believe your grandfather would have sent you without his protection," he said glancing at Aunt.

"No, I doubt he would," I said.

My grandfather never let me go anywhere. He was the very definition of overprotective. "I do miss your grandfather," he said quietly. He looked sad. I vaguely remembered the way he and grandfather spoke to each other. Wanting a little taste of home, I leaned in so Aunt could not hear and said: "He spoke of you fondly, though in his last days of illness he may have given away a few interesting tidbits about a cat and a chamber pot, which I promised never to mention."

His eyes brightened, and he squinted at me.

"And yet you have mentioned it," he said.

"Only to you who shared in the confidence with him, and I must say I do feel I've unburdened my conscience knowing you know I know," I said, curtsying.

"Eva, let us not linger in the lobby when intermission ends," Aunt Claremont Hull called warily over the woman with the nasal voice who moved toward me. Well knowing my tendency toward impertinence, she looked unnerved at what I might have said to make the old Earl smile. Standing up straighter than necessary, she brushed me out of the way with her shoulder so Lady Garrett could introduce us to her son, the most eligible bachelor in town, who finally arrived to meet Julia.

Lord Devon looked at me being brushed aside and I could see in his eyes he already missed speaking to me. This made me smile. My grandfather would keep me by his side if possible. As a few of the groups clustered around us moved into the theater, I re-situated myself next to his grandfather. I couldn't be bothered with the duke and left him to my cousin.

"Do you live primarily in London, Sir?" I asked, focusing on the elder. "No, I come for Parliament and leave for my sanity," he whispered. A laugh burst from me, but I managed to cough to cover it up when Aunt looked at me sharply.

She jerked her head to indicate I move forward to an introduction, the fear in her eyes unmistakable that I would embarrass her. Unable to avoid the introduction that would prove my abject inferiority to my cousin, I politely stepped around the nasal-voiced woman and Lady Garrett. I turned to Duke Garrett. I choked over the breath meant for my lungs. Recognition sparked in his eyes as I took a deep gasping breath in, trying not to hack a cough. He did not mistake his box after all.

Chapter Three

In the paused moment of humiliation, an eternity passed. I stared at the man I'd just spent two hours with. I'd never found myself caught in such a compromised position.

I prayed he would not say anything about the matter in front of Aunt. She would relish any reason to send me home.

Duke Garrett stared at me blushing, and I thought I saw something like vindication in his eyes.

It was made worse by Julia trying to talk to him, which delayed Aunt's civility.

His looks were his own; his eyes dark and intelligent, his straight clay brown hair parted deeply to the side and pushed back just enough to show his widow's peak in the most fashionable style. He was on the taller side of average height, and trim so his waistcoat cut an impressive figure. He looked as any fit young man of twenty-five or twenty- six would, and though his collar and cravat sat high on his jaw, none of his chin came forward.

His expression frowned deeper into frustration the longer he waited for Julia to stop talking and my aunt to do her duty.

Disgrace did not cover what I felt, seeing his lips tighten in a line of disapproval. Finally, Aunt, feeling Julia rambled a bit, introduced me, simply to stop her.

"Your Grace, this is my niece Miss Eva Grey, Miss Grey, The honorable Duke of Surry, His Grace Jonah Devon William Garrett."

I tucked my chin politely, my face burning with the shame Aunt so feared at my presence. He barely attempted a bow. He brushed past me to help his grandfather manage the stairs. When we finally made

it to the box, the stage below us moved with
life. Since I no longer had to hide, I turned to look out
on the audience. A sea of heads restlessly grew into a
torrential wave as people flooded toward their seats. I
grew light-headed and felt overwhelmed.

Awed by so many people in one place, I must have
teetered. A strong hand grabbed my arm so I did not
go over the side of the box. Startled I moved back and
Duke Garrett released my arm but watched me.

"Excuse me," I said bowing, while Aunt glared at
me. "First time in London, my girl. You will get used
to it," Lord Devon said. He patted my arm. With so
many people stuffed into the small viewing space, I
quietly slipped into my original seat in the curtain, this
time holding to it like an anchor.

Duke Garrett glanced at me, no doubt disgruntled at
my escape. I didn't dare look back at him as he took
the prime seat in the middle of the box to the sound of
Julia's honeyed tones addressing him. Julia's
distraction turned insignificant. Nothing could keep
him from noticing the lights glaring off opera glasses
turned in his direction to get his attention. Such was
the curiosity of the quality in observing the newly
titled duke. Many could not believe it when they first
heard that the Garrett family line endured tragedy.

The Twelfth Duke of Surry took his two sons to
visit their holdings in the West Indies, meaning to
leave his second son to oversee it. That would provide
him an income after his brother inherited the
estate. Despite being warned of his imprudence, the
conceit of the twelfth Duke challenged any tempest to
batter his new state-of-the-art screw-propeller
steamship. Could any gale resist such a challenge?

Four months ago, the Twelfth Duke and his heirs
were officially proclaimed dead. The whole kingdom
buzzed in anticipation over the obscure nephew who

would inherit the title and estate. He never came into society.

The Twelfth Duke's nephew, the son of a youngest brother, grew up with the title of gentleman in name only as he could not inherit anything but an education and a few family trinkets from the Garrett line.

Until that is, that sudden storm broke a whole branch from the family tree. Unexpectedly, the providential young man was declared the Thirteenth Duke of Surry, with all the wealth and acclamation that came with such a title. The new Duke, His Grace Jonah Garrett, spent his youth with his mother's family, namely his maternal grandfather, Lord Devon, being overlooked and ignored.

Now, I sat near His Grace while every eligible lady and her mother attempted to get his attention, the sea of faces ever bobbing in our direction. Not just the eligible wanted to look at the newly titled duke. The working class, who generally favored the lighter experience of burlesque which encouraged lively audience participation, joined us. They helped Shakespeare's words along by whistling and jeering.

Thankfully Duke Garrett didn't appear much different than the rest of the le bon ton. Many found him dull and the play old-fashioned. They left after a short time to visit the saloon. It took a great effort, but I managed to eventually ignore all of this.

Instead I savored my moment in theater. I made the necessary introduction for Aunt. I could do nothing more to help my cousin marry the duke so I couldn't be sure of another chance to take in a play. I leaned forward and grasped the edge of the box. I committed every word and action to memory. Because of our incredible vantage point, I could make out the words the actress cried out, playing her part so convincingly. I lost track of everything except the chaos happening on the stage. After the play ended, Aunt Claremont Hull and Julia walked with Duke Garrett and his mother as wealth and privilege parted the way for them. Aunt could not have basked in any brighter light. I walked slowly with Lord Devon, who insisted on introducing me to every man over the age of fifty he came across.

Many took a polite interest in me. My grandfather had been one of the most pronounced philosophers of their time.

I responded appropriately when addressed and was pleased when Lord Devon handed me up into my Aunt's carriage, ignoring his grandson's attempt at helping him. I snuggled in next to Miss Bolton who had come straight to the carriage after the play and was freezing.

Aunt managed to wheedle us an invitation to family dinner at Lord Devon's terraced home. We drove around Grosvenor Square for a time to be sure the family made it home before us.

When we finally stopped outside Lord Devon's home, Aunt said: "It is certainly one of the older houses, and not nearly as grand as Lord Holland's corner mansion."

"The Holland estate is, of course, the grandest of our acquaintance, but few could compare, considering its individual design.

"Certainly Mother, you can respect we are in the very heart of the quality; there is none of the middling sort here," Julia defended as if the home were already hers.

"The northeast heart," Aunt chuckled to herself, "but this part of the evening does not signify. Our trip to the theatre has solidified our standing among the elite, despite your father's good-for-nothing older brother." Miss Bolton flinched next to me. No doubt she had never heard Aunt talk about the head of her family in so disrespectful a way. I often heard Aunt begrudge her husband his reclusive older brother, and instead was insulted for poor Lord Devon and his home. Her assessment of the situations seemed rather rich considering her home was not placed with such distinction. She lived nearer the fashionable, yet, older neighborhoods of St. James Square.

I said nothing. Still, having made the observation, from this point on, my mind would not stop comparing her home to that of Lord Devon's. Both were true townhouses, the terrace design connected them to their neighbors. Both facades were in the classic style, though Lord Devon's townhouse looked dimensions larger. Uncle's façade formed straight lines of columns and windows that stood at attention in perfect uniform. Lord Devon's home curved and moved to hint at the Rococo whimsy over the columns. The straight, spiked gate outside Uncle's house meant to keep intruders out, while Lord Devon's home welcomed his guests in with the most charming arched gateway lit in the warm light of an entrance lamp.

"I'm sure you can go down to the servant's entrance," Aunt Claremont Hull said to Miss Bolton after we alighted the carriage. The latter quietly bowed and walked around to the servant's steps to the basement.

I watched Miss Bolton go, horrified. Aunt would never have sent her lady down, but instead, insist she eat with the housekeeper. Aunt watched Miss Bolton out of sight, then stepped quickly to the door. She feared Lady Garrett may change her mind if we did not make haste. The butler let us in, and Aunt, with no cloak, was ready to be shown to the family before Julia and I could get our bonnets off. As I tried to get the knot that I made earlier out of my bonnet strings, I looked around the old-fashioned home. The house emanated a charming calm, while my uncle's home tirelessly kept in the height of fashion, held tension suspended in the air. "Julia, help Eva," Aunt snapped, tired of waiting for me. Julia pulled at the ribbon twice and I was free. We were shown into the drawing room but did not even sit before the family escorted us into the dining room. The dining room was longer than it was wide. A light currant-red covered the walls. On one side, huge golden frames held pictures, still and breathless and ancient. On the other side, a marble fireplace glowed with vivacious movement.

A large table occupied a majority of the room that the six of us did not fill. Especially after a footman quickly took away a place setting that was clearly meant for Uncle.

Despite our being invited to a simple family dinner, the linen was fresh and bright, and the silver reflected the lights. Aunt Claremont Hull was given the seat of honor at Duke Garrett's right, and Julia sat on his left. Lady Garret, our hostess, sat at the head of the table and I was placed on one side of her with Lord Devon on the other.

This seating suited me fine. Julia's duke still seemed annoyed, and Lord Devon doted on me. Lady Garrett smiled easily at Lord Devon and I speaking about my beloved grandfather who passed on the previous summer. Lord Devon and I were all comfort and ease as a continuation of the old friends. Lord Devon's wrinkled eyes squinted in concentration when I spoke, so like my grandfather. It was only one of the many mannerisms the lifelong friends shared. It warmed me and made me lonely in one turn. The meal ended with our side of the table animated in lively conversation, and the other in awkward silence. After dinner, we left the grandfather and his grandson to their port.

In the drawing room, Lady Garrett and I discussed the frost of the last week, and how her roses were faring considering how chilly February turned out to be. This room also had a large fireplace and the comfortable heat made me feel drowsy.

Until the men joined us. Lord Devon looked at me in such an amused way, there could be no doubt he knew how impertinent I'd been to his grandson at the theater. Being jolted awake by humiliation, I agonized over my behavior. I betrayed Grandfather, who would have expected me to treat his old friend's grandson with respect, more because of the connection than his new title.

I wanted to leave. Aunt did not. In an attempt at lingering, she suggested she was so inspired by Shakespeare that we ought to do a reading of our own.

"What part of the play particularly inspired you?" Duke Garrett asked, tilting forward to engage in the discussion. Aunt froze. She'd not heard a word of it, as all her efforts went into being seen. Unfamiliar with the play she scrambled to say anything.

"We were speaking on our drive from the theater of fairies blessing us with good fortune to be invited into your lovely home Lord Devon, were we not Aunt?" I asked, unable to even look at Duke Garrett.

"Of course," she bowed, and then with a look of perplexity she finished, "Though I am not certain what the donkey's head had to do with it all."

"Bottom simply had a poor translation of his name, or perhaps a correct interpretation of his character." I said. "I personally think Shakespeare must have targeted an actor who did a very poor job playing one of his roles." I tended to ramble when nervous. My

aunt squinted at me. I could see she didn't know if I
was being impertinent so, I quickly shifted and said,
"Aside from Mr. Phelps' portrayal of Puck, Hermia
was by far the finest performer. I have heard she is a
rising star."

Duke Garrett flinched and looked at me, and I
looked away thankful Miss Bolton went below to the
servant's quarters for her meal. His Grandfather
agreed with me, and instead of shooing us out of his
home, as he should have, he called a footman to get
him the play so we could review it.

I sat with Lord Devon for a long time discussing the
play. Julia and Aunt spoke with Lady Garrett. Duke
Garrett bobbled back and forth between the
conversations as he was spoken to by Aunt or Julia but
wished to put in his view of our subject matter.

The whole room stopped to listen when Aunt said:
"I am surprised Your Grace. I would think the Duke of
Surry would have a home in town."

"My uncle's widow resides there," Duke Garrett
said tersely.

"Yes, but she cannot expect to keep the place for
long, especially if you were to marry."

"I have given her leave to stay as long as she
likes. She is to have use of the house in the country as
well, until she can move into the dower house," he
said.

"Well, that is almost too generous," Aunt said. She
sounded put-out and anyone could see she meant for
him to not only take the house back from the widow
but establish Julia there as soon as the arrangements
could be made.

I turned away from the spectacle Aunt made of
herself and worked very hard not to think of how I
used my grandfather's connection to lure his friend's
grandson into such a predicament. I felt even more

uncomfortable as Lord Devon paid me many kind attentions, when I clearly did not deserve such civility. He pushed for my opinions, truly interested in what I had to say. Too soon to have learned any sobering lesson from my behavior, I lost myself in discussing the play with Lord Devon. We disagreed about the role of Puck. I believed him a device used to complicate an uncomplicated situation, proving, in the end, love is best left alone from outside sources. He thought him simply the comedy relief. "Does love ever really grow so complicated?" he finally asked when I persisted. "I can only speak to the subject theoretically considering my experience on the matter is limited to the stable hand who broke my horse when I was fifteen, thereby gaining my adoration," I said.

"But my father squelched the thing quickly, so my understanding is limited."

"I can't say I remember complications in love, old man as I am ,"Lord Devon said looking wistful. "I remember a deep love for my wife after she had my first son. We got on well, and I was very sorry when she died after so many years elapsed."

"I am sorry for your loss," I said touching his arm, quieting the other discussion in the room.

"Many years have passed. Almost all my friends have left me," he said looking over at his daughter who looked back compassionately.

"And yet, if you still mourn, may I not still be sorry?" I asked. The older man smiled at me, and for some reason, Duke Garrett nodded at me for this. I nodded back awkwardly unsure if that were wrong because Julia glared at me.

Unwilling to get involved in her pursuit of conquest, I refocused on my discussion with Lord Devon. "Throughout the work, there is always something complicating love. Hermia's father, Puck, then the wall in the ridiculous play. All devices, and if I may add, ridiculous devices, divide the lovers," I said.

"Most of Shakespeare's works complicate love for some reason," Lord Devon said. "I suppose it could very well be a device, like Ophelia or Lady McBeth. I did not bother finding meaning in the comedy." We ended our argument when Lord Devon insisted I read the few passages that convinced me, so we could decipher.

Duke Garrett moved in, closely listening to me read. Finally, the older gentleman agreed I may have a point, while Duke Garrett thought I must. Julia agreed with the Duke simply to be agreeable. "Well, my dear, my box is available to you as long as you are in town," Lord Devon said to me. I felt Duke Garrett stiffen. The poor man wanted to be rid of me, especially after I had been so rude to him in his own box. I wavered, unable to pass up the opportunity that my country theater fell short of. I served my purpose so I would not be asked back to London by my aunt.

"It would be an opportunity for me, as my father isn't likely to come to town in the near future," I said, hoping Duke Garrett would insist I accept, despite he owed me no such civility.

"No, your Grandfather had to be summoned. Though I do wish your father would come," Lord Devon said.

"Who would summon a simple country Baronet?" Aunt said with a laugh. "It was prone to happen on occasion," Lord Devon said giving her a quick side glace with an air of the same contempt that surprised me when they were introduced. I could not allow the subject to change without seizing the opportunity.

Looking to Duke Garrett apologetically, I gripped the soft wood of the curling sofa arm and said: "I should dearly like to see another play if it would not be too much of an imposition."

"Of course not. It would be a pleasure to have you and your enthusiastic opinion of the text," Lord Devon said. Thankfully he did not bother to consult his grandson about an interloper invading their box – he probably had much to say on the topic. As I had been looking to Duke Garrett for his assent he moved in and held out a hand for the beautifully embossed leather-bound play. I stood and passed it to him.

"The tragedies start next week. Mr. Charles Kean will play Hamlet. He is spectacular, though he only does dramas," Duke Garrett said. He opened the pages of A Midsummers Night's Dream, between us.

To exclude Julia from the conversation he lowered his voice. Speaking quietly to me finished, "If your friend were to invite you to Tea again, I will not say a word to the contrary."

My mouth dropped open. "I…I am sorry…I was so very impertinent to you," I whispered as he flipped through A Midsummers Night's Dream as if he were looking for something.

"It was refreshing," he said glancing at Julia's simpering looks of adoration, "I enjoyed the first half much more than the second."

"As did I," I agreed. A small smile turned his lips up for the first time that evening and his dark eyes danced in a way that lit his face. I thought it a more natural look upon his face than the scowl he had thus employed.

"Thank you for not exposing my secret to my aunt," I said.

"Not at all. If you can manage an afternoon visit to your friend tomorrow, the final showing will be much quieter and the donkey's head less offensive," he said. He smiled as if his mood turned.

Aunt noticed the smile. She came forward, nudging Julia toward us, and the conversation ended abruptly. I took my seat by Lord Devon and indulged in reading for him the passage opened by Duke Garrett before handing back the play.

He tried to listen and rebuff Julia's extremely sweet advances at the same time. I found it amusing that he had me read the passage where Hermia, who is loved by Demetrius, but hates him, explains as much to her lifelong friend Helena.[i] She, in turn, wastes her unrequited love on Demetrius because he hates her.

Perhaps I should have stopped at the end of the passage, as it appeared he meant to tease Julia as well as me, but could not help reading the next, inflecting my voice higher and lower to imitate the actresses on the stage. "The more I hate, the more he follows me, 'the more I love, the more he hateth me.'"[2]

I felt certain the brunt of the joke was on me, so I took my comeuppance in stride.

Lady Garrett, who did not know I'd been so belligerent to her son, noticed my words and could only correlate them to Julia's simpering manners.

There was a reprimand in the look she gave her son the further I read. I thought it best to turn away from any passage in which the two women interacted, and instead read Tatiana, the fairy queen's lullaby. The evening ended when Lady Garrett claimed exhaustion and we were forced into our carriage by excessive bows and nods.

Chapter Four

The next day, before I could write my acquaintance from Dorsetshire to see if she could receive us again for a quarter of an hour in Cheapside, Lord Devon wrote to invite me to the final performance. He explained that his daughter and grandson would be on visits, then a tea, but he would enjoy reviewing the play again after our discussion if I could be spared.

Aunt, seeing an opportunity for the relationship to be strengthened without having to listen to the older gentleman's unfailing interest in Shakespeare, agreed readily. She gave me a stern warning about the virtues of a reserved, even silent-until-questioned sort of lady.

The morning passed quickly enough in shops buying trinkets for the ball that evening. The afternoon, however, would not pass. I could usually lose myself for an hour or two at the pianoforte, especially when Julia played her flute. Since Julia was working on a pillow with an intricate poppy on it to go with Aunt's décor, she could not play with me. For some reason, Aunt could not tolerate me playing alone, perhaps because I played the old masters. Aunt spent the winter redoing her drawing room. She happened to find some silk poppies that looked so real she had to have them. Enamored with the poppies, she papered the drawing room to match them. Then she covered chairs, sofa, and a table, in the poppy red dish orange, and they looked as if autumn stole the color from the deciduous room. The huge intricate rug beneath the table held a dizzying pattern of the reddish orange and cream to match the window coverings. The cost of redoing the room rivaled that of any of the great houses.

Aunt took great satisfaction in telling her friends how much her renovations had cost while displaying the poppies on a table near the pianoforte. The pianoforte she would not let me play. We sat in silence at our sewing when we heard someone enter the house. The door to the sitting room swung open and Edmund walked in. My cousin was a young man whose father kept him in a very respectable fashion. Since he left his father's house a fortnight before I came, he had started to experiment with colors and patterns. His tailcoat was blue like his fathers, but his waistcoat had become more colorful and his full light hair taller over the few weeks since his departure.

The more time and money he spent at Brook's tables, the more ostentatious his fashion became.

"Eva, how is your pillow progressing?" Edmund asked. He moved toward me after nodding a greeting to his mother and sister.

"Fair, I think if one slants it ever so carefully and squints a touch, he can tell it is a rose," I said, showing him.

"I think you had better call it a pattern and try to finish it into a box," he said, his huge blue eyes waiting for me to engage in his banter.

I could not disappoint him: "Perhaps if Julia were to trade me, she could make something out of mine and I could diminish the beauty of hers," I said.

Julia looked at me placidly, but Aunt snapped: "Don't you dare Eva! She has been working that for some time and I intend to show my friend when she calls."

"I suppose you will have to keep on trying then," Edmund said, giving me eyes that I'm sure were meant to commiserate, but they were overly dramatized and embarrassed me because Aunt saw him do it and looked downcast. Everything about my cousin Edmund could be construed as overdone. He lived on a constant stage performing for anyone who would give him their attention.

When we were children, and he would visit Grey Manor, I would often seek my room for a reprieve after a few hours with him. As I only saw Edmund in small increments and only on occasion these days. I found him excessively more amusing than my other companions and could not help giving him my full attention as an old friend, among all the newness of my experiences. Uncle entered the room looking for Edmund.

"Are you ready for me, sir?"

"Let us linger a while," Uncle Claremont Hull said. "Julia I would have tea."

"Of course, Father," she said jumping up with a surprised look at her mother. Uncle rarely ever joined us in the afternoon.

"Now's your chance, Eva. She left her work unattended," Edmund said. Aunt lurched to protect Julia's work as if I would reach for it. We all stopped and stared at her almost fall out of her chair to keep it safe. Recovering, she straightened her skirts and smoothed Julia's work on her lap. Uncle watched her with a look he would give a fly buzzing around his food. I had long observed with curiosity the incompatibility of my Aunt and Uncle. Uncle, who was several years Aunt's senior, most likely had not looked so much older than her when he was thirty-four years and she seventeen. Now, however, her timeless beauty that snared the Earl in the first place continued though she was several years over forty. He had grown thick with age. His face and body sagged in most places as he passed sixty. As his body matured, he developed into politics and crusaded for the betterment of the country. Meanwhile, Aunt's timeless frame kept occupied with the petty concerns of a seventeen-year-old.

"Eva, how was traveling to London?" Uncle asked. I hoped he had not noticed me examining him.

"Very well, I thank you," I said dropping my eyes. I had been here five days; such a discussion was outdated.

"How was your grandfather's old friend Lord Devon, and his honorable grandson?"

The Lark

"The elder remembers my grandfather's acquaintance with kindness, and the younger wishes to be better acquainted with Julia."

This made him smile, but it faltered quickly as Aunt started to add to my flattery of her daughter:

"Yes, well Julia's looks cannot –."

"What else have you seen since you came?" Uncle interrupted with a glare at his wife.

"Mostly the inside of the dressmakers shops," I answered. He gave me a wry smile and took up his paper. Aunt misinterpreted the comment as me being ungrateful.

"Yes, what is the good of having wealthy relations if they cannot put you to advantage once in a while."

"And I thank you, Aunt," I said dutifully, but irritated.

Uncle said, "Eva can fend for herself just fine."

"You must not discourage her from enjoying this turn in town on our charity," Aunt said. "After this she will likely live in the country as a spinster. Her only hope will be to die young, so as not to sink further into poverty."

Uncle set his paper down in astonishment.

Edmund turned to me. With an intensity that would keep me up at night, he said, "I will always take care of you Eva. You will never want."

This peek behind his mask confused me, and I could not recover right away. I said: "Th…Thank you Edmund, but–"

"Yes, we will certainly buy your grandfather's estate from you when the burden of upkeep becomes too great," Aunt said. It was no secret Aunt Claremont Hull wanted Grandfather's large cared-for estate, over her husband's small house in the country. Her husband was the Earl after all. Her deceased sister only married a poor country land owner who managed the lowly gentry title of Baronet. Their child should not be expected to carry on the beautiful estate of Grey Manor, especially if I were to die a spinster.

"I think you are mistaken my dear," Uncle said. "Eva will not be required to sell Grey Manor. Though I do think she will need help managing it when her father passes. Marriage and an heir to inherit ought to be your goal." He looked at me over his spectacles until I nodded simply so he would stop. Then he looked to Edmund, and I couldn't be sure what was going unsaid between them.

"It is unfair to set up her hopes," Aunt said. "I do not believe most of the men in London are aware of the estate she will inherit, and with no dowry, she can hardly be a temptation, especially among our acquaintances. Yet, in the country, there is no one of sufficient standing to marry her. No, her chances are very low."

"I think she ought to feel secure in the idea that we will take care of it all when the time comes," Aunt said. She looked sternly at Edmund and I could see something going unsaid between them.

"Mother, please," Edmund said, his face becoming serious.

"Eva, have you no income—no dowry?" Uncle asked, growing heated. I stammered in reply. Only then was I certain he knew very well I had. Both my father and Miss Bolton expressly forbid me to ever mention my fortune, especially in Aunt's presence. Clearly Uncle did not have the same scruples. Somehow, I became the center of a push and pull between Uncle and Aunt. I couldn't say what either one wanted from me. This was not the first time they showed themselves at odds; rather, they were continuously at war, and chose to put me in the middle of this particular battle. The outer bell rang, saving me from answering.

"Come Edmund, let us depart before the ladies swamp us," Uncle said. Picking up his paper, he slipped through an obscure door at the far side of the room that led

The Lark

to the servant's space, so he would not be seen escaping. Edmund followed with an apologetic head nod. I smiled for him, unconcerned with Aunt's ranting as I'd heard the same several times since arriving in London. Aunt clearly meant to give me my place among her elite acquaintances.

After a couple hours of ladies coming for visits, I was ready to be the one going. Aunt spent the whole time pretending to act sly about Edmund's attachment to Lady Alice Holland, all the while encouraging gossip in that direction. Aunt described Julia's time with Duke Garrett until a bell rang and the footman came in to inform me Lord Devon's carriage waited. I scrambled to put on my outer things and Aunt said to her most recent friend visiting: "She does not even need her lady, who will have to work a bit harder to make her charge presentable for the ball this evening."

"She is lovely enough not to need much finery," the woman said, embarrassed, as they usually only talked about people not present.

"Perhaps," Aunt said, raising her nose up. She continued justifying her actions to her friend who didn't seem to care about my chaperone situation. "I am confident, leaving my niece in Lord Devon's care. Even her father would approve the arrangement. The elderly gentleman has been acknowledged as such a close friend of our families to most of the Ton at the performance last evening. I do not hesitate to assign him the role of guardian."

I left, incapable of tolerating my Aunt's using my relationship with Lord Devon to garner attention.

"Ah my dear, are you prepared for the theater?" Lord Devon asked as his servant helped me climb into the carriage.

"Everything else is utter drudgery," I said. We spoke all the way to Drury Lane, excitement pricked me as

26

I was to see the play from start to finish without interruption. We were met at the carriage and escorted into the theater, every attendant on hand to care for the aging Earl. We were acknowledged by the few other fashionable people who went to the theater solely for the performance. I sat in the middle of the box, eagerly watching the stage. Only moments into Theseus's first speech the curtain parted and Duke Garrett slinked into the box and sat enclosed by the thick red velvet curtain so as not to be seen.

"Good afternoon, my boy," his grandfather greeted.

"Papa," he replied. Then to me he nodded, "Miss Grey."

"Your Grace," I answered. "Is this amusing to you?"

He smiled at my tone, willing to be teased.

"Only as I think of your seat in the House of Lords must, in fact, be free of drapery, but then I suppose you need not be so shy when discussing matters of state?"

"No, I've found it is necessary to be stared at in that venue," he agreed.

"Then I suppose your friends would be ashamed you are in the theater at such an hour?"

"Rather, their sisters would all find it necessary to attend, not to mention the light in which you would be seen." He looked back to see if he missed Miss Bolton's presence, but said nothing else at her absence.

I flushed. "I suppose you mean to imply," I said, "the Ton would see you in the role of chaperone for your grandfather and me? Which in turn would lead to speculation as to what my true relationship with Lord Devon really is?" Duke Garrett squinted at me, amused. I asked: "Would they find my attempts to entrap your grandfather brilliant or scheming, do you suppose?"

"Ah my dear, entrap away. I have heirs to spare and my fortune has been divided as if I were already gone,"

Lord Devon said, grinning. "With so little temptation, I suppose your grandson ought to stay hidden in the curtain."

"I suppose," he said chuckling. Then we all turned to enjoy the play that we felt was presented just for us. At an interval, I sighed. I had no idea my trip to town would be so satisfying.

"I think Hermia played better today," Duke Garrett said, turning so the curtain was at his back.

"As do I, especially when she was threatening Helena. I think perhaps the actress playing Helena thought herself in real danger. She played the scene better as well," I said.

"You read very well," Duke Garrett said.

"Will you be recommending I tread the boards soon?" I asked.

"No, but a private venue, a reading or a Christmas party, would be just the thing for your talents."

"Oh sir, I think Shakespeare's words lent me their charm, for I assure you I've none of my own unless being sharp-tongued can be considered an advantage."

Both men laughed for me, and I noticed the younger had gone from scowling the night before to a jovial sort whose rosy face generally looked poised as though he anticipated joy in the next moment. I liked to watch him. His look of satisfaction was contagious. Being caught examining him, I looked away.

"I suppose after we review *The Taming of the Shrew*, you may read a few lines as Kate for us," Duke Garrett said.

"Though some of the passages are diverting in themselves, I do not like that play," I said, looking down at the stage as if to find a tormenter.

"Most of Shakespeare's plays have some offense to modern sensibilities," Duke Garrett said, "but for a man to starve a woman until she behaves in the way he sees fit is inexcusable."

"Yes," I said. "I have heard the Tamer tamed is entertaining enough," Duke Garrett said.

"I do not believe a man should oppress a woman, nor the woman a man," I said, uncomfortable with the serious turn in the discussion.

"There is some of that on both sides in most relationships," Lord Devon said.

"Certainly, there are also relationships that sit well-balanced, neither one tipping the scale in their favor over the stability of the other?"

"I believe it is more a matter of learning to balance until it is your turn to tip the scale as life dictates," Lord Devon said, patting my shoulder, "You really are the Lady your grandfather claimed you to be, and so I suppose, we in this box are the exception, and I declare it a steady surface."

I laughed. "Thank you, Sir," I said.

"Where did this animated love for Shakespeare come from?" Duke Garrett asked me.

"I can say with authority it came from the same place yours did, my boy," Lord Devon said.

"From you?" he asked. "Yes, I convinced her grandfather to recite in school; the two of us would practice for hours. We grew extremely attached to the words."

"That is correct. Grandfather would often express a wish for you to come and play act with him. I spent hours learning the words so he would prefer me to you."

"And in the end, did he?" Lord Devon asked.

"In Shakespeare, he enjoyed me reading the female parts more than you, but in cards, he always preferred you. Your pockets are deeper than mine," I said bowing my head to him.

"Had I known the matter being disputed, I would likely have come and debated it," he said.

"Why did you not come in recent years?" I asked.

"We ... had a disagreement," he said. He glanced at Duke Garrett.

"I am sorry you did not reconcile before he passed," I said quietly.

"No sorrier than I can be. Especially considering the situation has reconciled itself. I will be with my old friend soon enough, and he will have the pleasure of being right," he said with a teasing smile.

"Not too soon, for I understand tragedies are to be acted out, not lived through," I said.

"I will endure the season for you, my dear, and to be sure what your grandfather and I quarreled about is securely resolved so I might face my old friend without trepidation," he said. I turned and kissed his cheek as I had when I was a child.

"Ah, I was right in my desire for perseverance," he said, grinning at his grandson who laughed.

Tea was brought in and we sat in light-hearted discussion on the poorer performance of Helena when compared with Hermia. Duke Garrett regaled us with an impression of Helena when she claimed if she were Daphne, she would chase Apollo. His impression was done as flamboyantly as the curtain would allow, and his dark eyes held laughter. The early evening passed indulging in Shakespeare. I felt certain I could endure the next three months bowing down to Julia, with just this memory. Though Lord Devon made it clear he meant to invite me to see the gambit of Shakespeare's productions as long as we were both in town.

Duke Garrett left as the curtain closed on Athens. Lord Devon and I sauntered out without a care in the world. The players came out to meet us and we spoke at length to the young actress debuting as Hermia. Lord Devon offered to sponsor her if she were to continue so flawlessly in her performances. I delighted in seeing her joy.

30

Chapter Five

"I suppose you will attend the ball tonight?" Lord Devon asked after we were back in his carriage of velvet scented in mothballs.

"Yes," I said trying not to sound despondent, "though unless you plan on dancing, I will not be guaranteed the pleasure of seeing you except at supper. My cousin will not leave that venue."

"No, I expect not. I am no longer a dancer, though in our youth your grandfather and I could be counted on to stand up for many sets," he said.

"Yes, I can believe that. Grandfather taught me to dance with enthusiasm," I said.

"Oh dear. I shall tell my grandson to watch for his toes if means to ask you," he said.

"He is most sought after and I will have to find my own drapery tonight. I doubt he has anything to apprehend."

"Come, my child. It cannot be as bad as that?"

"My dance card has one name on it, and he only added it that he might court my cousin through me," I said.

"I may still have a set in me," he said.

"Or, if you invited me, I would, as the insignificant daughter of a poor country Baronet, be allowed a round of whist with you after supper. I doubt my aunt would object to having me out of way," I offered.

"Your uncle may," he said.

"Not likely. The Earl does not notice many occurrences beyond those of a political nature. I do not think he even knows my cousin Edmund is showing a marked attention to the Marquess of Stratford, Lord Holland's daughter. Uncle barely remembers his own daughter; I am not sure how his wife's country relation can capture his attention."

"Your uncle is not dictating his heir's courting practices?"

"I do not believe so," I said.

"Who is this your cousin courts?"

"The Marquess of Stratford Lord Holland's daughter," I repeated, noticing Lord Devon's surprise. Then I asked: "Do you know my cousin Edmund?"

"I have heard him spoken of, but I do not know him," he said.

We were quiet for a moment, but then Lord Devon, incapable of being satisfied on the subject, asked: "Is it just a trifle flirtation or is it likely to develop into something?"

"Aunt has encouraged gossip in that direction. I do not think there is a firm understanding between them by any means but if she can force one with gossip until the lady is honor bound, she certainly will."

"Ah, I see. And your uncle is oblivious of the whole thing?" he said.

"I believe so. He does not seem to notice much aside from his political crises."

"He does not even attend to you?"

"No, certainly not," I said with a little laugh.

"Is your Aunt… is she unkind to you?"

"She feels it is her duty to keep me in my position, especially when Edmund is present."

"I am sorry my dear, I'm surprised your father left you so unprotected in her care, though I am certain he relied on your Uncle to protect you."

"Do you know my Aunt?"

"Your grandfather often wrote to me after her visits," he said.

"I see," I said, smiling for him because he seemed truly upset.

"Well, Uncle cannot be bothered to look out for me, and Aunt Claremont Hull is… diverting in her set downs. Even this morning she indicated my death would be a blessing, so the family may not be burdened by a spinster."

"You are a beautiful woman, and I assure you, when the time comes, you will have no trouble marrying."

"You forget I am educated, too, which almost made my mother a spinster. What is the likelihood of meeting with another quirky Baronet who would wish for such a wife?" I asked.

"Oh, posh child, your uncle should take greater care with you," Lord Devon said. He patted my hand to reassure me.

"I did not mean to imply he is inconsiderate of me; he spoke to me just this morning in a very attentive manner. He is just far more concerned with Viscount Melbourne possibly relinquishing the role of Prime Minister. Uncle will be in the room set aside for political rhetoric, not noticing how many times his heir dances with the same lady, let alone to wonder whether his wife's niece is enjoying the ball."

Lord Devon seemed to consider this. Then he said: "In that case, I would be honored to invite you to my card table, but I must know, did your grandfather teach you that skill as well?"

"Yes, why do you ask?"

"He was a notorious cheat!"

"But I am uncommonly good at it and as a team, it could only serve to add weight to your purse. As long as you do not question your sudden fortune," I said in return. The old gentleman laughed so vigorously it turned into a cough.

"Are you well?" I asked as the carriage stopped in front of my Uncle's townhome.

"Oh, just a tickle," he said, but I could see sweat coming from his temple and a purpling around his lips as though he wasn't getting enough breathe. I knew he would be just as reluctant to discuss his health as my grandfather was toward the end so I nodded and said: "I will try not to be so clever in the future."

"Oh, my dear I'd rather die at the quip of a clever woman than live in the drudgery of a dull one," he responded.

"When the Peelers come around I will take full responsibility then, but let it not be too soon," I said, more concerned than I had been with our joke.

"One cannot always control the reaper, but I will do my best," he said.

"I will see you tonight," I assured, kissing the old man's cheek trying not to look at him as a nursemaid would. That always set Grandfather in a slump.

"Yes, my dear," he answered patting my hand, but he did not look well as he sat back to observe the park across from my uncle's door.

Chapter Six

I took my leave from Lord Devon as the coachman came to open my door after having claimed Miss Bolton to escort me in. Miss Bolton and I walked quickly toward Uncle's door. The crescent shaped building in the park where Uncle Claremont Hull lived began to grow dingy from the soot of factories. The massive interconnected structure had a lovely park in front and large stables to the rear making it an ideal home for the season. Most of the townhomes were rented, very few people in this neighborhood bought like Uncle had when he inherited his title. His house certainly was not blessed with originality but served its purpose. Aunt Claremont Hull was in a fashionable enough neighborhood, while Uncle, being close enough to Parliament, could participate with ease. Uncle had a country estate, but spent little time there and had made little effort to improve it despite his being financially capable of doing so, though as far as Earldoms went, he was sorely lacking in assets. Most of the family holdings went to his older brother, a Marquess. Yet, as far as younger brothers went, Uncle did very well for himself.

"Are you vexed?" I asked Miss Bolton who walked very fast.

"Your aunt has played a trick on us, not wishing you to wear one of the gowns you brought; she insisted you wear the one she bought you, which came only this morning. It is full of creases, and will make you look frumpy," she said.

"Why does she insist?" I asked.

"She says you will clash with Julia if you wear the one your father bought you," she said.

"You do not believe that the reason?" I asked.

"Never mind, but I will not allow you to wear a creased gown like a country bumpkin, even if the blasted thing is not dry enough to be worn," she said.

Sounding like my grandfather in a rage, she left me at the door of the drawing room and climbed the stairs toward our room.

"How was the play?" Aunt asked when I entered the room.

"Very good thank you," I answered sitting on her burnt orange sofa and rubbing the velvet against my hand, so I did not have to look at Julia. Without waiting to draw my attention, she asked loudly:

"Did Lord Devon mention where Duke Garrett was?"

"No," I said uneasily. I did not mention I could see very well for myself where he was.

"We drove the park all afternoon hoping to see him, but His Grace never made an appearance. It was not entirely a waste of time. Mr. Percival was particularly attentive to me," she said.

I nodded but said nothing. Mr. Percival was a handsome and charming younger son with little fortune and no property. I had no doubt his attention was all for Julia's large dowry. I looked over at Aunt as she stood up and excused herself. She looked down on me as she always did, with annoyance, making me feel my company made her go. When Aunt, a rare beauty with impeccable manners, married an Earl two times her age, my mother, her older sister, was at the time resigned to be a spinster. Aunt assumed her older sister would be her companion in their later years and took my mother with her to a house party at a lovely estate in Dorset Shire. The beautiful and ancient Grey Manor was the seat of Grandfather's family for hundreds of years. A distant relative built the estate after he was made a Baronet for services rendered to the Crown in the Year of Our Lord

1490. Grandfather and his father had done much to improve and build upon it until the glorious estate rivaled any of the great houses in the country. My mother recalled her first two weeks at the manor, and her introduction to my father as the best of her life. She and my father became great friends and after much correspondence, she ended up married to him for love, the year after her younger sister accepted the earl. My Aunt believed her sister married the son of a country Baronet who'd been land rich, but otherwise poor.

Aunt mentioned several times my mother married simply because she had no other choice. It was the perfect match, the lowly Baronet's son, and the aging spinster with a decent dowry to keep the beautiful estate afloat. She never suspected my grandfather chose to live in a quiet style. Instead, she assumed he lacked the fortune to do otherwise. My grandfather, an extremely educated and philosophical man, circulated many successful essays, which in themselves were quite lucrative. They earned nothing in comparison to what his family retained over the years. If she knew the truth of it, even suspected the girth responsibly invested and maintained over years that Grandfather passed onto my father and even myself, she may have been more impressed by her sister's match. As for father and me, we'd return it all to have Grandfather back.

As things stood, Aunt resented her sister for the whole unfortunate connection. My mother died of a lingering illness when I was nine years of age, and so Aunt transferred her antipathy to me. The disconnect between us was only strengthened as I was raised by Father and Grandfather with only the quieter influence of Miss Bolton to keep me from losing all air of civility. I was always meant to be Julia's companion, but after our sixteenth year, the disadvantages of being raised by two doting, and scholarly men started to show in my impertinent responses to every question posed of me. With Uncle's fortune, Julie's season would far outweigh the pomp of Aunt's. Therefore, Aunt found very little use for me to be a part of that. Until that is, she learned last fall that my late grandfather's closest acquaintance, Lord Devon, had a grandson who inherited a Duke's title and wealth. When Aunt found I could be of use to her, only then did she remember the intended companionship she promised my mother would exist between Julia and myself, to ease her comfortably into her grave. Aunt spoke to me as if I were the most blessed of creatures for her generosity. I only smiled demurely in return.

"Edmund said to tell you he would see you this evening. He had to leave before you returned," Julia said in my direction. I smiled at the thought of sharing a quip or two before he scurried off to be the partner of the fashionable lady he courted.

"I will be glad to see him," I responded. I returned to my sewing in quiet contemplation. A genteel lady trained herself to be silent in her repose. I imagine aunt tired of my voice quickly when she instructed me thus. I only saw Edmund in company. Since I'd come to London this season, Aunt insisted he be rented a flat for himself near a friend of his, so we were not staying under the same roof. He seemed as friendly to me as ever. His mother prevented our meeting frequently, carefully keeping him from any relationship that could not put the Earl's heir to advantage. Edmund and I had, at one time, been great friends despite his being three years, my senior. I suspected a few times he harbored a juvenile affection for me. After we both came of age Aunt stopped bringing Edmund to the country in the summers while Uncle finished up his session in Parliament. Instead, she spent the season in London, only coming to the country with Julia when she could no longer tolerate the smells in August. Edmund came only for two weeks in the autumn with Uncle to enjoy shooting game with Grandfather. He had not come at all since grandfather's funeral.

"Can my maid do your hair this evening, Eva?" Julia asked. She felt Miss Bolton made me look above my station with her intricate twists and ringlets.

"Surely, I cannot look too extravagant this evening," I said.

"Well, I thought perhaps Miss Bolton could do my hair tonight," she said.

"Oh, well, in that case, I'm sure she would be delighted," I said, not allowing my smugness to show. Two evenings previous Lady Pennington complimented me on my hair, even lacking the luster of jewels. I did not think Miss Bolton could sculpt Julia's fine golden hair to compare with my thick tresses of chestnut hair.

"I suppose we should get started," Julia said.

"I am already tired. How do you keep up these long days?" I asked.

"Excessive amounts of tea. I will send for some while we dress," she answered.

I said nothing. Miss Bolton, to allow my dress to dry from her steaming, did a lovely and extensive job with both our coiffures. Her intimacy with my hair could not be denied when the two were compared. Julia looked more angelic than usual if possible, but the long thick ringlets down my back could not be ignored. I relished them, and felt trivial in the same turn. Why did I need something to compensate for being put lower than Julia in every situation? Grandfather told me so often if I were stalwart in my duty to myself, my family and my country, I need not ever feel degraded, even in the company of royalty. Since arriving in London, I felt delinquent in my duty to him, needing such a reassurance as beautiful hair.

Chapter Seven

Long after we dressed, Uncle's carriage arrived at the door. My uncle, of average height and well into his sixth decade, also tied his cravat high, but his chin jutted over his starched collar and worked it very hard to stay stiff and upright. As we drove, he seemed agitated and his jowls sagged with displeasure like an old bulldog.

"Julia, stop looking out the window," he snapped.

"Sorry sir," she said. She abruptly dropped the curtain and looked at her mother.

"Is something distressing you this evening?" Aunt asked.

"Has Edmund made a conquest?" he asked, glancing at me uncomfortably. Aunt smiled smugly, her ageless face taking on pleasure.

"I am certain he will speak to you soon," she said. "He is quite a favorite of Lady Alice Holland, and has proved worthy of her exclusive attention."

"Have you been encouraging the match?" Uncle asked, astonished.

"She is a lady of the highest pedigree. I did not think you could possibly object," Aunt said.

"You should have consulted me," he said turning from his wife, disgruntled. He shoved the window covering open as the carriage slowed, and peered out to see how long the line in front of Lord Holland's house was. It was long, and he sighed in frustration the whole time we waited. Aunt and Julia glanced often at each other, and I tried to stay small and out of his way. After the carriage finally stopped in front of the door, Uncle did not wait for the footman, but opened the door and pulled himself out onto the footplate. Then declared his extreme annoyance at the footman for not being there. Lord Holland had one of the grandest free-standing mansions in Belgravia. His grandfather worked feverishly during the revolt of the American Colonies and was granted the title of Marquess of Stratford. The first Marquess of Stratford never considered settling the eight miles outside the city on the holdings granted him, and instead became the center of London society. The family invested in a free-standing mansion in the up-and-coming area of Belgravia, instead of a terraced house in Mayfair. The grandeur of the area grew more affluential with every group of terraces built. The Holland family ended up with one of the most imposing estates in London, settled in the most fashionable of neighborhoods. With so much more space than his counterparts in London, Lord Holland entertained often and in return expected his autumns and Christmases to be filled with invitations from the titled Lords to their country estates. If the invitations did not come, they would not be invited back to his escapades the next season. Uncle had avoided the nicety so far, his country estate neglected as it was. Aunt often expressed it was starting to be noticed.

We stepped out of the carriage, toward short flat stairs lit by rows of torches. The estate emanated with light from four stories of lit windows, and the clean white exterior glowed as if it might ignite. Uncle escorted us into the grand entrance hall. The marble glittered from a crystal chandelier. The ladies were shown to the women's dressing room where I found Miss Bolton, who arrived a quarter of an hour earlier. Julia asked Miss Bolton to put the tall feathers in her hair, which left her no time to put any final touches on me. It did not matter. Nothing could improve the dull yellow gown trimmed with a color of brown that somehow clashed with my hair.

The dress Aunt chose could not be considered charity but rather bullying.

Uncle picked us up from the women's dressing room within minutes after we'd been deposited there,

The Lark

clearly impatient to get to his discussions of the day's
Parliament session. I waved to Miss Bolton wishing she
could join me in the ballroom. She spoke of the balls she
had been to in the days of her season. I felt guilty she had
to stay behind, to be available if I needed her. We were
greeted by the Marquess and his family standing in the
hallway. Lady Alice was singled out by Aunt and almost
ignored by Uncle's slight bow, with no inclination to offer
her his hand. We were directed to the various rooms of
interest. Uncle left us at the door to the ballroom with very
specific instruction to send Edmund to find him when he
arrived. We gladly relinquished his protection and gave
him to his brandy and politics. The air around us felt more
breathable and even Aunt visibly relaxed a little.

I walked into the ballroom behind Julia and
stopped. My mouth opened, but no sound came out as my
eyes were drawn upward. The barrel-vaulted ceiling
looked like a tortoise shell lined in gold with pictures
painted on each segment. Six panels, two arching inward
on the top of each wall, were painted with intricate scenes
of the Iliad; the most gripping being Achilles in his chariot
triumphantly pulling the body of Hector. The center of the
ceiling was a huge painting of Zeus standing on a cloud in
the act of throwing lightning at Poseidon, who was
conjuring a wave. A series of chandeliers hung from the
ceiling. Golden wall candelabras lit every corner of the
room. The accents on the walls were adorned with gold
leaf. Oak floors shined, and made the whole room
shimmer. Huge arched doorways led out to a veranda
overlooking the lovely and extensive garden. "

Eva," Julia whispered.

"Huh?" I asked. "

Close your mouth," she said.

"Sorry, Julia," I said pulling my eyes away from the
ceiling. The ballroom was not overcrowded, nor
extravagantly decorated; anything beyond a few flowers

would be ostentatious in the beautiful room. Lord Holland was very selective about which of the titled members of society attended his balls, rumors being that he wished to tempt a Royal Duke or a member of the Queens Court to one of his gatherings.

A very large man stepped up to us. His height was excessive, but he also had such girth his arms were the size of Julia's waist. He bowed to her and put a hand out expecting her card without even having to even ask.

"I am available for a quadrille Sir," she said sternly. He bowed his head looking for the set she mentioned.

"Sir Victor, may I introduce my cousin?" she asked. He did not bother to glance at me but nodded.

"Miss Eva Grey may I present Viscount Victor Harley?" I bowed.

The man barely acknowledged me as he put his name down on Julia's card. As he handed Julia her card back, she said: "My cousin Sir, Miss Grey, is a wonderful dancer." The bull of a man glanced at me, bowed and walked away. Both Julia and I were bright red.

"Sorry Eva," Julia whispered.

"No, you are too kind," I said back, trying to hold my head high. Many men came to ask Julia for a set. Her card filled quickly. She found ways to almost force a few of the lower nobility to fill in some of my insignificant sets before dinner. Julia looked around. She'd held back one dance for Duke Garrett. I spotted him long before she did but said nothing. He spoke to a young man I did not know. He was engaged in their conversation and his face took on a pleasant expression when he considered what the other man said. Half a dozen young women stood at a polite distance waiting for Duke Garrett to move. Every unattached young woman in the room would do whatever it took to be introduced to the young duke, who already inherited his title, and was under the age of thirty. When

Julia finally saw him, she smoothed her muted sapphire dress and nudged me.

"There he is. Come with me Eva. You can ask about his grandfather."

"Oh, I do mean to wish him a good evening."

Julia looked at me.

"The grandfather," I said.

"Oh yes, of course," she said. As we approached, I felt a tug on my glove and turned to see who could be using such poor manners. "Edmund," I said. He wore a black coat and white tie that transformed him into a very handsome young man from the boy I knew only hours ago. His dark blond hair and ripe blueberry eyes set off his evening wear but looked out of place while his white-gloved hand pulled on my glove as it had when we were children.

"Darling Eva, and how was the theater this afternoon?"

"Better without the crowd," I gloated, pulling my glove back up. "I suppose you quoted along with the players until those around you were ready to fling you into the pit?"

"That is something I do only for you," I said with a curtsy.

He laughed. "Eva, whenever I think of you it is in the country. It is disconcerting to find you in London in such a scene as this."

"Disconcerting, like I am tailing you?" I asked.

"No, rather it is a rare pleasure."

"It may not be, for the first person to see you, is to charge you to go find your father," I said leaning in.

"Yes, I can well believe it and will not hold that against you." "Kindness at its very core," I said. "Lady Julia Claremont Hull, Miss Grey," A familiar voice addressed us. "Your Grace," Julia cooed, "may I introduce my brother Earl of Somerset, Viscount Edmund Claremont

Hull. Edmund, this is His Grace the Duke of Surry Sir Jonah Garrett."

"It is a pleasure, I have heard you spoken of," Duke Garrett bowed.

"And I you," Edmund responded. Julia gracefully hinted her dance card was almost full until the Duke bowed politely and asked to see it. He put his name down for the mazurka, the only dance left, and the first couple's dance of the evening. "You'll dance with me before supper won't you Eva?"

Edmund turned to me and asked. "I am not fashionable enough to be danced with before supper," I said handing him my card, "Perhaps one of the after-supper dances will do after you have favored all the top ladies with your hand."

"Would that leave you free to dance with me before supper?" Duke Garrett asked and bowed taking the card from Edmund. Edmund looked up at Duke Garrett and then his outstretched hand where he had been considering my card with excessive exaggeration. His eyebrows contracted in annoyance. I stopped, feeling myself blush. Dance with a duke?

"Did your grandfather warn you about the thickness of your socks?" I asked.

"He did, and I assure you my boots are sturdy," he said. "Very well, but as you see, I only have the next set and the dinner open. I cannot think you are available for either of those."

"I have not an engagement for the next." He bowed waiting for me to assent.

"Thank you, sir," I said, bowing back. Julia's mouth dropped as he wrote his name in. Had she known that, she would have found a way out of her commitment to Mr. Percival. Not that the line dances were as intimate, but rather bathed the ladies leading the line with attention from the room when Julia knew her gown and hair looked most

45

to advantage. "Ah, it is so good to see the young enjoying yourselves," Lord Holland said, while bowing to our group. "Thank you, Sir," Edmund said. He grasped the man's hand in an intimate way.

Our host then said: "Duke Garrett, there are many who wish to make your acquaintance, may I?"

"Please," he said bowing, but instead of leaving us, Duke Garrett said, "the ceiling is quite impressive Sir." Duke Garrett gave me a side glance, and I wondered if he had seen my awe when walking in.

"My father commissioned it. I find it inconsistent," Lord Holland said looking up.

"How so, Sir?" Edmund asked. "The Iliad does not reference the fighting between Zeus and Poseidon."

"It is theorized that all war on earth is just an extension of the war that started in heaven. I believe it is symbolic," I said.

They all turned to stare at me. I closed my mouth. A lady was not supposed to put herself forward in a scholarly way.

"I think you may be right, Cousin," said Edmund. "Lord Holland, may I present my cousin, Miss Eva Grey. She is the granddaughter of Sir Henry Grey, the philosopher," he continued, reverting back to a formality with me that had not been present moments earlier, and I could see he meant to inspire a good opinion of himself in the father of Lady Alice.

"It is a pleasure. Miss Grey, I will think on your theory, or at least have an answer for the next curious eye." I bowed my head. I wished my face did not turn red at the slightest provocation.

"Sir, shall we?" the host said, and Duke Garrett followed him. I did not doubt by the time he came back to me every one of his dances would be filled. Edmund left to finish off his dance card, and I noticed he did not put his name in on any of my dances. Did I embarrass him? Julia and I went to her mother. After a little more scrambling on Julia's part, she still hadn't managed to help me find a supper dance partner, and no one at all to dance with after supper.

"Do not concern yourself," Julia said, "there will be more people here by supper and if you dance as well as you always have, we will finish off your card."

"Yes, after supper a few of the waiters should be available," Aunt commented. Both Julia and I pretended not to hear her.

"Lord Devon did mention he would like a partner in cards after supper if it is not–"

"It would be better to dance, Eva," Julia said, "I will fend for you at supper."

"Thank you," I said.

"If not, I will arrange with Lord Devon," Aunt said, astonishing Julia. Very soon it was my turn to astonish Aunt. The first dance was announced, and a few strokes by the musicians signaled their readiness. "Shall we?" Duke Garrett said moving to my side bowing again with a hand forward.

"Of course," I said, but it sounded like a question. I placed my gloved hand in his, and the way they rubbed together lifted my heart in my chest. We walked to the very top of the dance floor while a few dozen eyes followed us. Only Lady Alice and Edmund were ahead of us, she the highest ranked lady to dance. "This is very disconcerting. Where is a curtain when it is most desired?" I asked. "I suppose we could dance near the window covering, but it would draw more attention to us, not less."

I smothered the mirth in the back of my throat trying to appear not to be laughing. We started with The Grand March. Duke Garrett paraded me around the room, and I sorely wished to be wearing my own turquoise gown that made me look much more elegant. Julia wore her delicate sapphire and Aunt thought them too close. I followed as Lady Alice led the ladies around the room. I look like a rotten egg in a hen house among blue, green and pink eggs. When that dance ended Duke Garrett and I came back together, and we started in on the Minuet.

I said: "The flourishes I must put on my steps will require all my mental acuity, especially if I am to aim for your toes."

"I did not know that would take such an effort," he answered.

"If it would suit you, I can manage a stony silence that will make us appear at odds," I said and turned out to walk around another couple, then finishing a full circle I went back to Duke Garrett, taking his hand again.

"I do not think that would suit," he said. "Shall we hide behind the acquaintance of our Grandfathers?"

"I suppose that will do."

Just then another couple turned out and swept by us and I said louder, "Yes, my grandfather's funeral was well attended."

Duke Garrett closed his eyes trying not to express his amusement out loud. "I think that might have been too literal an assessment of the situation," he said.

"Very well then, I will tell you that the young actress, the one who played Hermia with such conviction, has been promised a sponsor in your grandfather."

"Yes, I commissioned him to do so," said Duke Garrett, turning out again. When we rejoined hands, I said: "You missed the sweet joy on her face. It was something to behold."

"I suppose it is something akin to the shining on your face just now," he said.

"Oh dear," I said, refocusing my features. "I am trying for somber."

"That is absurd," he said, his bright, dark eyes watching my face. The natural smile I could not resist when his features were so employed came back. "You get me into trouble Sir," I said, glancing at Aunt as I turned out again. She watched us closely from her seat, beating her fan in front of her face to hide the glare I could see in her eyes.

When I took Duke Garrett's hand again, he said: "She wishes for you to be somber?"

"Isn't that the way a well-bred lady always looks?" I said, glancing around at the other women in the room.

He looked around and his eyes grew large. "You may be correct." "Furthermore, any man above a viscount in station is not allowed more expression than a disapproving eyebrow lift."

"Ah, like this," he said, demonstrating.

"That was very good, and appropriately timed, for now my Aunt has seen you disapproving me and can rest at ease that you will not burden yourself with my company, even for your grandfather's sake."

"That isn't a kind thing to say about one's self," he said more seriously.

"Oh dear, kindness is not a trait a duke can bother with. I do not know how we will ever elevate you," I said.

"What traits are allowed to a lower baron?" he asked.

"He can do whatever he wants, except, of course, come into this assembly."

"Yes, I was never invited before becoming a duke."

"Careful, that sounds like…" I stopped. What did his words sound like?

"That sounded almost wistful," I said, quickly recovering the steps I missed.

"I took the anonymity of my barony for granted. I was to take orders when the living on Grandfather's estate came available. Now I am…."

"I suppose you cannot give back the title of duke," I said when he did not expound further. "There is no one else to take it." I glanced up at him from the side, he looked down and smiled at me. It was a kind smile and a sweet look.

"Well then, we will be socially ridiculous together, I suppose," I said, squeezing his hand a little tighter, and he nodded. Our next dance was a quadrille, and the star formation we used was complicated. We left each other so often conversation was impossible, but the smiles and comfortable companionship we shared when our hands clasped back together, sent the time passing too quickly. I dreaded leaving Duke Garrett, but all too soon he escorted me back to Julia.

"Well, I have been disappointed," Duke Garrett said into my ear.

"Yes," I said looking up at him. "I wore my thick boots and they turned to be unnecessary."

"Only because you took the precaution; had you neglected it, I surely would have stepped thrice. To step on a duke is something, you know," I answered. "I expect better for your next partner. Is that he with your cousin?" he asked.

Julia and Mr. Percival talked while she watched us. I glanced at Duke Garrett. He looked almost jealous eyeing Mr. Percival. The incredibly handsome young man often doted on Julia. I should not have been surprised at Duke Garrett's reaction, but to find yet another man enamored with Julia frustrated me more than usual.

"Yes," I finally answered when he looked back to me for confirmation. "His thin boots should afford him a few tromps on the toes," he said. "They most certainly would, but he has not a title and it would elicit no scandal. It is not worth the effort."

"I suppose one does have to consider these things. I am flattered you saved the honor for me alone," he answered squeezing my hand in the most scandalous way. I smiled up at him wishing he was not dancing the next with my extremely pretty cousin.

Chapter Eight

I dipped my head to Duke Garrett when we reached Julia's side. He bowed back. Then he turned from me and extended a hand to Julia, and I felt forgotten. Julia looked at him serenely, a placid smile upon her face, just as a well-mannered lady should. I turned from them and focused on Mr. Percival, who walked me to the very bottom of the dance floor, where we the untitled stayed with our own kind. Many feminine eyes still followed us, Mr. Percival being the most handsome man in the room. His dark hair waved perfectly off his forehead, his face held a place among the angels. His perfection culminated in sky-blue eyes disarming every woman he looked at. His waistcoat cut in tightly and rounded his chest as it should. His muscular legs under his close-fitting breeches indicated he did not have to stuff his clothes to look perfectly proportioned. His attractive appearance and intimacy with the Marquess' family allowed him invitations to many gatherings someone in his station would usually be barred from. Mr. Percival danced with a perfect light step, which made my skill seem more considerable than it was. It would have been an experience worth having if he didn't plague me for Julia's likes and dislikes while the puffed sleeves on my ugly gown bounced. I welcomed the end of the set when it came, even though I had no idea of my partner for the next.

I did not see Julia and Duke Garrett. Apparently, neither did Mr. Percival. I expected him to take me back to my Aunt, but instead, he took me to the refreshment room and insisted I take a drink. I knew he did it to stay by my side so he could say a word to Julia when she returned, and I felt sorry for him. Julia had her sights set on a duke. After I swallowed some thick punch to appease him, we returned to the ballroom. We both spotted Julia, who came down from the top of the room where a duke and the daughter of an earl danced. Mr. Percival veered to where Julia and Duke Garrett talked to my next partner. They spoke about the upcoming horse races. Mr. Percival joined in. Duke Garrett turned to me and asked; "Is the punch worth it?"

"It is too rich," I said feeling a little sick.

"Are you well?" he asked, moving closer to me. "I am not used to such heavy foods all the time, at home everything is–"

"Duke Garrett, do be so good as to settle an argument for us," Mr. Percival said. "We are speaking of the Craven Stakes. They are saying 7 to 4 on Montreal, but I've had it that Scroggins has been training on the continent and may be worth a bet." "What are his handicaps?" Duke Garrett asked. He stepped forward in a way that nudged me into the group's circle, and I had to take a step to keep from leaning against him. I didn't know if it were the punch, or him standing so close that made my stomach lurch. I listened, feeling light-headed as he spoke of Newmarket in April. Julia also listened, but neither of us commented. She behaved like a lady, and my father supported local horses for political reasons, which would be unpopular in this group. I kept up the conversation with my next partner throughout our set simply by knowing how to react to each of his comments. He seemed more interested in talking about the races than dancing. Having a memory for names and numbers, I knew many of the racers and their statistics, which kept him questioning me. This would not have been such an inconvenience if I did not have to also concern myself with Julia's partner. Julia danced with a mammoth of a man, Viscount Harley, and they made up the other couple in our set. When he hopped the floor shook, and I slipped a few times. My partner scowled at the Viscount and then went on plaguing me for the racing record of Crucifix, a three-year-old mare of great promise. He did not consider the mental sharpness I needed to keep up his conversation and not get in the path of the enormous Viscount. It almost came to tragedy when the large Viscount missed his step and came cambering toward me. My feet were required by the music to occupy the space he clumsily inhabited. We collided over the spot. His solid frame claimed the floor and threw me backward. I stumbled trying to regain my balance. Duke Garrett, who was in the formation next to us looked as if he may leave his partner and come to my aid when I stumbled toward him. It proved unnecessary. Just before I teetered to the ground my partner, almost waiting for such a mishap, righted me, pulling me out of harm's way just as the Viscount stepped heavily where I would have been on the shiny oak floor. My partner took a deep, annoyed breath as the Viscount asked pardon. My partner turned me away while he continued with our conversation as if nothing happened. He took so much pleasure in my company, after we finished our dance, he rushed away quickly. I thought he might get a scrap of foolscap so he could write down a few bets he wanted to place.

Julia smirked at me and, glancing at the vast back of Viscount Harley, said: "You must be sorry he did not ask you to dance?"

"Or perhaps," I answered, "he felt badly for snubbing me, and meant to give me the honor of his company after all."

She laughed at the back of her throat and threw me an amused glance. I caught Duke Garrett's eye from across the room and he smiled at me as if he knew our subject matter. Julia and I went to Aunt to await our next partners. Miss Bolton and Father often argued about the races. I never thought amassing what I thought to be useless knowledge would keep me in easy conversation with all my partners. Knowing statistics and handicaps made the first half of my evening pleasant. Eventually, the pleasantness ended, and I had no more partners, even though the music was not finished playing. My last partner politely sat me next to Aunt who glanced at me with annoyance. The dance manager caught her eye, and Aunt made an exasperated sigh. He began looking around the room, and I knew it was to find me a suitable partner for the next set. It was the most humiliating practice and yet, he would do it. I watched him whispering to Lady Alice who then glanced at me and both started scanning the room. He saw Mr. Percival. He headed toward him. I felt nausea roll my stomach. The man did not realize Mr. Percival had already been my partner. I did not see Duke Garrett coming until he was almost before me. I thought he would ask me to dance again. He smiled as if he would speak, but Edmund stepped in front of him.

He held his hand to me with an extravagant flutter meant as a bow and said: "I insist on the next, Eva."

"Ahh," I stammered but took the hand Edmund gave as he pulled me up. We walked away before I could even nod to Duke Garrett. Out of the corner of my eye, I saw the hostess exchange a glance with her counterpart who was just about to tap Mr. Percival's shoulder. His hand retreated. Both stopped scurrying and relaxed. She even spared a smile for Edmund, and he gave her a gallant exaggerated nod in return. This brought hotter flames to my cheeks than sitting alone by Aunt.

"You really do look stunning this evening. You are one of the few women who can make that color of yellow work," Edmund said. My dress looked the color of white linen wet and spoiled.

"You are too kind," I said giving him a sarcastic side glance.

"I am not in jest, though I suspect my mother outfitted you for this turn in town, elegant but not as shiny as Julia's attire."

"One cannot upstage an Earl's daughter," I said.

"Unless one has a quick mind and a confident quip, then one can do nothing but upstage an Earl's daughter," Edmund said.

"Only in the eyes of her brother," I answered.

"And the newly titled duke?" he questioned with his eyes.

"It is a combination of Duke Garrett having few acquaintances in the room as of yet, and his Grandfather, Lord Devon, a theater enthusiast, who has taken a liking to me. And though the grandfather is in his seventh decade, I can only hope, since his wife passed on ten years ago, I have made a solid conquest," I said.

"I suppose stranger matches have been made," Edmund grinned.

"I am only using him for his theater box. I expect to jilt him at the end of the season and leave town in the shame of it all," I said.

"Yes, I suspected you the jilting sort," he said. We couldn't say more because we started the arbor march. Duke Garrett was the arbor with Lady Alice. I couldn't help wondering if Edmund was supposed to be her partner, but instead came to her rescue to be my partner. I again caught Duke Garrett's eye as I passed under his arms. I wanted to smile at him, because I felt sure he meant to ask me to dance before Edmund swooped in. Before the smile could catch in my eye, he looked at me with wonder. I moved too quickly to tell what he wondered. He was gone in the blur of other couples.

After our set, Edmund noticed the supper-room had been opened so he escorted me in. The large dining room had the enormous table pushed up against the far wall. I sat and watched guests pick apart the artistic towers of exotic fruit, intricate twisting bread and clover shaped rolls surrounding the soup. Many chairs and benches were set up around the room. Edmund piled my plate with all the exotic foods I simply had to try. Then he sat me as close to

The Lark

Julia as possible, thronged by her many admirers. He left
me to assist Lady Alice. I saw Lady Alice give Mr. Percival
a head nod. She took Edmund to accompany her so Mr.
Percival came and sat next to me. Again, we spoke of
Julia, as I removed my elbow gloves and set them on my
lap, placing my napkin over them so I could eat. I started
to suspect his interest in her more than just her sizable
dowry. He truly seemed to want to please her. This
development would interest my father, though his
enthusiasm for a social experiment seemed to have dimmed
since Grandfather passed on.

When I thought I could no longer tolerate more
conversation about Julia, he said: "You are from Dorset
Shire are you not?"

"Yes, Dorchester is my family's seat," I said.

"Do you go to the seaside much?" he asked.

"Yes, often, especially in the heat of the summer," I
said.

"I don't suppose you have ever sea bathed, but it is
a glorious practice," he said.

"You may be astonished what an ill-supervised
young girl would do at the seaside," I said.

"I suppose it would be something akin to a hoard of
brothers spending summer days with their grandfather at a
hotel in Brighton," he said. "Yes, I can imagine," I said
smiling at him until I caught Julia's eye. She watched us
from inside her circle of admirers. She looked as if I
injured her. I quickly smiled at her and said: "Julia bought
a new saddle for her mount this season. Have you seen it? I
think she said she met you at the park," I said.

"Did she," he said. He looked at her and she smiled
at us, she could not hide the relief when Mr. Percival turned
his beautiful eyes on her. This aggravated me. Did she
need every man to be in love with her? She planned on
marrying Duke Garrett, why did she have to keep Mr.
Percival's attention as well? Especially considering he was

56

one of the few men in the room low enough in rank to even speak to me. It didn't seem fair, not to him, and not to me. I would not bow down to this ridiculousness anymore. Uncle was right; I had more than sufficient dowry and a home to offer a man with none. Mr. Percival had a lovely charm about him, not to mention if I married him, I could just stare at him the rest of my life.

"Did you collect seashells from the sand?" I asked turning my full attention on Mr. Percival.

"Yes, I still have a few of the larger in my possession."

"I made a necklace out of a collection I gathered for my sister," Duke Garrett said sitting next to me and Mr. Percival. We both stared at him. As the highest ranked in the room, it was peculiar for him to be sitting with the lowest, but we said nothing.

"Have you ever seen a dolphin?" Duke Garrett asked.

"No, I've read about them," I said.

"That surprises me. The channel is teeming with them. I saw the most extraordinary pod when I crossed to tour the continent. They leapt from the water and flipped as if showing off for each other." Duke Garrett had my full attention. I found even the terribly handsome man couldn't keep my attention over this incredibly interesting man. I was starting to prefer Duke Garrett. Somewhere deep inside, I knew it very dangerous to indulge in this preference, but I couldn't help how much I enjoyed our conversations. Mr. Percival started to describe a fish he caught when Lord Devon hobbled up to us with a footman holding his food. Lord Devon grinned at me, and then at his grandson. He looked pleased.

"You must be doing well at the tables," I said. He only smiled wider. Duke Garrett stood, but Mr. Percival, knowing his place, said:

The Lark

"I am needed, please excuse me," and gave up his
seat to Lord Devon. He looked sorry to go. He seemed to
enjoy our conversation. It felt unfair he should leave us
simply because he was born after his brother. \

"Of what are we speaking?" Lord Devon asked.

"Sea creatures we've seen on our travels," Duke
Garrett said.

"On my trip to India to examine our family's
holdings there, I saw a whale," Lord Devon said. He told
us about it until my only wish in life was to see a whale in
the ocean shooting water up.

"Your Grandfather bought a fast clipper six years
ago before we ... when he ...."

"Yes, he went to meet with two philosophizers of
Europe to write his final essay," I said. "That is the trip I
was speaking of, the dolphins seemed to race the boat,"
Duke Garrett said.

"You were with him?" I asked, shocked.

"Yes, he was heading over to the continent and so
were we. He gave us a ride," Lord Devon said looking
abashed for some reason.

"He did more than that. He introduced us to the
French Philosopher Pierre-Simon Ballanche," Duke Garrett
said.

"He...he never spoke of you to me," I said
wondering how Duke Garrett, who would have been my
equal at the time, would not even be mentioned by my
Grandfather as a traveling companion. Lord Devon, seeing
my confusion said: "That is when we had our disagreement
which led to the breach between us. Him not mentioning
us would be my doing. I asked him not to mention our time
on the continent together, to anyone."

"Did you argue about Monsieur Ballanche?"

"I would rather not discuss it here," he said dipping
his head to me.

"Of course, excuse me," I said, but the curiosity burned within me and I wondered if I would ever know what came between the two. After a time, others joined in our conversation. The gentlemen of the group wanted to impress Duke Garrett. Each spoke of their own Grand Tour, and I enjoyed hearing all about the world I only ever read about. Spinsters didn't travel and I couldn't help thinking perhaps I would not marry after all. This thought came after Duke Garrett said, "Are you feeling better?"

"I…" He sat right at my eye level and he leaned in, close enough for me to smell the lavender he must use to sooth his face after he shaved. My stomach turned again, but this was not the unpleasant sensation of before. My insides squealed. I wished I could say something that would keep the look of concern on his face.

"I am completely recovered," I forced myself to say and he smiled, then turned back to hear what was being said. After supper, Julia and I went to the ladies dressing room, or rather a sitting room that had been set aside as a dressing room.

"How is your ball?" Miss Bolton greeted us.

"It has been like a dream," Julia said, spinning.

"I have enjoyed it much more than I thought I would, and my legs are quite tired. Have you eaten?" I asked Miss Bolton.

"Extravagantly. They even brought us some punch," Miss Bolton said smiling. I saw one of the other lady's maids glance at Miss Bolton disgruntled in a way that told me that was not the case and she was probably starving.

Then Julia gasped. The whole room turned.

"What, what is it?" I asked.

"You haven't a single dance for after supper," Julia said, horrified.

"Oh, yes, well …" I stammered. Lady Alice, who had been in her own part of the room, turned to look at me. The woman Aunt intended Edmund to marry was pretty enough, her light brown hair curled naturally and she had kind eyes that saw everything. If her slim nose hadn't peaked just a little too long she would be very pretty. "I am so sorry Eva. I forgot to fend for you," Julia said.

"I was so pleasantly engaged at supper, I did not remember my dance card once," I said.

"You could feign a headache and go home," Miss Bolton said as she fixed the feathers in Julia's hair. I tried to decide how Uncle would feel about this. It wouldn't be hard to take Miss. Bolton and I home if our carriage was accessible. The drive alone was only a quarter of an hour.

"There is a gentleman at the door for you," Lady Alice said to me politely. She looked just as humiliated for me as Miss Bolton. Lord Devon stood at the door of the sitting room. His kindly old grandfather face filled me with total relief.

"Good evening, Sir," I said.

"Miss Grey, I was hoping to engage you as my whist partner," he said.

"I would enjoy that sir," I said, then turning to Lady Alice I said, "I really am tired out, and would appreciate the reprieve."

"Of course, I will make your excuses," Lady Alice said. She looked relieved for me. I thought she would make Edmund a lovely wife. Perhaps one day Father would invite them to Grey Manor and we would become friends.

"Oh, and I don't think my lady has had anything to eat. Would you mind terribly?" I asked. "An oversight. I am certain my lady has had nothing either. I will, of course, see to it," she said.

"Thank you so much," I said offering the lady my hand. She took it and we shook. I spared one entirely fake happy wave to Julia and Miss Bolton. Then I left on Lord Devon's arm. "I see Aunt Clermont Hull has whispered a word in your ear," I said.

"She mentioned you have few acquaintances among the group." My face flamed. I leaned in closer and said, "Then shall we see what mischief we can make?"

"Let us make them regret they did not introduce you to their sons," Lord Devon said.

I walked away with him. I did not consider the ballroom when we passed. I wanted nothing to do with the fashionable people who wanted nothing to do with me.

At the card table, we worked flawlessly together and Lord Devon gave me all the money we won. I left very content with my evening instead of dreading dance after dance of scrounging partners among the elite who would pretend not to know me on the morrow.

Chapter Nine

While I slept most of the morning, fragments of the gabled ceiling fell on me. Miss Bolton worked them out of my hair while I breakfasted in my room. She muttered about wood bugs and my thick beautiful hair while she worked. When satisfied I was clean, and bug-free, she helped me dress. I left her quickly in hopes of escaping further examination. I found Julia in the drawing room of autumn surrounded by bouquets of flowers as if it were spring.

"What is this?" I asked.

"They are from the men I danced with last night," she said, then biting her lip she said:

"Those are yours." Julia pointed to a huge bouquet of fat pink roses that clashed abysmally with Aunt's poppy color scheme. I moved to the flowers on a side table. She eyed me sourly as I pulled the card from them and read.

"I cannot decide who enjoyed your company more, me or my grandfather. –Duke Garrett"

I smiled. "What does he write?"

"I think he is enamored with me."

"Come now you cannot seriously be hoping he will–"

"Invite me to another show? I think he will," I said, pocketing the note. "Oh, Lord Devon, of course. What a lovely man," she said breathing deeper.

"He ought to teach his grandson how to send a bouquet." She pointed to a lovely spray of assorted flowers that blended in with the rest of her offerings. Edmund came bounding through the door. "Good morning, oh, I've neglected my duty," Edmund said stealing a rose from one of Julia's bouquets and handing it to me.

63

"You are too good to me," I said. Julia looked at her brother with the same wary expression she always gave him, almost like she couldn't predict what came next.

"And these are for you," he said, looking at my large bouquet glancing through them for a card. "Lord Devon," I said. "My conquest is at hand."

"Is that where you disappeared to last night?"

"I was invited to play whist. Lord Devon needed a partner."

"How did you do?"

"I reduced noble men to tears, and made a little fortune for myself," I said.

"Now you will have something to serve as your dowry," Julia piped in. We both stopped and looked at her. Edmund glared. Julia pinked. "It was a good quip, Julia," I encouraged because she usually spent her wits desperately trying to smooth out the day so her mother might be in good spirits. "

What will you ladies be doing today?"

"I have a fitting for a new gown this afternoon," Julia said. "I mean to sleep late and eat finger sandwiches when I wake," I answered looking around expectantly.

"You are not off to the best start," he replied, beaming at me. "No, I suppose not, but if you offered to drive me to Covent Gardens it would be most refreshing."

"Shall I just drop you off at the front door of the theater?"

"I heard last night The Drury Lane Players will be setting the stage for Hamlet," I said. "I have also heard the theater manager, Mr. Hammond, is insisting Mr. Kean, who is to play Hamlet, rehearse—with the group."

"Yes, the Sixth Duke of Bedford died last year, and the committee is not sure his son means to be as generous to them, or rather his London steward does not mean for him to continue to support the theater. But there is high hope for Mr. Hammond as the theater manager. He has already brought back much respectability to the place," Edmund said.

"We saw a lion being tamed there last season," Julia said.

I groaned and asked, "Do you think Mr. Hammond will turn things around for good? I am so pleased with his selections."

Here Edmund just looked at me dumbfounded. "Sorry Eva, I can only tell you what I've heard among the gossip," he said. I noticed for perhaps the first time, Edmund never gave his opinion on anything. He only regurgitated what he heard.

"You are qualified to give your opinion. You've been educated in finances, and understand the committee, the temperament of the crowd and what is likely to tempt theatergoers," I insisted to Edmund, "In your opinion do you think Mr. Hammond will succeed in his endeavors?" Edmund thought for a moment. "No, Eva," he said, "I am sorry to say, only you and the last generation really want to see Shakespeare. I doubt he will make it through the season hiring actors he cannot afford, to watch plays only the educated wish to see."

"I appreciate your honesty," I said to Edmund, but I could not help my disappointment.

"Come, Eva, we are powerful in this country. Perhaps we should drive over to the theater. We will convince Mr. Hammond to turn Shakespeare's works into modern-day operas. With your musical talents and knowledge of Shakespeare, you could give them a boost. Perhaps we together could save Mr. Hammond," Edmund said. I wasn't sure if he was serious or not. I don't think he knew, either.

"Edmund, you know Father expects you directly," Julia said, quickly picking up her role as official family smoother. "Yes, I received a letter this morning and verbal direction last evening. He has something very particular to

65

say to me and must set appointments instead of having out with it. Surely, both have inspired me to make haste as you find me this morning. Yet, his man declares he is away, but will return by Tea, which I am to take with the family," Edmund said glancing out the window.

"That is odd," I said, "Uncle was not going to Parliament today."

"He may have gone to the apothecary. He has been coughing," Julia said. She often moved to the worst-case scenario and looked worried. I could not surmise whether she worried for her father or for herself under her brother's guardianship if anything were to happen to him.

"Come Eva, Julia, let us at least have a ride to Hyde Park while the weather is fine, and it is early enough we may give the horses their heads," Edmund said forgetting his noble quest to save the theater and Mr. Hammond, just like that. Julia jumped up to call the lady she and her mother shared, and we went to change into our riding habits. Julia was an exceptional horsewoman, and when she visited me at Grey Manor in the summers, we spent most of our time riding. Neither of us acknowledged as much, but we got along best when we rode. She pushed me and I challenged her. After we were properly outfitted, the groomsman brought our horses around to the front door. Edmund assisted Julia onto her horse. Julia looked like a heroine in a story, her dark blue riding habit contrasted beautifully against Pegasus's white mane. Edmund turned to help me mount my own chestnut colored horse, Avon, who turned jet black at his nose and legs. Edmund cupped my foot when putting it in the stirrup. He moved to smooth out my riding habit, and his hand caressed my leg. I flinched in surprise. He moved away. It happened so quickly, I could not be sure it really happened. Before I could examine him to see if he even noticed, Edmund sprung up on his large grey Arabian stallion and moved forward. He did not look at me, and I decided he mistook where my leg was and must have been embarrassed by his accidental breach of civility. We kept a sedate pace as was appropriate on the public roads. My beast started to dance along with Julia's as we rode through the three-arched entryway of the park. It took all my arm strength to contain Avon through the park. We heard the tromping of hooves before we saw them. Stable hands and groomsmen worked the speed out of the Ton's horses, so they would be tame enough to walk when the fashionable hour came. Upon entering Rotten Row, the energy of the other animals brought Avon's knees high in anticipation. Edmund fell into a trot. His Arabian cost more than mine and Julia's horses together. Living in London most of the year, he didn't bother to work the poor creature to its potential, and in return, the beast barely acknowledged his rider. Clearly, the intelligent animal could sense respect begat respect. Julia and I gave our horses their heads and galloped, throwing gravel and hide behind us from one end of the mile and some odds long row to the other. Julia outstripped me on our first run. By using less caution on the turn at the palace side of the row I came much closer on our second run. Many of the stable hands and the other nobility who'd come to ride stopped to watch us race. Julia was always in high spirits when she rode and I felt close to her like we were still the friends we'd been in childhood. On our third pass, her horse only beat mine by a nose.

Julia turned to me and breathed hard. "That was a good run, Eva."

"Thank you, Julia," I said.

"You both ride very well," Duke Garrett said. He rode up behind us.

"Oh, Your Grace, I did not know you would be here this time of day," Julia said, genuinely caught off guard.

"Yes, I've only just heard of the practice from my man. Your mount is fast, Lady Julia, and your seat on her is nearly perfect," he said. I clenched my jaw wishing to ride again, certain I could beat her this time. "Miss Grey, I should have known you ride, considering your first affections went to the stable hand who broke your stallion," he said giving me a side glance.

"I did not know you heard that confession, Your Grace. Sadly my affection for him dimmed and has since been lavished on Avon," I said leaning down to rub my horse's neck.

"The Bard's birthplace," he asked.

"Shakespeare is an obsession for Eva," Edmund said, riding up.

"Ah Sir, will you race?" Duke Garrett asked.

"No, Julia will beat us both," he said, having lost several times to Julia, despite his stallion being superior to hers. Edmund didn't even try anymore. Mr. Percival came bounding up. "Come let's ride," he encouraged. He drove his horse straight toward us and barely turned to the row so he didn't ram into me. A more handsome picture then Mr. Percival on his horse galloping away could not be painted. Yet despite his attractive seat that drew Julia's eyes, I preferred Duke Garrett's intelligent eyes. He watched to see if I would stare at the excessively handsome man like all the other ladies. I smiled at him instead. I did not regret it. I was rewarded by the glow on his face swelling my chest further. Julia finally turned back to Duke Garrett after she realized she stared at Mr. Percival. She dutifully gave Duke Garrett preference, but clearly wished to ride free. Duke Garrett nodded to her and moved his horse forward while Julia turned and moved into a canter. As her companion, I kept pace with her until she turned to me and grinned. We both whisked our horses to a gallop, but her horse jumped and moved with unbridled enthusiasm. She outstripped me by a few yards quickly. Duke Garrett kept pace with me until I nodded at him and whisked Avon again. Then he pulled ahead and chased down Julia who raced to beat Mr. Percival, despite his fifty-yard lead. We drove our horses, hooves blurring, before us. Duke Garrett soon abandoned decorum and raced Julia and me with enthusiasm. All three of us eventually outstripped Mr. Percival, who raced with more caution but never gave up the chase. We kept this up for over an hour. Duke Garrett usually won, having the advantage over us who rode side saddle, but on the few occasions Julia won, I cheered because she had the disadvantage.

After her first win she said: "Duke Garrett, you may want to start carrying a handicap."

"I do not think my pride can handle such a thing," Duke Garrett said.

"My brother and Mr. Percival have survived it," she said.

"Very well. I will find an impost if we arrange our next meeting," he said.

"That is very gentlemanly of you. The day after next if it is not raining," she said bowing her head. I could see the slight grin on her face indicating she won something from him. My jaw clenched with surging anger, which made me hate Julia to her very core. I could not stop this foreign unnamed anger from rushing up my throat, but I caught it before something catty about her handicap came out of my mouth. What was the matter with me? She rode with so much passion I felt inspired by Julia, and yet, I somehow hated her for it, too. Was this jealousy? My grandfather told me emotion blinded people. A part of me coursed with pain that froze my mind and burned my heart. The reaction held me captive in irrational repulsion of Julia, and the desire to run from Duke Garrett. If Julia carried her point and married him, I would go home and never wish to see either of them again. And not only that, but it felt extremely cruel of them. Though certainly if they married, it would have nothing to do with tormenting me

69

personally. Why did it feel so personal? I turned from their banter. Edmund, seeing us taking a rest, trotted up to me. I felt gratified someone remembered me. "The Life Guards left a few of the stumps they were jumping. Come with me Eva, I seem to recall you are exceptionally good at jumping."

"Avon is always ready," I said. I followed him and we jumped a few stumps in a row. Mr. Percival came with us. Julia and Duke Garrett eventually followed, but neither was enthusiastic about jumping. After we could no longer delay our return, we rode toward the gate of the park. Edmund came in and rode with me, while Julia rode with Duke Garrett and Mr. Percival speaking of their final race.

"Eva," Edmund asked. "Yes," I said.

"Will you sing tonight?" he asked.

"It is a gaming party," I said. "Of course there will be singing."

"I have heard some of the ladies insisting they will find a way," he said, and I knew he meant his particular lady but only answered: "Even so I doubt I will be asked. I am not exactly...." I hated to mention the gap that existed between our stations in life. It never bothered me before, I never really understood what Aunt was always going on about when she visited us in the country. Now the grandeur of an earl became significant in my estimations, and since coming to town it felt as material as any chasm in stone.

When I did not finish, Edmund said: "Come now Eva, your grandfather would never wish to hear you speak such."

"No, he would be very disappointed in my being..." I could not finish. It felt wrong to give my confidences to Edmund; his lady would not like it. Especially when I started to think I was growing vulnerable to the human condition and may find myself relying on him simply because he gave me the attention my susceptible heart craved. When it appeared clear I would not finish opening up to him, Edmund said: "You must be confident Eva; it is part of your charm."

"Thank you, Edmund," I said. "I will remember Grandfather's face whenever I find myself seated behind the throng."

"Oh Eva, it was unfair of them to bring you. My own jewel, smuggled away in Dorset Shire. You belong in the country."

I nodded uncomfortably at the way he leaned toward me. He knew the ideals of my grandfather. The status he pretended not to need in the country smothered him in the city. I could not help wondering if he wished me back to the country, simply to preserve my image of him there.

"I promise dear heart," I said with a sad smile, "I will return to my little hamlet, and when you marry Lady Alice, you may forget me. I will fade away."

"Ah my Eva, I never forget you. Sometimes I wish I could," he said more quietly looking at me with something akin to heartache. I looked at him confused. I did not notice Duke Garrett stop to wait for us until we were almost level with him.

"Come. You lag, and I happen to know if we ride quickly, we can perhaps take in different sort of play this afternoon."

"Ah what do you propose?" Edmund asked, shaking off his melancholy.

"The Royal Surry is playing a dramatization of Oliver Twist. It has been rumored at times Mr. Dickens attends the performance and shows his displeasure at the plagiarism of his work."

"Let's do go," I said, looking to Julia, trying to push back my loathing of her to be civil.

"I suppose, if Papa agrees."

The Lark

    With that we all rode toward Uncle's townhouse. Mercifully Duke Garrett stayed by my side, so I did not have to engage in another tête-à-tête with Edmund.

Chapter Ten

To my great surprise, Uncle agreed to the scheme, appointing Edmund mine and Julia's guardian for the outing. He sent a footman and Miss Bolton with us, so all was proper. The only instruction he gave regarded us being back early, for he required Edmund's company for a time before we went to the card party at one of the cabinet member's home.

The evening was important to Uncle's career, he did not wish to arrive more than fashionably late. Julia and I dressed for the theater and Duke Garrett called for us in his largest carriage. Uncle even walked us out, strangely satisfied when Duke Garrett handed Julia up, and Edmund helped me into the carriage. I took the seat next to the window and forced Miss Bolton to take the center so I did not have to sit by Julia. Miss Bolton looked at me shrewdly, but I looked out the window so as not to meet her eye. After we started moving, I remembered my manners and took the opportunity to introduce Miss Bolton to the group. My Abigail being only ten years older than me nearly looked a part of our outing.

"I knew of some Bolton's, in Sussex County. A barony I believe," Mr. Percival said after the introductions took place.

"Yes, my grandfather was quite prominent in that part of the county," she agreed. Miss Bolton looked out the carriage window to hide her blush. Her father was a second son and she was a fourth daughter. He was land rich but ran out of income before he could provide for her. Her brother and my father had been friends at school. After her father died, her brother was unable to support her, with the taxing weight of his growing family. He sent Miss Bolton, highly educated, to live with me as my governess when my

73

mother died. She would be with me always, whether we were spinsters together, or she one day helped me raise my children. We would always be together.

"Are you Miss Grey's companion?" Mr. Percival asked, pushing the issue.

"Her Abigail," Miss Bolton responded.

"But you are too high ranked to be Abigail to the daughter of a country–"

"Eva, give me a synopsis of Oliver Twist," Edmund said, glaring at Mr. Percival.

"Ah, a young orphan boy is starving and does whatever is necessary for food and belonging," I summed up, as I looked from Mr. Percival to Miss. Bolton, confused. Suddenly my relationship with Miss Bolton didn't make sense. Was she my superior? Did she need money so badly she agreed to be the Abigail of a lowly Baronet's daughter? Certainly, if she chose to be a companion to a titled lady, she could have chosen much higher in status. Not to mention higher pay with less work. I did not know what her arrangement with my father was. I took her arm, defensively grateful she stayed with me, even after I'd grown. Clearly, she had the skills and social level to go to a top family. I'd inherited so much, I would share some of my pin money with her. Only that relieved my conscience of the sacrifice she'd obviously made for me without my even realizing it. The carriage pulled up in front of the theater. The building was not so beautifully designed as the Theatre Royal, but it was large. Julia and I were far overdressed and stayed close to Miss Bolton who stood up straight, looking fiercely at anyone who came too close to us. She allowed Duke Garrett to guide her through the entrance. Edmund followed us, and Mr. Percival looked around nervously.

The crowd at this theater was not as refined as that of Drury Lane, and I supposed if my uncle understood where we were going, he would not have let us come. His head full of Parliament, and politics, he rarely looked beyond. Soon seated on a balcony, we watched as Oliver Twist came alive. Though the boy playing him was older than Dickens's protagonist, it was well done, and I would have enjoyed it immensely, but audience participation made that impossible. The audience became loud and unruly, even threatening and frightening at times when the lower classes saw something they did not like. Dressed as we were, we stood out, and every one of us grew visibly uncomfortable. If we had taken a tally, I believe we would have left at an interval. Instead we pretended to each other that we were enjoying ourselves while the orphan starved on stage, along with gaunt faces in the audience. For all the different social levels in our group, none of us had ever wanted. The jovial temperaments we'd walked in with dimmed. When the play ended, we walked out of the balcony as inconspicuously as possible. I felt Miss Bolton's hand on my arm as we walked. Her grip was tense and she did not stop looking around at the crowd thronging us. Julia whimpered and moved between us taking both mine and Miss Bolton's arm. Mr. Percival came up behind Julia, closer than propriety considered appropriate, and yet, none of us were uncomfortable with the action. Duke Garrett moved into my side and Edmund into Miss Bolton's. Edmund shoved a man away as he tried to divide him from Miss Bolton, and Julia shrieked. The man landed on another man and they started punching each other. Edmund took Miss Bolton's arm and hurried forward as the men started launching themselves in our direction. I felt the tug as a different man grabbed Duke Garrett's arm. He pushed the man back, proving a strength, I had not anticipated. Duke Garrett was not able to regain his balance before a man in front of us grabbed my arm, wrenching me away from Julia. Mr. Percival, close as he was, blocked his friend from reaching Julia. He did not mince actions and swung out expertly. The man dropped where he stood. Clearly more accustomed to the rougher crowds, Mr. Percival hit two more men until the crowd gave him a wide berth. The action saved Julia but jostled me further back into the horde. I connected eyes with Miss Boulton, who scrambled toward me but Edmond wrestled her toward the door. My assailant, a strong man who clearly worked in physical labor, yanked me by the arm.

"Bet a pretty girl like you'd fetch me a coin or two," he said, putrid breath in my face, dragging me further away from my friends. He did not seem concerned with pulling my arm from the socket, or even breaking a bone. I turned desperately, shoving the man away from me, using the other members of the crowd against him. Another man grabbed me, trying to pull me away from the first. I felt a strong arm around my waist, and moved to strike its owner, but looked over my shoulder to see Duke Garrett pulling me behind him with one arm, and planting his fist in the first man's face with the other. I ducked behind him but held to his jerking waist as he threw his fists, so the mob could not separate us. Before the men could come again, Duke Garrett pulled out a handful of coins and threw them in the opposite direction. The color of golden pounds caught in the air, and everything went silent. The spell broke and the crowd skittered toward the coins. Duke Garrett swayed like a wave hit him at the onslaught but did not budge. When the crowd loosened up, Duke Garrett pulled me to the side of him, putting an arm around me. My arms stayed wrapped around him so that I could not be pried away again. He almost carried me back to our group, all heading quickly out the door. Back on the street, we stepped out of the way of the doors spewing people from them. Duke Garrett turned me to look at him. He put both hands on my shaking shoulders, and I forgot everything except the way he searched me.

"Are you—"

"Thank you, thank you," I said, trying not to cry.

"We need to get out of here," Miss Bolton said sternly, watching the door. Duke Garrett nodded, but instead of letting Miss Bolton take her place at my side, he gestured for her to move in front of us with Edmund and took my arm above my elbow. Julia curled into Mr. Percival who kept one arm around her and quickly moved her forward, outstripping us all. We did not wait for the carriage to come to us. Duke Garrett directed Mr. Percival forward while keeping a strong hand on my arm. Mr. Percival led us down the street where the carriage waited. He looked cautiously into every shop door and alleyway, tense and ready to strike, like a stray cat. We said nothing as we moved, but Julia cried and I shook. Mr. Percival did not let go of Julia. He looked to be half carrying her. None of us thought his protection of her improper, considering the look on his face. No one would come near them. Edmund followed his sister, taking Miss Bolton's arm, but both seemed to be on the high alert and neither seemed the worse for wear.

"Are you all right?" Duke Garrett asked in my ear, and I could not be sure who was in higher distress, me or him.

"I think so," I said.

"I… I cannot imagine… I did not mean for this to–"

"This was not your fault. I wished to see the play immensely," I said looking up at him.

"Everything in my makeup as a gentleman tells me that I just put you in harm's way. I have no right to your good opinion," he said.

"You saved me, I … I do not know what I would have done without you," I said. My breathing increasing as I tried not to cry, and I leaned back into his shoulder. For just a moment he pulled me in closer, moving his grasp to my other arm so my back rested against his chest. Any onlooker would have supposed I stumbled into him, but I felt embraced in the action.

He said: "I cannot forgive myself." He released me, stepping to the outside of the walk to shield me as a man on his horse flew by us.

"I do not remember you forcing me into the theater and making me watch a play," I said.

"No, perhaps not, but I put you in my carriage, and –"

"That is using the term 'put me into your carriage' very liberally. If you had not brought me, and I chanced to hear of it some other way, there is every possibility I would have persuaded Miss Bolton to do so. What trouble would I have been in then?"

"Please do not ever go back to that place," he said moving closer to me in a protective stance.

"I can promise you I will not. You must promise me you will not harbor these feelings of self-deprecation over the matter."

"How can I not?" he asked.

"Why must you?" I returned.

"I want to…I do not know how to live up to the responsibility I have been given, but I am certain bringing you into a riotous situation was not acceptable in my duty to you."

"You take too much upon yourself," I said.

"I swear I will do better by you from now on," he looked at me intently.

"Eva, do not fall behind," Miss Bolton snapped, turning back to retrieve me. Duke Garrett took my arm and we proceeded forward.

"This dukedom must be weighing heavily on you," I said.

"I do not, or rather I cannot, disappoint those counting on me. I feel like a lie. I am playing at being a duke instead of actually being of use to people."

"You are doing better than you can know. I heard you argued in favor of England's moral obligation to allow China to rid themselves of their massive opium addiction. Uncle called you a fool for arguing against the fight with China. He does not care if the drug is addling all the Chinese's brains, he wants his tea. But I thought it very noble of you."

"They all think I've lost my faculties, but I've seen the effects of opium. It is nasty, and dependence on it ruins people. It is not legal here. Why shouldn't China have the same protection for their own?"

"I am proud of you," I said turning to look up at him.

"Yes, I can imagine this is my finest moment," he said tilting his head forward to beckon me toward the coach because now Edmund and Miss Bolton eyed us.

"Perhaps life cannot always be measured by the moments without turmoil, but rather the moments we fight our way through the turmoil, instead of giving up."

"Ah, Miss Grey, who is very wise, will not allow me to be overly critical of myself. Was there ever a woman your equal?"

"My aunt will tell you how far above me Julia is if you'd like to confer with her on the matter," I said squirming at how insecure I sounded mentioning my cousin.

"I do not like your aunt," Duke Garrett said bluntly. I could not respond. We were at the carriage. Mr. Percival loaded Julia in. Duke Garrett kept his hand on my arm until I was safely into his carriage.

Chapter Eleven

Miss Bolton put an arm around me as I slid into the carriage next to her. Edmund climbed into the carriage, reaching out to squeeze my hand.

"Can I do anything for you, Eva?" he asked.

"No, I have come to no harm, thank you."

He nodded but did not let go of my hand. "I am so glad."

"I am whole," I said nodding and sliding my hand away. I sat as far back in my seat as I could. Miss Bolton sat close to me and the menacing scowl on her face could not be ignored. We drove away. Her grip on me tightened. I started to fear she would insist we leave for my father's home within the hour.

"That was unacceptable," Miss Bolton snapped as she put an arm around Julia who shivered as if she had a chill.

"I should have patronized the theater before I suggested it. I apologize," Duke Garrett said, looking abashed. I could not bear Miss Bolton, whom I loved so well, glaring at Duke Garrett.

"I feel like I took home the point," I said.

"What point is that, Eva?" Edmund asked.

"Human nature, and how the same amiable qualities are in the finest lord and the dirtiest charity-boy," I summed up.

"Oh, Eva," Miss Bolton said.

"Mr. Percival, I think you may have the most impressive amiable qualities I've witnessed. I was distracted by the gentleman who was so desirous of my company. How many men did you drop to the ground?" I asked.

"That is not clever," Miss Bolton said over the top of Mr. Percival responding: "A few," and coloring.

"Do you play at fisticuffs?" Edmund asked, glancing over at the man he sat next to.

"I had my education at school," he said.

"As did we all," Duke Garrett said. Edmund didn't seem to understand the two, but considering each grew up without the benefits of an Earl as a father, they must have shared some understanding only school boys could. "Remind me never to wager against you," Edmund said.

We were quiet for some time then Duke Garrett addressed me. "Dickens started a new series last week in "Master Humphrey's Clock." It is entitled The Old Curiosity Shop. Have you read it?"

"No, Uncle does not subscribe to anything aside from the political news," I said.

"My father will collect them for me." "You may borrow mine," Duke Garrett said.

"I will get her a copy," Edmund said, glaring.

"You need not go to the expense. I already have one that I am finished with," Duke Garrett said. It looked like he was baiting Edmund, but to what end I could not tell.

"It is no expense for me. I have money enough to live on and support my cousin with whatever she may need," Edmund snapped.

"Yes, but the expense may grow tiresome with the flowers I have heard you are sending Lady Alice. I dare say you may empty the hothouses entirely," Duke Garrett said.

"That is my business and a gentleman does not interfere with another gentleman's affairs," Edmund snapped.

"Yes, precisely. So I will be happy to send Miss Grey my copy of *Master Humphrey's Clock*," Duke Garrett countered.

81

"She is my cousin and I will get her a copy before you can have yours sent so do not even bother with the kindness," Edmund said, gritting his teeth.

"I uh… Thank you Edmund," I said to stop the fighting, but I could not help the slight smile I gave Duke Garrett. Did he see me as his affair in the same way Edmund saw Lady Alice? When the carriage stopped, Duke Garrett climbed down and offered his hand to me. He took my hand in one of his, and my elbow in the other, the action brought me in close to him as I stepped down. I could not stop the smile from erupting on my face.

"Thank you," I said with little breath, certain he could feel the heat I radiated. Unconsciously I reached up and straightened his cravat that had gone askew in the brawl.

"Thank you," he said. He looked just as red as I did. Miss Bolton and Julia came next, but Edmund, who looked anxious, jumped out over his sister. Edmund took my arm and pulled me away from next to Duke Garrett.

"Good evening," I said quickly. I walked away.

"I'll wish you good evening, with the promise of seeing you tonight," Duke Garrett said as I tried to look back at him, with little success. The bruise on my arm throbbed acutely where Edmund pulled me, in the same manner as the brute at the theater had. Climbing back into the carriage, Duke Garrett left to take Mr. Percival to his lodgings.

"I need my horse," Edmund said, turning to his father's footman when they were out of sight.

"Father wished to speak with you," Julia reminded him.

"He should have been home when he scheduled to meet with me then," Edmund returned.

"You can send her a note making your excuses," Julia said. Miss Bolton and I grinned, but then I stopped. Edmund looked at me, with an intensity that burned.

"What can I do?" he asked me, as if I could tell him. Confusion colored my face. How did I know where his duty lay?

"I suppose you must decide which consequence you most wish to avoid," I said. Then I turned to go into the house. He had no right to put me in the middle of his relationship with his father or the lady he courted. I was his lowly country relation whom he clearly did not mean to court. Yet, he spoke and looked at me as if he did mean to. Even worse, he meant to scare off Duke Garrett, who did not seem to mind my lowly heredity. Julia and Miss Bolton entered after me, but Edmund did not.

Chapter Twelve

At the entrance hall, Julia took Miss Bolton's arm. She seemed to need human contact, so we all ascended the stairs to the third floor where the family bedrooms were. Miss Bolton and I entered her room and helped her out of her boots and dress. Her bedroom was the coloring of a white puppy with a light pink nose. The bed looked like a large white throne, only longer so she could lie down. Her pink bedding matched the curtains. The dressing table, mirror, and other chairs and pictures were all white with pink accents. The room was delicate and fine like Julia. Julia laid down talking about all that passed until she finally fell asleep. Miss Bolton took me up the stairs to the room we shared in the gabled section of the roof. Our cots were pushed against opposite walls. A tall window occupied the center of the wall. My overly large roses decorated a small dressing table that sat in front of the window. Our trunks were at the foot of the bed. A wardrobe had been shoved into the corner across from the stairs, but it did not fit, nor did it seem to belong. Miss Bolton sat me in front of the dressing table and helped me expose my arm where the brute had grabbed me. It bruised into long dark fingers just above my elbow.

"I think you will have to be a touch old-fashioned this evening and cover it with full length gloves. One of your older dresses with high sleeves will do for them."

"I like my pink," I said.

"As you should," she said smiling. "Tomorrow I will adjust a few of the three-quarter sleeves with lace to cover the bruising sufficiently. Let us get through this evening before we worry about it," she said. She examined my arm again.

"I am sorry about today, Myra. I should not have been so insistent we go," I said. She stopped and closed her eyes.

"When that man took you, I was left so helpless."

"He was so strong I could not get free of him," I said, shivering.

"I would have died if anything happened to you. How could I face your father knowing you were harmed? Not to mention your grandfather haunting me for all my days."

"I promise I will use more caution," I said.

"Thank you, Eva," she said.

"Myra," I asked as she released my corset so I could relax.

"Yes dear," she said putting a cold cloth on my arm. "Are you too high in station to be my Abigail?"

"No dear, we are ... your aunt would only allow you to come with a lady's maid ... not a companion for a motherless girl ...."

"Why would she not allow the woman who raised me in my mother's place?" I asked, leaning against her.

"People would talk. As your mother's sister, she should have taken on responsibilities that she has not. It would be obvious to her acquaintances she did not do certain things for you if you came to town with a companion," she said.

"I am sorry you have to do so much here," I said. I looked at her hands burned and withering from the work required of her.

"Do not concern yourself. I assure you I would never have let you come alone," she said. She pushed back the hair on my forehead to kiss it.

"I could hire another Abigail if you wish."

"Would we get her a pallet to sleep on the floor between us?" Miss Bolton asked looking around the small space.

The Lark

"I suppose there isn't room," I said.

"No, dear. Besides, your aunt would not ... your grandfather meant for me to protect you. Especially if anyone ever found out how much money you could be worth," she said.

"Do you wish for some of my pin money? You could have whatever you want," I said.

"I already have all I've ever wanted, dear," she said.

"Um, my father pays you well enough?"

"Extravagantly, besides, I have a family. I have a comfortable home. I am respected and welcomed at family dinners. After my mother died, I needed a family. You and your father are my family. Please try not to worry about what Mr. Percival said."

"I will, but I don't want you to feel like ... I want you to...." "Be a part of your family. I am dearest. Now put these thoughts from your head and take a rest. We must start to get ready in half an hour."

"All right. I love you," I said, lying down.

"I love you, too," she said.

"Today was scary."

"Yes it was," she said taking my hand. "It was terrifying."

"Please don't blame Duke Garrett; he has a tendency toward over-blaming himself."

"I will try. The greatest kindness I can show His Grace is not to tell your uncle, nor your father, about this," she said.

"Yes," I agreed, feeling myself growing drowsy. The next thing I knew, I awoke, feeling better. Miss Bolton still slept on her cot, so I crawled out of bed quietly. I sat at the dressing table and examined the bruises on my arm that had only grown in intensity while I slept.

I found a letter from my father on the table that had not been there before. I sat quietly near the window and read: *My girl, how goes your season? Have you taken*

86

pleasure in witnessing the pomp and lifestyle of your cousins? Do you see much of Edmund? He is a particular favorite of mine and if you do see him, let him know he will be invited for Christmas if he chooses to come. How do you find the duke? Is he as awe-inspiring as your Aunt seemed to think he would be? My father would have been intrigued to know his friend's grandson rose to such a position, considering the interesting grandeur that is suddenly heaped upon one who inherits a title they were not trained for. Pray send word of the anomaly that I may better understand his dilemma. Indeed, Kant himself would certainly be intrigued in the idea of a situation changing so dramatically. Do you think the man's new experiences will rewrite his persona? Is innocence to be left behind, perhaps rewriting his moral code? His posteriori knowledge will, no doubt, improve him in the eyes of the Ton, but perhaps degrade him in the eyes of God where he stands as the cobbler's equal. Even if they get the duke, darling, don't let them get you. See through the glamour, and set downs, the intrigue and wealth. Do write and divert me with such ideas, proving you are still immune to them. I am miserable without your discussion. I even consider whether to take a house in London to spy on you whilst you improve your own posteriori knowledge. Oh darling, do not let them ruin you, and the perfect indifference myself and your grandfather strove to place in your sense of morality and reason. As always your loving father, LG

I smiled at his perfectly written nonsense and answered immediately. "Dearest Papa, I suppose I must own not having my dance card filled as it would be if I were an earl's daughter does put a damper on my social experience, but is not this experience enlightening? The duke whom you expressed interest in remains an echo of his time as an insignificant baron, and even dared to dance with the earl's lowly country relation, in a room full of

87

nobility. He is a fan of Dickens and took a group of us to a plagiarized production of Oliver Twist. I like him, but don't concern yourself. I do not see his disinterested attention toward me as anything but a favor to his grandfather. Still, I am excessively proud of him for making the gesture. His grandfather is marvelous. If you come to town simply for the re-acquaintance of that man, it would be well worth the ride. Most of Aunt's acquaintances are what you would expect. The pretense of perfection, swallowing up the glimpses they give at individuality. Though I am reluctant to say that is who they are simply because that is the experience they are having. My cousin Julia at times dares a little wit, but only when her brother is present and her mother is not. She could be moderately clever if she gave herself the chance. Edmund, as always, is diverting in small doses, but is so often called upon by his father he cannot be examined in more than the one-act play which suits him. I cannot help at times giving into the unflattering experience of being of a lower station than my cousin. I am making a concerted effort not to lose myself to the sensation. I am perfectly capable of seeing the greater reason of the philosophers I have studied. I feel the tutelage of my dearest loved ones. You and grandfather will not be undone by my season in town and I remain ever yours, EG."

I closed my letter and sealed it. I felt deceitful for not admitting my mortification at not having partners to dance with, or my growing complex when Julia was around Duke Garrett, but I did not want to worry him. He always expected more than honesty from me. He expected my confidences on every subject. At times, my upbringing felt like an experiment of the human mind. My father spent years studying. Everything we did had to be educational and something that forced the mind into occupation. Yet, for a man who prided himself in sense, he also shifted toward romanticism at times, a notion my grandfather found rather appalling in his heir.

Chapter Thirteen

I woke Miss Bolton only when it was time to tighten my corset. She couldn't believe she'd slept so long, and turned to my dressing with vigor. She barely had my hair up into ringlet's when I was called to leave.

"Do try to eat something," she said and I nodded. I put on my Palette Sac before Aunt could see I wore my own salmon gown that showed my figure to full advantage and brought out hints of red in my dark hair. Most importantly, it allowed for the gloves that fully covered the very distinct fingerlike bruises on my arm. Julia climbed into the carriage and sat next to me. We looked at each other, and I smiled. She returned my smile, almost proud we had a secret between us, and seemed in higher spirits than when I left her.

"Did Edmund make an excuse for his departure?" Uncle asked when the door was closed, and he was free of the servants.

"He apologized profusely to you, Father. He sent his most sincere–"

"That will do Julia," he dismissed. Fumbling in his overcoat he said, "These should get you through the evening. They are only betting shillings since the ladies are participating." Uncle handed Julia and myself each a purse full of coins, "if you lose too quickly, they will have parlor games, I am sure."

"I will not bet extravagantly, sir," Julia said.

"I have a knack for charades," I said because they looked to me as if I should be required to say something.

"If you lose all that money–"

"My Lady," Uncle Claremont Hull interrupted, "there are many of my acquaintance who asked if Eva will be allowed in our venue. She plotted so well with Lord

90

Devon at Lord Holland's ball last evening they are hoping for a chance at their money back."

"Then you will be sure to lose, Eva," Aunt scolded.

"I think you must make up your mind. Should she win or lose?" Uncle asked. Aunt thought for a long moment and then said: "Lose slowly."

"Take them for all they are willing to part with and I will double your earnings," Uncle said.

I smiled. "This night is our first invitation to Lord Harley's home," Aunt complained. "Yes, and he is a relic who has far too much luck at the club. Eva should take his money if she can."

"I have met his son before," Julia said before the conversation could turn into an argument. "In fact both Eva and I danced with him last night at Lord Holland's ball."

I looked at her confused. "You remember, the very large Viscount," Julia said with a glint in her eye. "Ah, yes," I said realizing I'd almost been trampled twice since coming to London.

"Yes, his eldest son, the Viscount, is away."

"His horse must be a sturdy creature to carry him very far," I said.

"Eva," Aunt snapped. Uncle laughed. Julia smirked.

"I apologize ma'am. I swear it is out of my system and I will not mention the poor creature again."

"You will not mention the Viscount at all," Aunt said, "I believe Lord Harley has another son who does not mingle often in society. This may be an opportunity for you unlike any other, Eva."

"His second son will be there," Uncle said, "he does not mingle as often as his brother because he is working for Oxfordshire as one of the newest, and youngest MP's."
"MP, what is that?" Julia asked before I could be brought up again.

"An elected Member of Parliament in the House of Commons," Uncle said slowly as if he did not expect her to understand.

"I did not know you associated with members of that institution," Julia said.

"It is true. In the past, I have been occupied with the House of Lords, but it would seem tides are turning and soon the Lords will not be able to wipe our noses without permission from the House of Commons," he said irritated. "This evening must go smoothly."

We all nodded. Aunt glared at me as if she thought I would single-handedly ruin everything.

At Lord Harley's, we were shown into a terrace home not far from Uncle's. The footman took our cloaks, and when Aunt saw my dress, she glared at me again. I felt pretty when I checked my mirror before we left. Aunt took that from me. I felt ridiculous and old-fashioned. We were greeted by a large gentleman, almost the size of Viscount Harley, but he slouched at his rounded muscular shoulders and his robust belly hung over his tight breeches. His cheeks were rosy, his eyes bright and he held himself with an amusement that his son, even on the dance floor, lacked. His second son also greeted us. He stood as high in stature as his father, but the resemblance stopped there. An extremely trim man with rim glasses, he nearly drowned in his breeches.

"Lord Harley, Mr. Harley, you know Lady Claremont Hull. May I introduce my daughter Lady Julia Claremont Hull," Uncle said.

The younger bowed extravagantly, his thin body folding like a card table. "And this is my niece, Miss Eva Grey," Uncle said.

"Is this the daughter of your brother, Sir?" Lord Harley asked, watching me.

"No," Aunt said. "She is the daughter of my sister, and her husband the Baronet of Dorsetshire."

"Yes, the son of the philosopher," he said, "but her surname." "She is no relation to the past Prime Minister," Aunt said.

"Actually, I believe she is distantly related. We hope her father is to come to London. I would be happy to put him in your company that you might ask him of the relationship," Uncle said.

"Yes, and perhaps Lady Claremont Hull would find it of interest as well," the older man said looking closely at my uncle who gave half a smile, "And is your brother, Lord Hull, to come to town?"

"No, he passed away last year. That is why we spent the little season and winter in mourning," Uncle said. I turned to look at him. I had not heard his older brother died. Did my father know? He could not. We would have sent our sympathies if we knew. As a woman, I was not allowed at Grandfather's funeral, but Uncle came. He wore his heredity and as they followed the hearse to the churchyard, he even marched with the primary mourners. I felt sick I had not even known his brother died. I made a mental note to write to Father as soon we returned home. Then, in the strangest action, the older man bowed extravagantly to me folding himself over with a great effort. I curtsied back looking to Uncle feeling something was unsaid. We were invited to explore the rooms until we found our game. Lord Harley took up his place next to Aunt Claremont Hull but turned back to be sure I followed him with Julia. Uncle Claremont Hull took up the rear. We went into the large drawing room, papered green, a huge golden framed looking glass stood on the wall across from the fireplace. The looking glass could not find the furniture that ordinarily occupied it, but instead reflected six foreign tables set up with cards.

"I would very much like to play quadrilles," Julia said looking to me to confirm I would be her partner. I smiled and nodded in agreement, feeling important to her. We were halfway through the room when a strange and abrupt movement caught my attention. At the very back of the room, Edmund and his lady both stood from their table.

"Lady Claremont Hull," Lady Alice said, moving toward our group. Edmund followed behind her.

"And you are here, are you sir?" Uncle asked. He pushed around Julia and I to glare at his heir.

"Yes, excuse me, Sir," Edmund said bowing. Uncle waited as if an explanation should have accompanied his apology, but none came.

"Miss Grey," Edmund said, not even acknowledging his mother or sister. His formal address was undone completely by his overly familiar examination of my person,

"Perhaps you and Julia would like to make up a quadrille with Lady Alice and myself?"

"You forget sir, we are three. My younger sister will make up the fourth," Lady Alice said speaking a touch too loud, and in a higher pitch than she normally used.

"Excuse me, Miss Grey." Julia and I both looked over at the younger Miss Holland, already engaged in a game of whist at a different table. She seemed to be the only one in the room who hadn't noticed the altercation.

"I would have Edmund as my partner at Speculation, making your teams even," Uncle commanded. "Come, Sir."

Lady Alice looked from Edmund to his father. Speculation didn't need partners. She gave Edmund a haughty raise of the eyebrow. She clearly thought he ought to make his excuses to his father.

Perhaps Edmund could not defy him twice in one day because he said, "Of course Father. Please forgive me, Lady Alice." As Edmund slid past our group, he paused and looked apologetically at me. Uncle practically shoved his son past us. I looked at Julia for an explanation, but was stopped when Lady Alice said: "If we are to admit another, I was hoping you would join our group, Lady Claremont Hull." Her loud, high-pitched voice betrayed distress and made it clear she did not mean for me to be of their group.

"Of course, my dear, I would be honored," Aunt said. She turned and pushed Julia in front of her, walking them both toward the table in the back. Julia kept glancing at me unsure why her mother would leave me alone in a stranger's home. Lady Alice leaned toward me and said:

"I do so desire to be in Lady Claremont Hull's company, for there ought to be an intimacy between us superior even to yours. You understand Miss Grey?" Her tone had turned as icy as her facial expression. What happened? She was so amiable to me at the ball.

"Of course," I answered, unsure what I was supposed to do, separated from my group. Clearly embarrassed by Lady Alice and my Aunt, Lord Harley said kindly "Miss Grey, we have parlor games set up in the library, or if you would join us in the dining room, we play Speculation."

"Or perhaps she will consent to be my partner," Duke Garrett said from behind me. I turned, along with those at the tables he called over to get my attention. He was framed in the doorway. I felt him a magnificent sight but could not explain the tears at the back of my throat. I tried to smile, but my heightened color gave me away. I could only bow my head in ascent and complete gratitude. I walked quickly toward Duke Garrett weaving through the tables of players. Both Aunt and Julia looked up from their table but could not leave Lady Alice nor the hand being dealt them. Duke Garrett stood with the younger Mr. Harley, and I wondered how much of Lady Alice's snub he witnessed. It must have been all because when I reached him he said to Mr. Harley: "Miss Grey played last night with my grandfather and he claimed her to be a most successful strategist."

"In that case, I insist she join our table, Duke Garrett."

The younger Mr. Harley bowed his long body in half and I was much reminded of a stick breaking. "I will join your table as well, son," Lord Harley said, winded, having followed me with great effort, and much apologies to those he rammed into on his way to the large doorway of the room. He looked as if he would give me his arm, but Duke Garrett already extended his arm. I glanced once more toward Lady Alice, trying to understand her. We had been so civil last evening. I caught her eye. She glared at me with malice. Her overly large nose made her look like a bird of prey. What had I done to deserve the lady's ire? Duke Garrett turned me, and I felt him squeeze my hand in the crook of his arm. I leaned into him as we walked toward the dining room, and my anxious heart relaxed. I breathed in his scent of lavender and felt the world right itself. Both Uncle and Edmund looked up at our entrance. Uncle looked confused, Edmund chagrined. I smiled at them both and allowed Duke Garrett to pull out my chair.

"Are you familiar with Speculation?" Lord Harley asked, taking the seat next to me.

"Yes, my grandfather was a cards enthusiast," I said.

"I enjoyed his work," Lord Harley said.

"What work did her grandfather do?" The younger Mr. Harley asked.

"Her grandfather, Henry Grey the philosopher, built on many of Kant's ideas," the elder said.

"The experience is the man," the younger Mr. Harley ventured.

"Yes, among his earlier works he built upon that to be quite prolific," the elder said. "Dealer antes six," he said putting his coins in the pot, "and four to the rest."

We all put in.

"I am sorry my oldest son is not here to meet you, Miss Grey. I think you would enjoy meeting him," Lord Harley said.

"I believe we have crossed paths," I said quietly. Duke Garrett cleared his throat, and I smiled knowing he understood my quip.

"Really! Capital!" Lord Harley responded. "Victor is no philosopher," Mr. Harley said, and he sounded like Julia when her father wished for Edmund unless he needed his tea poured. "I did not refer to him because he is interested in philosophizing, but rather that he might beat her at cards. I have heard she is quite impressive," he said bowing to me.

"I am better pleased with Mr. Harley, who is interested in philosophizing with me, and won't begrudge me his anti," I said, grinning mischievously.

"Here, here," Lord Harley said laughing. Duke Garrett gave me a look like I might have crossed a line. Mr. Harley chuckled but seemed to be deciding if he should be offended.

"You are a clever thing," Lord Harley said.

"Thank you, and in all seriousness, if your eldest son is as pleasant a fellow as your second, I can only hope to further our acquaintance," I said bowing slightly to the son before me with my most charming smile. Mr. Harley smiled at me, and I glanced at Duke Garrett to be sure I had done enough to fix the situation. He gave me a shadow of a head nod, and I knew he was pleased I recompensed my insult so quickly. Feeling content, I happened to glance at Uncle who sat in my line of sight at the other table. He stared at me. His face looked out of sorts. Had he heard me insult his friend's son after he'd told me how important this

The Lark

evening was? I quickly looked down at the four cards
accumulated front of me, hoping we could play instead of
talk. Mr. Harley seemed a little too sensitive for my sharp
tongue. Lord Harley tipped his card to a five of hearts.

"Who will buy it?" he asked.

"I will, Father," Mr. Harley said. Both Duke
Garrett and I looked at him wondering if he was playing by
some obscure set of rules we did not know. Duke Garrett,
who sat directly across from me, grinned, and I could not
help a smile to answer back. My smile fell. Behind Duke
Garrett, Uncle examined me. He looked very
concerned. We locked eyes and Uncle shook his head in
the negative. I looked down immediately trying not to be
humiliated. Did he think it inappropriate of me to smile for
a duke? Perhaps he worried I was setting myself above my
station? I tried to shrug off his obvious reprimand, but
Lord Harley, who seemed fascinated by me, had also seen
my uncle's look and watched me to see how I reacted. I
refocused on our game and won the round with an eight of
hearts. On our second round, Mr. Harley revealed the Ace
of hearts that could not be beaten. Just then Uncle and
Edmund's companions, two older men, looked out of sorts,
stood and excused themselves.

"We have lost our game. Perhaps we can join
yours," Uncle, said moving over. I could tell from the
disgruntled looks on his retreating companion's faces, he'd
done something to provoke their moving to the third table
in the room.

"Of course," Lord Harley said.

Duke Garrett stood so two footmen could pull the
tables together.

"That is not necessary. Edmund, you sit next to Eva,
and I will sit by His Grace," Uncle said bowing. Duke
Garrett and I stood and the footman adjusted the chairs. It
was snug, but not terribly tight, as Lord Harley must have
his tables made to fit his girth. Duke Garrett looked

98

disgruntled, and I decided he did not like Uncle so close as he dealt.

"Ah, bad luck old boy," Edmund said when he turned over a two of spades. Duke Garrett looked like he wanted to say something. Instead, he caught my eye, which was not hard because I watched him. I looked at him with commiseration, but when he saw my concern, his face turned mischievous. Duke Garrett looked at his card, then to me, then flipped his card in his fingers. With the lifting of his eyes, he indicated I should buy his card. I squinted my eyes and gave him a slight head nod indicating I would not be taken in. Then I made a slight glance to Mr. Harley who proved himself a novice at cards.

"Nobody will buy the card," Edmund snapped. I turned to find Edmund watching me.

"Very well," Duke Garrett said, and he laughed like he won anyway and put the card in front of him. No other spades showed so Uncle flipped his card revealing a heart, and Mr. Harley the seven of spades. Edmund tried to buy it at two shillings, and Mr. Harley looked inclined to oblige until Lord Harley clicked his tongue.

"My boy, the game is half played and that is the highest card so far. I will pay six shillings," Lord Harley said hinting to his son the value of his card.

Mr. Harley, a quick learner examined his father and the growing pot and said: "I will keep it. Thank you, Sir."

I flipped a diamond. "Miss Grey have you been to London before this season?" Mr. Harley asked.

"No sir," I said.

"Did you say your father was coming?" Lord Harley asked. "In a letter I received today, he said he may," I said.

"If you asked him to, he would come," Uncle said. I nodded, knowing it was true, but I could not face him. I could not brush off jealousy nor rank distinction, not to mention the affection growing inside me for a man I knew I could not have.

"When did your grandfather pass on?" Lord Harley asked.

"Last June," I said.

"Yes, your father ought to come soon," Lord Harley said looking to Uncle who nodded. An awkward silence held. Lord Harley appeared determined not to explain his sentiment.

"Miss Grey, what has been the most diverting part of the London season? Have you been to a ball?" Mr. Harley asked politely.

"I am very indebted to Duke Garrett's grandfather. Lord Devon has taken me to the theater. I am very fond of Shakespeare," I said.

"Ah, then this is your year. The court has determined the only way to find the next Shakespeare is for his works to be performed."

"Yes, Drury Lane is doing Hamlet first," I said. I turned over a heart and set it down. I hated games that I had no chance of winning except luck and deep pockets.

"What play did you see?" Lord Harley asked.

"Midsummer Night's Dream," I said.

"I'm not familiar with that work. What is it about?" Mr. Harley asked.

"Truth, reason, and love keeping little company together," Duke Garrett quoted almost verbatim.[3] I laughed at the back of my throat.

"That about sums it up," I said. Uncle grew a little red, and I thought he might ignite, but I could not be sure why. "I understand you are an MP in the House of Commons," I said to Mr. Harley, knowing my Uncle who seemed keen on watching me, would perhaps lend his attention elsewhere if I brought up politics.

"Indeed, my grandfather gave me a little-used property that was not entailed in Oxfordshire. I was very fortunate to win the seat," he said.

"With all the changes occurring I suppose the House of Commons is in need of leadership," Uncle said.

"The conservatives will push us back two centuries if we are not careful," Lord Harley said.

"The radicals will have the uneducated masses voting if we are not careful," Uncle said. I noticed Mr. Harley look down uncomfortably. He looked to Duke Garrett who gave him a sly smile of sorts. It was a meeting of the older ideas, while the younger voices seemed content to save their opinions for the arena. I turned over the Jack of Spades.

"Oh, what good luck," Lord Harley exclaimed. "I will buy it from you, Eva," Edmund said.

"How much," I asked, leaning back so I might examine him next to me.

"All my cards," he said.

"I will give you thirty shillings for it," Duke Garrett said.

"That is more than you can win," I said, ready to laugh, but Duke Garrett looked serious and very annoyed. "Yes. Well," Edmund said pulling his coins from his pouch, intent on outbidding Duke Garrett. "I will keep my card," I said looking between them. Uncle looked as well. Neither of us knew what to think. After I won the pot, Edmund picked up my hand in warm congratulations.

"How is Lady Alice this evening?" Duke Garrett asked. As if the very name pricked me, I pulled my hand away.

"She is well," Edmund said flushing, but he set his hand very close to my arm on the table. I worried he would pull on my glove as he did at times. Miss Bolton pinned it at my bicep, but it barely covered my bruised arm. Any slight jostle and the purple-black finger marks would be exposed. I did not want to make that explanation, so I shifted away. Edmund moved as well, his fingers coming so close to my glove, I felt sure he would grab it in the next moment.

"It is warm in here," I said, standing before I could be dealt into the next round.

"Perhaps you would be my partner in quadrilles after all," Duke Garrett said standing.

"Actually, I believe Julia meant for Eva to be her partner," Uncle said standing.

"You are mistaken sir," Duke Garrett said. "I saw Lady Claremont Hull and her daughter teamed up before we came hence, leaving Miss Grey with no table to play at." He pulled my seat away so I could escape.

"It is so," Lord Harley confirmed, "but to our benefit, I have so enjoyed getting to know you, Miss Grey. I would have you back in this home again. Please consider it a firm invitation when your father comes. I am very desirous to meet him."

"Thank you, Sir," I said nodding to him and scooping the last of my coins into my purse. I looked at Uncle to see if he would stop my retreat since Duke Garrett meant to come with me. Uncle glanced at Edmund waiting. Edmund ground his teeth, but kept his face toward his card, unmoving. Unwilling to make a scene, Uncle nodded with a disgruntled air, but his glare toward his son's head could not be mistaken. I took Duke Garrett's arm unsure what just happened. He moved me just as quickly from the dining room as he had the theater earlier in the day.

"Are we going to play cards?" I asked as Duke Garrett moved past the drawing-room door.

"Let us try our hand at the parlor games," he said. "It is a little warm in both those rooms."

"Yes, you are right," I said not wanting to be snubbed by Lady Alice again. "It feels like there is an added tension this evening does it not?" I asked.

Duke Garrett just smiled at me with an exasperated nod and said: "You look very lovely this evening. Is that a new gown?"

"No, rather an older one," I said.

"Yes, well it is flattering," he said glancing at me, but then quickly looking away. I leaned into his arm. He thought I looked pretty. We started our own game of Dominos. Though many people joined us in the library after they could or would gamble no more, Duke Garrett did not allow anyone else into our game. The library smelled musky like leather, and Duke Garrett could strategize as well as myself. I grew extremely comfortable in our situation. I started to think perhaps Uncle was right. I was crossing a line. This thought came after I sat back waiting for Duke Garrett to make his move and dreamt of a snug little room all our own where we could indulge in many more evenings of Dominos.

Chapter Fourteen

The next morning Uncle was in a right state. He sent his footman twice to retrieve Edmund personally but found he was out both times. Finally, he sent a note stating if Edmund did not go to Lord Pennington's political party that evening, he was cut off. Uncle refused to leave the drawing room and instructed the butler to turn callers away. Aunt became sulky without her morning's gossip and started to quarrel with Uncle for quarrelling's sake. Aunt could not make headway in her argument with Uncle. He was clearly put out and meant to push her out as well. Looking for some reprieve, Aunt started in on me.

"Eva, if you start to weary of the pace in town, you need not stay the whole of the season."

"She will stay the season," Uncle snapped at Aunt.

"She is my relation, not yours," Aunt snapped back, "and she is starting to make some of our more intimate friends uncomfortable. Lady Alice refused to play cards with her last evening."

"Did you see the way Edmund looked at her when she entered the room? He could not even attend what the lady was saying," Uncle said.

"That is why Lady Alice forgot her civility."

"Yes, Eva should have kept her wardrobe as I instructed."

"She ought not wear anything that would set her to advantage?" Uncle asked, looking at Aunt, who tried to ignore him to glare at me. He finished, "I seem to recall a time when it worked to your benefit."

"Even more reason Eva should return to the country, at least until after Edmund is married." I watched the two, stunned. Is that what happened?

"Eva, we arranged to ride this morning, did we not," Julia said quickly, seeing there was no smoothing when her parents worked themselves into such states of aggravation.

"That may be best," Uncle said, "you will take my man with you, though. I will not be uninformed where my own family is concerned."

"Yes Sir," Julia said, confused. We were ready quickly, wishing to be out of the house. As we mounted our horses, a chilly wind started. Neither Julia nor I mentioned giving up the ride because the sky mimicked Uncle and Aunt, and we'd rather be tossed about by mother nature.

"We best move quickly before the rain starts," I said.

"Yes," Julia said. We kept our pace a little faster than appropriate, but few people were out to witness us, so we chanced it. As we rode, each of us tried to pretend nothing stood out of the ordinary, though Uncle's man behind us made my skin crawl. Duke Garrett rode up to us at the entrance to the row.

"Ah, I did not think I'd see you today," he said. "I could not find a handicap, please excuse me, Lady Julia." He eyed Uncle's man, who looked like a rat, a man all points and angles. His limp arms barely extended and ended in long curling claw-like fingers that held his reins.

"It is of no importance. We need to get our exercise before the rain falls," Julia said. She glanced self-consciously at Uncle's man and then kicked Pegasus hard. The plume on Julia's riding hat thrashed in the air wildly. I started to chase her, and Duke Garrett followed behind. I felt apprehensive with Duke Garrett racing us. I rationalized he always focused more on winning Julia when we raced, and I didn't think anything underhanded in our meeting him. Would Uncle disapprove Duke Garrett's attention toward Julia, or did he think that connection more appropriate? Somehow everything felt underhanded with

105

Uncle's man watching. Soon I forgot the pointed face trained on us. With prudence abandoned, I delighted riding through the wind until my hair started to fall free and pushed dangerously against the ribbon chinstrap of my topper. I could barely open my eyes against it. The March morning promised to deluge us, and Julia rode hard, like she was being chased. When I could no longer catch my breath against the gale, I stopped to adjust my habit that whipped wildly. Duke Garrett stopped next to me while Uncle's man followed Julia for one last lap.

"I thought you would follow Julia," I said. I glanced quickly to ensure my dress was draped correctly. When Duke Garrett didn't answer I looked up from my task. I stopped. He watched me with an intensity that made my chest expand rapidly.

"Is everything all right?"

"You look like some wild mythical creature," he said, his horse pranced to stay near me. I laughed, unsure how to respond. "I cannot decide whether you are more elfin or fairy-like."

"I prefer pixie. They tend toward making mischief," I said raising my eyebrows at him.

"Yes, I suppose so," he said. He glanced up to see where Julia was. My heart dropped when he stopped to watch her ride. I wondered if he would describe her as an avenging angel in flight; she was such a magnificent sight on her flying white horse. Duke Garrett turned back and noticed me watching him. I blushed and turned to watch Julia, certain the stinging in my eyes was due to the wind.

"Did Julia mention where Mr. Percival is today?" Duke Garrett asked. He kept his unnerving glance at me.

"No, he must have been kept in by the weather," I said.

"He must not have thought Julia would ride," he said, watching me.

"Well that is his loss. This wind is glorious," I said as a gust burst over me, picking up my hair and whipping it around my face, playing with me.

"Yes, it is," he said. He circled his anxious horse around me because the animal would no longer stay still. Julia rode back to us. "I suppose we must go home," Julia said looking at me.

"I suppose," I said. Duke Garrett saw the reluctance between us, but only said:

"Please allow me to accompany you." Julia nodded and we trotted to the entrance to the park and back to Uncle's house. Duke Garrett kept trying to stay to the right of us, but brush overlying the back road we took made it awkward. We ended up with Julia and me on each side of Duke Garrett.

"How did you enjoy cards last evening?" Duke Garrett called to Julia so she could hear him over the wind.

"Very well, Your Grace. And you?" Julia responded.

"It was a pleasant evening, though Lady Alice Holland looked out of sorts," Duke Garrett replied, turning to me. I quickly looked out toward the sound of a bird fighting against the wind. It screeched in fear of the storm coming. I could not find the lovely lark to calm my racing heart.

"She was rather displeased. Edmund has been her companion since the end of last season. It is hard for her to compete for his attention," Julia called, glancing at me.

"Yes, but certainly your father had precedence last evening," I yelled and looked away again, certain if I could find a lark fighting against the wind, we could fly away together.

"Certainly," Julia said with a laugh.

"I enjoyed our game of Dominoes, Duke Garrett," I called. "I think you may have let me win."

The Lark

"I am not ashamed to admit you outmaneuvered me. If you had not, I may have let you win. When a lady looks as you did last night, she ought not lose," he called back, leaning his horse toward me to be sure I heard him. But the wind quieted suddenly and even my uncle's man, riding at a respectful distance, must have heard me say:

"Or rather the impish pixie ought to lose. The loss would be an adequate check for her pride."

"I think you were set down sufficiently for that not to have been a concern," he said, examining my face to be sure I had recovered.

"I think her set downs were rather a confirmation, perhaps even a compliment of how far to the advantage she looked, especially to the plainer daughter of a marquess," Julia said leaning across Duke Garrett to goad me. I smiled at her. I liked it when Julia engaged in our banter.

"Come now," I said, "I am not the sort who can carry such compliments with grace. I shall lose my charm in conceit. Perhaps we should instead let Julia be the very pretty one. I have grown rather fond of my role as the impertinent one."

"You are uncommonly set to advantage on that score," Julia said.

"We all must have our charms," I said and they both laughed for me. I realized Julia smoothed me, being sure her parents had not done injury to me. It was pleasant, and I liked how Julia could catch onto my joking tone to be sure I was comfortable. That seemed a greater proof of her gentility than any dowry could offer. Julia really was a lovely soul, her external charms nothing to the internal. Duke Garrett kept the light banter going, and I found I preferred him laughing to every other of his expressions. When we made it to the house, Uncle's man quickly moved to help Julia down from her horse. Duke Garrett came and raised his arms to me, not even bothering

108

to take my foot down. I slid down into them. I was very close to him.

He asked, "Do you think your father will come to London?"

"I …ah…I can request for him to if you would…I would," I looked up into Duke Garrett's eyes and he leaned toward me. I thought he might kiss me right on the blustery deserted street. I did not find out.

"EVA!" Uncle hollered from the stairs. Duke Garrett and I jumped and he let go of me. We walked around the horse.

"What are you doing here Sir, before a decent hour?"

"We were riding Papa. Your man was with us the whole time. It could not be deemed improper," Julia said.

"Eva, Julia, go inside. We will be unavailable until the political party this evening. I suppose you have been invited to that event, Your Grace," Uncle said.

"Yes, Sir. I have been working with Lord Pennington, Lord Harley, and his son rather closely on the Vaccination Act," Duke Garrett said, bowing to us.

"Good day to you then, Your Grace," Uncle said snidely, sending him off with a snap of his head like he would the dog. I shrugged to him apologetically and he smiled as he turned back to his horse. I sorrowed to see him go. He felt like the only ray of sunshine on a stormy day.

Chapter Fifteen

The bitter day drew into a biting evening. In the cold weather, Uncle and Aunt grew more out of sorts with each other as the evening fell. Privately I thought perhaps we should send our apologies to Lord Pennington. No one else even mentioned giving up the party so I dressed and climbed into the carriage as I should. The moon, covered in black clouds, gave a slight glow and seemed determined not to expose itself to the night. House lights and carriage lanterns worked harder to compensate, but could only do so much when the sky was covered in black ink.

We arrived, and the footman helped Uncle, Aunt, and Julia step down to the darkness-shrouded ground. I started to climb from the carriage after the others but was forgotten. I paused, unsure if my foot would find solid ground. Uncle turned back to give me his hand and glared at the footman, who apologized. I dropped from the carriage into the darkness. Uncle guided me onto a soft patch of grass. I thanked him.

"Eva," he said as we walked to the door.

"Yes, Uncle?"

"Be very modest in your behavior to Duke Garrett," he said.

"Yes sir," I said. I was certain the glow of my face could be seen through the dark night. The door opened and a sliver of light lit my path up the staircase. The butler welcomed us in, but I wished him a little less efficient when he took my warm outer clothes and left me with only a wispy gown and flimsy gloves.

Noticing the chill on my arms, the butler said: "The drawing room is heated, Miss."

"The discussion must be politics," I said. He only bowed in response. Julie smirked but quickly wiped it away. Lord Pennington stood in the hallway just past the entryway, speaking to Lord Devon. He was an established member of the political community. Lord Pennington, a fit man of sixty with his steely hair slicked back and his mustache flawlessly waxed, stood up straight while Lord Devon, stricken with age drooped, but each man held himself in such a manner they could be distinguished even at a distance as men of honor. Lord Pennington played a part in distributing the funds of Parliament, but as this was never fully explained to me, I only knew Uncle valued him. Uncle looked forward to being welcomed into his house, and always invited Lord Pennington to his supper parties. Though my Aunt and Julia dreaded the evening, the idea of a political discussion intrigued me because it meant I would hear Uncle's views. My father said at times Uncle sided with the Tories, but he was very quiet about it. I wanted to listen carefully that I might report back on any of his opinions. I thought Uncle brave for not bowing to popular opinion, but hoped he did not believe, like some of the Tories, the lower classes should starve to death if they could not work. We proceeded to the drawing room, but the door was blocked by Lord Devon. My grandfather's old friend spoke to Lord Pennington in quiet, but urgent undertones. I looked behind his frail frame in hopes of seeing his grandson, but my view was obstructed, and Duke Garrett could not be seen. The men turned at my uncle clearing his throat. They each exchanged bows with Uncle, but Lord Devon held his shaky arm out to me. My Uncle held my arm, not relinquishing me.

"I'll walk my niece in, Lord Devon. I would like her on hand for our discussion tonight."

"Of course, Claremont," Lord Devon said, "but if I might be so bold as to claim her for a supper companion, my daughter has found an old friend, and everyone else is paired." Uncle looked annoyed but glanced at Lord Pennington who beamed like this was the perfect solution. Uncle bowed his accent. I stopped. I looked from Uncle to Lord Devon. They had not been introduced. Did they know each other? Their interaction was tinged with familiarity. The strain in their mannerisms indicated some previous acquaintance. But if they knew each other, then surely my aunt would not have needed me to make the introduction. I took Lord Devon's shaky arm and moved into the drawing room. There were many well-dressed people in the large room. Many chairs and sofas were added to the room, most of which were occupied by women while their male counterpart stood near them. Lord Devon headed for the fireplace, the chills upon my arm. We were stopped before we could warm ourselves.

"Ah, Miss Grey! It is such a pleasure to see you again," Lord Harley said, going out of his way to take my fingers in his large meaty grasp and shake hands with me.

"Thank you, Sir," I said bowing to him and to Mr. Harley, who left his conversation to join his father in welcoming me. Wrapping his twiglike fingers around mine, he shook hands with me. I tried to be attentive, but Duke Garrett stood by the fire and happened to look up and smile at me.

"My oldest son comes back into town in four days. May I count on you to accompany us to the theater?"

"I will have to consult my Aunt. I do not know if we are free."

"Yes, well. I have a box at Covent Garden on Friday of next week if you are available," he said. I could not imagine being stuffed into a box with the Harley family. I smiled and bowed without committing.

"The play is *Much Ado About Nothing*. The very talented Mr. Charles Mathews is playing Benedick opposite his wife, Madam Vestris, who will play Beatrice. Both are insistent about historical accuracy. Mathews is applauded as one of the top comedic actors. You must come," Lord Harley said.

"Lord Harley, you will have to discuss that with her Aunt," Uncle snapped.

"Oh, come on old boy, you did not think you could keep her all to yourself, did you?" he said, and he winked at me, his overly large cheeks moving his whole face. I could not have stopped the smile that spread across my face if I tried. A jollier soul I'd never met.

"I only heard of that production this morning," Lord Devon whispered. "Shall I see what we have to do to get in?"

"Yes sir," I whispered back. Uncle looked at Lord Devon whispering to me and squinted suspiciously.

He turned from us and continued to say to Lord Harley: "Did you see the number of people estimated to have taken the railroads in the past few weeks?" Lord Harley reluctantly engaged in the conversation about the steel death traps. Lord Devon led me to the settee, but I helped him into a chair before I sat next to Julia and across from Duke Garrett.

"You went to the theater yesterday, I understand," Lord Devon said.

"Yes," I said and left it at that. Julia looked away, glancing timidly at Mr. Percival, who stood across the room debating something with Mr. Harley. He looked once at Julia, caught her eye and lost his point completely. She looked down embarrassed. Did Julia favor Mr. Percival? His handsome face and figure could not be compared. She looked at him often, and she did not like it when he and I spoke together. This made me sad for her. Uncle would never accept such a suitor for his daughter. The more I thought about Uncle's reaction to his attentions toward me, the more I knew he meant for Duke Garrett to court Julia.

Lord Devon persisted in inquiring about the play. Julia spoke of Oliver Twist. I told what of the story was left out. Duke Garrett looked chagrined about the whole thing, but it did not stop him from putting in the details I forgot. Edmund came into the room last, and as Lord Holland had not been included in the invitation, he sat near us and tried at every turn to add to our conversation. When dinner was announced, Duke Garrett came to assist Lord Devon in standing. I leaned into him, shoulder to shoulder, and took the older gentleman's arm to help support him. Our combined efforts pulled Lord Devon up. Once up, I noticed Lord Devon had the most devious grin on his face, and I thought perhaps he had not needed so much help.

I tried to look at him with the reprimand I knew Miss Bolton would wear, but my energy went into trying not to laugh when his face feigned innocence. Duke Garrett looked like he wanted to laugh as well. He put his arm out to Julia, whom Lady Pennington arranged to be his dinner companion after much contriving on the part of Aunt Claremont Hull. Lord Devon and I paused and waited for Duke Garrett to pass. Duke Garrett spoke to Julia, and she leaned toward him in a way that felt too comfortable, too familiar. When he passed me, he smiled with her as though they shared a secret joke, but then turned his smile on me as if I should join into their intimacy. I felt a little ashamed, and confused that Julia's escort showed me so much attention. I glanced at Uncle and turned away from Duke Garrett dutifully.

When we finally started to move forward, Lord Devon felt heavy upon my arm, and I wondered if he were well. At the door to the dining room, we waited for Uncle and Aunt to pass. Uncle glared at Lord Devon. I looked to Lord Devon to see if he was offended, but he had the smuggest look of satisfaction on his face. I stared at him in wonder. He answered my wonder with a charming smile. I felt sure of one thing. Lord Devon and Uncle Claremont Hull knew each other, perhaps even well. They were in the middle of some game, and I did not know the rules. Was

Lord Devon using me as a pawn in this game against Uncle? Uncle looked very put out as he took his seat on the other side of the table, much nearer the host. Did he think I was setting myself up for heartbreak, or scandal? If I were too low in station for a duke, why didn't Uncle agree with Aunt to send me home? But then, if country gentry ought not to be interacting with a duke, why did Duke Garrett stop to smile at me? Perhaps he had not been a duke long enough to know any better. I did not understand the attention. Not to mention Lord Harley's interest in me. Nothing made sense.

Then it did.

I looked up at Lord Devon. He smiled back down at me as he attempted to pull my chair out for me. I quickly looked away while I sat, pushing the chair out further as I went. Lord Devon sat next to me, though he should have been much closer to the head of the table. Did Lord Devon steer his grandson toward me for my wealth and holdings? Perhaps even Lord Harley know about Grey Manor, and all I stood to inherit? The titled did not take such interest in a poor country relation, but what about an extremely affluent one? Julia spoke of an American heiress tempting suitors last season. Perhaps I stood higher in station than Aunt supposed or wished to admit. I could believe dishonesty and manipulation of my Aunt, but Lord Devon loved my grandfather. He influenced his grandson to be kind to me for my grandfather's sake. My Uncle, whose concern was justified, felt the gap between us made any interactions immodest on my part for receiving them.

He was right. I needed to stop this naive affection from developing any further. It really was ridiculous in my position to think his manners to me could mean anything. Then again, I wasn't just making up a flirtation where nothing existed. Duke Garrett and I got on well. I felt important when I spoke to him. I felt valued. If the two of us could potentially be happy together, why did fortune and title factor into the matter? Could a man be disinterested in a title to favor a clever girl? Sometimes I thought that is why my Grandfather did not tell me about my inheritance. He wanted me to value myself, and not the great wealth he meant to pass along to me. I would write my father and ask if Lord Harley, Lord Devon, and by extension his grandson, knew of our holdings.

"You are very quiet this evening," Lord Devon said.

"Yes. Sorry sir. I have to keep my mind clear so I might be able to soak in all the new political ideas. If I do not give my father a long and accurate letter, I will be a disappointment, so I must not say anything clever."

"That was, in its self, moderately clever," he informed.

"I did not mean for it to be. I can hardly be blamed if you found it so," I said pursing my lips at him playfully.

"Very well. Shall I tell you I watched the Drury Lane Players set up this afternoon? Or will it be too distracting?" he asked.

"Were they in right form?"

"They were extremely boisterous and though I do not wish to offend," he lowered his voice, "I suspect they were half-rats." I laughed out loud drawing Aunt's glare and then clamped my mouth shut.

"Perhaps the drink will help their performance?" I asked quieter because all the older men in the group already seemed to be watching me with something akin to fascination.

"We will have to see tomorrow. I mean to ask your aunt for your company to watch them rehearse," he said.

"That would be very kind," I said. "And will the curtain be occupied as well?"

"I suspect," he said with half a grin. I grinned back. I smiled with barely a nod at Mr. Percival, who escorted the youngest daughter of the house to her seat. Then he sat on the other side of me, and across from

Mr. Harley. Aside from the few people I knew like Mr. Percival, Lord Devon, and Duke Garrett, the party around me changed. It was not like Lord Holland's ball, where no expense had been spared for the titled and wealthy to show off their frivolity. These were serious, older men who all had something somber to discuss. They were the influential and educated who climbed from many different class sets to work tirelessly up the political ladder. Most of the women quietly listened but never contributed. Lady Pennington would on occasion venture an opinion, but as Lord Pennington's second wife, and the daughter of the Chief Justice of the Common Pleas, she could get away with such things. Her father was a baron who distinguished himself. I was the granddaughter of a renowned Baronet. Perhaps I was not so out of my element in this group as Aunt implied. Still, I could not imagine what Uncle had to say to me, or rather, what he felt I could contribute. During the main course, I found out.

"My niece, Miss Grey, may be able to shed some light on this subject," he said.

I looked up. "Pardon me, I was engaged in conversation with Mr. Percival and Lord Devon," I said.

"I was speaking of Mr. Bentham's book on Parliament reform. You have read it?" Uncle asked.

"Yes, Sir," I said feeling my stomach drop. I did not care for this line of questioning. I learned early in my acquaintances that I was not like other women, and it was not wise to prove my intelligence in too great a quantity.

"Do you think, in the name of Parliament reform, Queen Victoria should, as Mr. Peel does, get rid of her Whig Lady's-in-waiting?" he asked.

"Queen Victoria made it clear last year she would not. I thought that is why Mr. Peel rejected the job of Prime Minister when Lord Melbourne meant to retire over the slaves in Jamaica," I asked, unsure how the two were connected.

"Yes, but last year her lone adviser was Lord Melbourne," Mr. Harley said. "Now she is married and Prince Albert is ... he may persuade her that Mr. Peel's concern at having well-known Whig daughters and wives always at hand may have merit."

"Can anyone really believe the queen's companions will keep the country from a peaceful transition of power, if transfer it must? Is our current political system really so fragile?" I asked.

"The ruffians are growing restless," Lord Pennington said. "I read this morning that a group of nobles were assaulted while attending the theater yesterday. And though they left unscathed before the peelers arrived, and have not been identified, it does show a certain irreverence on the part of the lower classes. They may not be satisfied with their situation, and insist on revolution."

"If Mr. Dickens is to be believed, they are all ready to rob us and leave us for dead," Mr. Harley said. No one responded to this. I subconsciously reached out to cover my arm. No one said it aloud, but everyone must have some knowledge of what we experienced at the theater. We all knew of the horrors that occurred in France. How long would the worker bees keep supplying the queen with honey, before they realized they were being cheated?

"I don't know about that, but we should have the advantage. The Whig Party's kept order for hundreds of years," said a rather boisterous man, with a smashed face aged in liver spots, who sat two seats up and across the table from me. I only smiled hoping to be done with the conversation.

"Eva," Uncle said, slowly reviewing the facts as if I could not possibly understand the words for myself, "Queen Victoria and Prime Minister Melbourne are certain we can reform without war and unnecessary losses like the French. Setting the Queen's attendants aside, do you believe a peaceful transition of power can take place?" he asked.

"I hope if it must take place, it can be peaceful," I said trying to stay neutral. A strange curiosity crossed Uncle's face. He asked: "Do you like Queen Victoria?"

"Very much. My grandfather corresponded with her a few times, and though she has made her share of youthful errors, at her heart, I believe, she wants what is best for the country," I said.

"I thought you might like her; the two of you have more in common than you know," Uncle said. I flinched. He often of late implied at my inheritance, tempting me to admit to it. Tired of his condescension, I said: "Yes, we both favor reform without the bloodshed of revolution. Our country is headed for change. We have all seen the French lose their brothers, simply for the working man to have a say. Not to mention what happened in Manchester. One cannot deny industry will continue to make commoners wealthy, giving their children the opportunity to be educated. Educated men will want to vote."

"That is a very bold declaration. What is your parentage?" the boisterous man across the table asked.

"Her grandfather was the philosopher, Baronet Henry Grey. He proclaimed himself a speaker of truth and reason," Lord Devon said.

"Ah, yes. I've read his works extensively," Lord Pennington said. He looked at me with far more interest, "and so you align yourself with the philosopher Kant's school of thought. Man can only define right and wrong by duty?"

"I do not," I said shortly. Uncle and Lord Devon looked at me in surprise. "My grandfather believed so. However, among our tenant farmers, there are those who abandon duty, and live in the shadow of avoiding their consequences, they do have a place. Though, I would not

119

align myself with Mister Betham's utilitarian concepts, either."

"You have shocked me," Lord Devan said. "Certainly we would not wish our soldiers to desert their duty, though the consequences may well be death."

"Yes but then why is the heir never required to be a soldier anymore?"

"I do not question such things," Edmond said.

"No, because you do not need the pay," I said smiling at him, but it made Duke Garrett frown so I stopped, "but duty dictates every man capable of fighting should defend his home," I said.

"The consequence of his death would bring about many consequences to those dependent on his earldom," Lord Pennington said. "Utilitarian as that may sound," I said nodding.

"So when you deliberate a choice, it is either duty or consequences; many hope when the two intersect," Mr. Harley asked. "And in the day-to-day when neither can be significant what can we do but enjoy personal preferences," I said.

"Your grandfather and I argued the point, but he did not concede that consequences could gauge morality," Lord Devon said.

"Yet he lived his life avoiding consequences," Uncle snapped angrily.

"Grandfather and I discussed it many times, duty and consequences, to no avail," I said trying to calm Uncle's ire. "I did love him and he loved me, and since his duty was always first to me, I cannot think his opinion lacking in any way."

"Beautifully done, allowing for all opinions to be of value whether you share them or not. That you inherited from your mother," Lord Devon said. I smiled shyly at this idea. Until he asked again: "I meant to ask you if your father plans to join you in London?" I paused in perplexity, concerned Lord Devon was losing his mental faculties. He asked me this question several times. The whole table leaned forward to hear, and I almost thought he asked simply so they could all hear the answer.

"He has gone back and forth several times; I suppose it will only do to say perhaps. I do not think I could give you a definite answer unless he showed up at my Uncle's door."

"Well, he has not changed in the least," Lord Devon said. "I would certainly be sorry to find anything of the kind when we are reunited," I said. I flinched when Uncle let out an exasperated sigh. I looked at him confused.

Uncle, having my eye, said: "I would like to ask your opinion about women's suffrage. I am very curious if you will try to vote, Eva." Everyone stopped to stare at me. Duke Garrett, who'd been watching me carefully during these proceedings, though at an inconvenient distance up the table, stayed poised ready to join the fray should I need his assistance. He tilted his head at me perplexed. I was surprised Uncle used such bluntness to force me to admit my wealth.

"Can you vote?" Mr. Harley asked me, confused.

"I inherited sufficient land from my grandfather, which would entitle me to a vote. In fact, I could run for a seat in our borough in the House of Commons if I were a man. Though it is outlawed in Parliament, locally women who own land participate in the vote when the area requires it," I said to clarify, but hoped I did not give too much away.

"How extraordinary," Aunt said sternly through clenched teeth. "I would not be the first woman to vote," I said looking away.

"No, though it is always such a scandal when it occurs," Aunt said, folding her arms across her chest glaring at me. I did not say anything more, for fear she'd send me home before I could see *Hamlet*, and perhaps

Much Ado About Nothing. Uncle looked at Aunt. His older eyes seemed to calculate how she would react if he said it out loud.

Lord Devon said it so Uncle did not get in trouble: "Indeed, Miss Grey, your mother voted, did she not?" Aunt shot him a look of deepest dismay.

I cleared my throat. "She simply carried her father's wishes to a proxy. Her father was ailing but felt very strongly about the measure being voted upon," I said. I did not mention her father was in a state of incapacitation at the time. Everyone looked interested in this answer, except Aunt, of course, who looked furious.

"That is almost voting," Mr. Harley said.

"This was before the reform," I said trying not to sound offended by the action.

"Earl Grey had to include the prohibition on women, simply to get it to pass," Duke Garrett said.

"Well, times are changing when a woman can inherit the throne of England," Mr. Percival said.

"Certainly, Mary and Elizabeth would disagree. There are many ancient titles created during the Tudor's rule which a woman can inherit, though her husband plays the all-important role, just as Prince Albert will, now that he has married Queen Victoria," Uncle said. He watched me, but I simply turned to my food. I allowed Mr. Percival to recapture my attention, unsure what Uncle expected me to say.

Chapter Sixteen

When dinner finished, the women removed to a conservatory to await the men. It was a huge room with arched windows. In the center of the room, a statue of a Grecian woman with a vase over her shoulder poured water into a lovely fountain putting a warm mist in the air. Pillars stood around the room with plants growing up them. Lush growth took over the room in the corners. I wandered over to the card tables to see what games were available.

Considering it would likely be a long intermission before the men joined us, I thought I would like to play something to occupy my mind so I would not keep replaying the dinner conversation over and over. We all looked up in surprise when the men stepped down into the room before the card tables had even been decided. Lady Pennington showed compassion on me and quickly insisted I be Julia's partner at whist on the furthest side of the room from the men, arranging it so Aunt could partner with herself. I agreed, pulling out a chair to sit.

"Julia, Eva, please join us," Uncle called from a group of chairs across the room where the older men were settling in. I looked to Lady Pennington, but she looked at Julia. Terror showed in my cousin's eyes at this unusual request. Lady Pennington, unable to keep us at her tables when Uncle insisted we make haste, looked to me. I felt her put Julia's comfort in my hands. This made me feel competent. Julia came in close to me and I took her arm when she trembled as we walked over to the group of men. I looked for Duke Garrett. He watched me speak throughout dinner with an encouraging smile and bright eyes that made me feel supported. Now he sat next to his mother behind the group of older men. She kept talking to him, which drew his attention away when I wished he would give me a sign of encouragement. Uncle set out two chairs. Each was separated as if we were about to debate in Parliament, except we faced the men instead of each other. Uncle indicated I should take one, and Julia the other. Julia reluctantly let go of my arm and sat gingerly in her chair. Aunt, after Lady Pennington alerted her something was amiss, came over questioning why Julia left her. Uncle assured her the young ladies were needed for only a short time, and she would more fully appreciate cards.

When she hesitated, he said something to her in a whisper. It must have been unkind because Lady Garrett, who was close enough to hear, glared at him. Aunt looked cast down but left. The older men all sat around us pulling their chairs in like they were getting ready to pass judgment. The younger generation, being excluded from them, settled by Duke Garrett and his mother. Edmund, Mr. Percival, and Mr. Harley all sat at the edge of the group and looked just as confused as we did.

"Eva," Uncle said, "Do you mind if we examine you?"

"Examine me?"

"Yes, we are curious to see how much you understand of your education," he said. I glanced at Lord Devon. He grinned at me and winked.

"All right," I said, relaxing. My uncle proceeded to quiz me in mathematics, botany, history, conjugating sentences, memory, and comprehension. He stayed very basic and could not stump me even when he delved into the realm of intermediate. He then quizzed Julia. I was sorry for my cousin. She had not the education I had, and despite my own feelings of inferiority often plaguing me, when it came down to it, I felt it unfair to expose her. Then it was my turn to be embarrassed. They asked Julia to perform all the tasks of a hostess. She flawlessly planned out meals, paired wines, explained table settings and correctly used the titles of all the aristocracy in attendance. Miss Bolton, being more studious, had given me all the talents a lady should possess, not to mention propriety and manners, but never being mistress of an estate, knew little of what Julia valued as knowledge. I could only answer to the tastes of my father and grandfather, never having been exposed to such things.

"This has been most demonstrative. Thank you, ladies," Uncle finally said.

"I'm not sure I understand what is happening," I said.

"We are very interested in a subject we have discussed for many years."

"Women, if I am not mistaken, sir," I asked as it was the only commonality Julia and I shared.

"Yes," Uncle said. "It started before I was even twenty. My older brother, Lord Hull, was intrigued by a woman claiming to be a philosopher, who proposed females were only inferior to men because of their lack of education."

"Mary Wollstonecraft," I said.

"Yes, but she turned out to be an immoral lady and was discredited," Uncle said, "And for many years we forgot all about the debate. Then we met two sisters. The younger was a rare beauty, raised by a very proper governess, with manners and decorum the Ton had rarely seen. The older was something of a peculiar creature," he said looking to me.

"Claremont, this is not appropriate. You questioned her, and she is clearly unaware of the circumstance," Lord Devon admonished, suddenly looking uneasy.

"My mother was the peculiar creature," I said. Grandfather described her in such a manner many times, though when he said it, he meant it as a compliment.

"Yes," Uncle continued, "your mother's father had no male heir. Many times, he depended on your mother to oversee the property, giving her an extraordinary education for a woman. Making her bold enough to carry a vote to a proxy, even when your grandfather slept and could not be woken for his opinion."

This caused a bit of commotion among the older men. The smashed-faced man even exclaimed: "Outrageous!"

I clenched my jaw and held my hands in tight balls at my side.

"Just after my marriage to your aunt, my older brother The Most Honorable Marquess of-" "Lord Claremont Hull," Lord Devon said loudly, reminding my Uncle of some impropriety he committed. I could not see Uncle's breach, and the interaction only confused me further. Lord Harley licked his lips, watching the two men excitedly as if he were at a race he'd bet on. Lord Pennington watched me with a pity and apprehension that unnerved me.

"I married the younger sister, and your father the older," Uncle continued.

"You know this though; it is nothing new," Lord Devon almost shouted, addressing Uncle and not me.

"Yes," I said, discomfited, looking back and forth between the two men. I didn't think Lord Devon capable of anger, but he looked livid. His aged face creased and spittle came out of the corners of his mouth when he spoke with such force.

"Your father," Uncle continued, "argued that his wife was just as capable of improving her mind as he was. He felt Mary Wollstonecraft, despite her immoral life, may have been right. Your mother was extremely wholesome, so it did not follow that the education of women naturally led to immorality."

"I should think not," I said unsure how correlation could be made between the two.

"Yes. Well," Uncle said, "we argued it many times, me proposing that a man has no right to interfere in a woman's education, my older brother stating that a woman could share her husband's burdens if she were educated."

"And eventually you just happened to have two baby girls to experiment upon?" I asked. I glanced at Julia. She did not look up.

"Yes," Uncle said. He seemed relieved, as if my finding out my life was one long experimentation into the female mind should not offend me. The evening suddenly made sense. The men looked at us as if we were circus freaks. Uncle allowed me to ramble on during dinner, never letting on that I was the stage show and it would only serve to enhance the men's amusement for the evening. I looked across at Julia. She now examined her fingernail, no longer interested in the conversation. An extra sheen showed in her eyes, and she shook a little.

"I do have to admit, you are spectacular," Uncle said, not noticing his daughter's discomfort. I could not help thinking he could learn a thing or two. "I know many of my contemporaries would not believe you exist unless they saw it for themselves. Especially your ability to restructure ideas your grandfather held fast to shows your capacity not only to learn but philosophize with original ideas, like the most scholarly minds."

"Clearly the female mind can be cultivated as well as a man's, even more so in the case of a foolish man," I said, glancing at the smashed face admiral, and folding my arms combatantly. Thrown off guard, Uncle cleared his throat. I hoped this would stop the conversation. Yet even if it did, Uncle's offense could not be undone. Especially to Lady Garrett who sat next to her son, eyes wide, following the conversation with a look of outraged indignity.

"Yes," Uncle said recovering, "but like a fish out of water you no longer have a place. What good does your education do you?"

"I... I have no place?" I asked, looking at Uncle. He nodded. I looked at the men around him. They each looked away. Lord Harley moved his mouth as if to say something, but nothing came. Even Lord Devon could not answer right away.

I turned to Duke Garrett. He teased: "Your seat among us looks very sturdy and well-occupied to me." I gave him half a smile, but it quickly fell.

"My son would certainly desire your company," Lord Harley interjected, glaring at Uncle.

"Certainly, you have a place. Your mother was a very successful and happy wife and mother. Your father will not consider marrying again he is so devoted to her memory," Lord Devon said, recovering himself.

"Devon, you must admit, her mother would never have been the appropriate choice if my brother had raised his heir in his proper station," Uncle said. "What?" I asked. The words he'd just strung together did not make sense.

"Claremont, it is not your place," Lord Devon said sternly.

"This has gone on long enough. Everyone knows but her. It makes her a target," Uncle said. "Eva, did you know my older brother, Lord Anthony Henry Grey Hull, is, among many other titles, The Honorable Marquess of Dorset Shire." The breath caught in my throat. I shook my head. I recognized a few of his brother's names intimately.

"Dorset Shire has a marquisate?" Edmund asked.

"No," I said adamantly, "my grandfather's seat would have afforded me an introduction to a Marquess in Dorset Shire."

"Yes," Uncle said, "It was granted to a well-titled family who was loyal to the crown and defended the southern borders before the standing army could be organized.

"Your brother, who never comes into society, lives in Dorset Shire," I said with little breath behind it, hoping someone would belie his words. No one did. Apprehension pushed me back in my chair. The spacious comfortable building that encompassed everything I knew to be true, started to crumble around me. Too many coincidences played in Uncle's words. Too many happenstances in my life confirmed his declaration. When Uncle said: "Well, he lived in Dorset Shire. He died last year." My heart squeezed in spasms. How could this be?

"Father! What are you saying?" Edmund asked. "Simply that my brother preferred to live in the country, and among the landed gentry he preferred to be known by the oldest title he possessed, the Baronet Grey of Dorchester."

I looked away, numb from head to toe. My eyes started to water. I could not cry – the most feminine of responses would not be respected in such a group of old wolves ready to strike. I hated them all for knowing who I was when I did not. I hated them for toying with me, instead of just telling me. I would not cry for them. I swallowed. "Wait, Uncle Grey is your brother?" Julia said, confused. "No, Julia," Uncle said rather shortly. She couldn't understand as easily as I could.

"He is implying my grandfather was," I said, just to give myself back the value he'd taken from me.

"How is that possible?" Julia asked. "My father," Uncle said slowly, "had a son from his first marriage. Long before he inherited the title of Marquess, my father's first wife died. Henry was twenty, and he was granted the title of baronet, and since it was not a courtesy title, but his actual title, he was called that from then forward. Father remarried and had a second son, me, of course. Upon my father's death there would be two major titles to occupy, the Earldom in Somerset, and Marquess of Dorset Shire. My older brother had more interest in being a scholar than a nobleman. And so, my father, through a series of letters patent, was able to split the inheritance between the two of us."

"Eva is the daughter of a marquess?" Edmund said, sounding angry for some reason.

"I suppose she cannot give the title back," Duke Garrett said. I barely heard. My whole existence shifted. My head swam in this one declaration.

"Grandfather was a Marquess?" I asked, disbelieving, despite so many little examples from my childhood and even beyond slipped into my mind confirming it. I felt Uncle unreliable. I looked at Lord Devon. He ticked his head back and forth trying to decide what to say.

"Father, tell her the truth," Lady Garrett said, astounded he would pause.

"Yes, he was The Most Honorable Lord Anthony Henry Grey Hull, though it is your father's place to mention it," he confirmed.

I looked away, saying: "I suppose he should have mentioned it before sending me to London with Uncle as my guardian, instead of himself. Perhaps in one of the many evenings we spent alone in each other's company for years he should have mentioned it."

"Here, here," Edmund said, appearing even more agitated than I was. "How did he keep up the ruse?" Lord Pennington asked. "I met Lord Hull on a few occasions, but certainly never associated him with the philosopher Henry Grey."

"In town, he was Lord Hull, in the country he was Sir Henry Grey. Few of the Gentry in the country cared for his noble titles. They respected his ancient title of gentleman and baronet far more than they could a relatively new Marquess. My older brother maintained his responsibilities in the House of Lords, with as little effort as possible. He cared for the people in his portion of the county with great skill. I often voted proxy for him when he did not make it to London. He kept active enough in Parliament to ...." Uncle's voice trailed off as background noise to the commotion happening inside my head. A vine strangling the column next to me made me feel as if I could not breathe. My grandfather valued much of the social change that occurred in the last forty years, and I couldn't be sure why he hadn't appeared at Parliament. Or had he? The long trips he took in the spring, bringing me back candy, gloves and new specimens of plants to grow in his massive conservatory.

"Why were we not told?" Edmund snapped, regaining my attention. "My brother made me swear not to say anything ... he ... the circumstance was ... unavoidable," Uncle said cryptically.

Lord Devon said angrily: "Now that Henry has passed away, you need not respect Lawrence's right to – he's her father. You had no right—"

"Eva is the daughter of a Marquess," Edmund snapped again. The air caught in my throat. Was I the daughter of a Marquess? Upon my grandfather's death I learned we were much wealthier than I'd ever supposed, but a Marquess? I was not a Miss, but rather a Lady?

"Mother!" Julia called, standing up. The noise of the fountain in the middle of the room had kept the card players oblivious to our conversation. Aunt, upon hearing Julia's tone, came quickly across the room, Lady Pennington on her heels. Before Uncle could stop her, Julia addressed her mother.

"Eva is the daughter of a Marquess?"

"No. That is ludicrous," Aunt said.

"Rather not," Uncle said, sounding tired.

"Baronet Sir Henry Grey was my older brother. That is why I took you and your sister to meet him just after we were wed."

"No, he was your neighbor, not your brother. You, you didn't –"

"Consider, my dear. We lived in London, and my seat is in Somerset. Neither are in the proximity of any of Henry's homes," Uncle said.

"Why did he not attend our wedding?" Aunt asked. "My mother, for a time …," Uncle started.

"Your mother caused problems between you and your brother? Well, that is not a shock, is it?" Aunt said furiously. Uncle's eye fired up and his jowls swung.

He said quickly: "My relationship with my brother had been strained for many years after our father died. That was the case when we married."

"So," she said, "you pretended he was not your brother so your mother would not know we had been introduced?"

"I meant to introduce him as my brother, but you met him in the country, where you held the Baronet in little regard."

"I did not," she insisted, her eyes burning into his.

"You suggested his estate too far above the representation of his station, and that the crown ought to insist he give it up to an Earl or higher, clearly meaning myself, and by extension you. After that, he insisted you never know," Uncle said looking at her with something that bordered on deepest regret.

"Anna knew?"

"Your sister knew she was to be a marchioness one day."

"She never…."

"You ridiculed her for her choice in husband often, and yet, she never said anything, out of respect to my brother," Uncle said with a vacant stare. This obviously had burdened him for some time.

"How did she … capture the attention of a Marquess, in one fortnight?" she asked. "Your sister and her clever mind impressed my eccentric brother so much he encouraged his son to marry her," Uncle said.

"Yes, but we went to his properties on several different occasions," she insisted, refusing to believe her sister married above her in station.

"He never seemed to be there. When he came to town, you saw only your sister's father-in-law, who was not invited into society, instead of my brother, who chose not to mingle in society," Uncle said.

"Does that mean Eva is…."

"Lady Eva Grey Hull daughter of the Marquess of Dorset Shire," Uncle confirmed, "that is if her father chooses to take his title."

I remained in silent shock for a full minute. "I suppose that is why every one of you has asked if my father is to come to town," I finally said.

"Yes," Lord Devon said.

"So much so, that you have told me all this in hopes that I will go write him a scathing letter immediately demanding he come," I said to Uncle.

"He must at least claim his title, and soon. My brother's seat will no longer be kept in honor of mourning," Uncle said.

"Would not Edmund inherit, sir?" I asked. Edmund sat up straighter.

"No Eva. The settlement was based on the son of his mother, Lady Harriet Grey, our father's first cousin, who brought much into the marriage herself, all of which I could never inherit, and the son of my mother Lady Florence Claremont, which would be myself, then Edmund. You are the only heir of my brother's line. Unless your father remarries and has a son, the Marchioness title will go to you."

"What?"

"It is a very complicated matter," Uncle said. I could see him winding up again. To talk about my identity, my life, as if he had every right. I cut in sharply: "I find it very convenient my trip to town is taking place eight months after my grandfather's passing, so that we may be out of mourning when clearly you did not need me to make Lord Devon's acquaintance."

"Yes," Aunt snapped, "now it appears that you could have introduced us to Lord Devon yourself, despite your declaring many times that only Eva could give us the desired connection."

"Excuse the deception," Uncle bowed.

"You had us bring the child here under false pretenses, letting her think she is–"

"It did concern me how low you kept her ...."

"My father did not wish to come to town. You will force his hand," I said trying to stay on the offensive.

"Would your father have consented for you to come to town if he did not mean to eventually come himself, my wise girl?" Uncle asked.

"I suppose not," I snapped, but quieted. I happened to glance at Mr. Percival who had a hand to his mouth and his eyes trained to my side in concern. I followed his gaze and saw Julia trying to hide tears dripping down her face. Her arms were folded in on herself, like perhaps if she curled in tightly enough she would disappear. Uncle followed my gaze, glancing at his daughter. Uncomfortable with the sight, he turned to stare in disgust at his wife. Aunt paced, close to hysterics, mumbling about deception. This was enough. I do not remember standing, but I was. I quickly moved to shield Julia from the group. Duke Garrett stood and took a few steps toward us, but stopped when Uncle scowled at him.

"Where are you ... are you leaving? Duke Garrett asked. I looked at him over my shoulder. He looked concerned for me. No wonder he showed so much interest. The daughter of a marquess was a prize after all. No, I was angry. He was always kind to me... but is that because he knew? I stopped. I needed to think. I would not put myself to advantage if I did not leave.

"I suppose we will retire," I said, bowing toward Duke Garret. Still using my body to block Julia from sight I turned to Uncle Claremont Hull and my tone grew harder.

"Your family may need a private moment to digest this, Uncle, who turns out to be also my father's Uncle. Is there something grander I should call you now?"

"Ah..." he stammered unsure what to do with my anger, and not at all ready to leave the discussion of his experiment.

"Apparently, I have a letter to write," I said, pulling Julia up and turning her to the door as she wiped at her face and shuddered deeply. Aunt must also have seen the advantage of a hasty departure because she turned and followed us. Lady Pennington walked us to the door.

"Yes, of course," Uncle said. He stood reluctantly and turned to thank our host, who already nodded to his footman to call our carriage. Lord Pennington followed us through the house to the entryway.

"It turns out I knew your grandfather. I always had the utmost respect for Lord Hull. I am sorry you were not given the proper respect in my home due to your station," Lord Pennington said to me.

"It was my father's ruse. Neither he nor anyone else can shift blame upon you," I said.

He nodded and after consideration said: "I have always enjoyed the company of clever women. I hope you will consent to enter my home again on a more pleasant occasion."

"Thank you, Sir," I said bowing to him. He bowed to me, then excused himself to return to his guests. He did not bow to take leave of Uncle.

Chapter Seventeen

The ride back to Uncle's house was a very quiet one. Aunt gave Uncle the silent treatment a child in her eighth year would appreciate, and Uncle ignored her indignant huffs. Julia's snivels were harder for him to ignore. He glanced at her uncomfortably as we entered Uncle's house.

"Miss Bolton has taken a liking to Julia," I said. "Perhaps she can be called to her room with some tea."

Uncle nodded to the footman and he left. Julia did not bother taking off her outer things but went directly to her room. Uncle took me into his library. The wet night kept the moon from peering in and the smoldering fire only gave off a slight glow. The lamp Uncle lit illuminated a spot on his desk with paper, pen, and inkwell. I sat at the desk in a shadow. I stared at the cone of light over the sheet. It took me some time to form a thought. No words came.

Uncle loomed behind me in the darkness, his heavy, fiendish presence skulked over my shoulders and neck. I could not think. All I wanted at that moment was to shut Uncle out of my intimacy. Finally, I just regurgitated all Uncle told me and asked for an explanation. Uncle sent for a horseman, who stood by waiting for me to finish. The gaunt rider assured Uncle he would traverse the eighty miles in two days. Uncle gave him an extravagant amount of money promising the man he could keep whatever he did not use on horses and food. He also offered the rider a bonus if my father confirmed him making his time.

Miss Bolton waited for me outside the library. "
Is Julia ... ?" Uncle started.

"Asleep. She was worn out," Miss Bolton said, her arms folded and her eyes on fire. I walked away from their interaction and felt Miss Bolton follow a step behind, as she always did. The granddaughter of a baron was always a step behind me. I suppose I should have known my heredity surpassed hers. When we reached our room, she put a hand on my shoulder. I pulled away.

"Did you know?" I asked.

"Of course," she said.

"Myra, why did you not tell me?" I whispered, my tears dripping freely like the rain splattering on our window.

"Your grandfather was not only my employer, but the local government, and my brother's benefactor. I could say nothing."

"That is why you stayed as my lady's maid, though it was beneath your station," I said.

"Look at my hands that were once soft and gloved, now burnt from the effort of steaming your gowns. Do not take that tone with me, as if I did something wrong. I am not mistress of myself, but neither would I shun any task no matter how derogatory to protect you, child."

"I know the sacrifice you have made for me. Sorry, Myra," I said. "How much does my father know?"

"All, though I cannot answer to his feelings about it. We never speak of it, except to cover the pomp when it became too obvious. Your grandfather insisted you grow up without the burden. He said it would ruin you," she answered.

"That I can easily believe. Of all the revelations of the evening, that is the man I knew," I said pulling my boot roughly from my foot as I started to do more for myself when it was just the two of us. I did not want her help, but she had to release me from my corset. When she held out my chemise, I let it drop over my head. I laid down and turned toward the wall.

"Eva, your father, he…."

"Don't defend him to me, not tonight Myra," I said.

"But he…."

"Please, just let me think. I cannot speak anymore this evening," I said. She said nothing else but instead prepared herself for bed. Her ability to be silent was deafening. I held my breath to hear her, and finally, she made a few sounds in her struggle with her corset. I stood up and silently helped her out of it. Then I could turn over and go to sleep. In the morning Miss Bolton did not leave my side. She watched me as if I might lose my mind. I relished the sound of Edmund entering the house simply to have a distraction. His distraction did not prove comforting.

"Your Ladyship," Edmund said with an exaggerated bow.

"Very amusing," I said. "Where are the Earl and his Lady?"

"Mother has a headache and refused to come down. Papa left for Parliament," Julia said.

"I see," Edmund said, picking up a newspaper and hitting it against his leg. He turned to me. Making me feel like a fool, he asked: "Eva, you really did not know your father is a marquess?"

"She was shielded from all," Miss Bolton defended, folding her arms.

"You knew all," Edmund said turning to her, "not only knew but helped conceal all."

"What could she do, Edmund?" I asked. "Give up her position?"

"I would never leave Miss Eva unguarded," Miss Bolton said, and there was something accusatory in her look. Edmund clenched his jaw at her. I was reminded of the last time Edmund came to Grey Manor. He often tried to send Miss Bolton away. At the time I had almost thought he wished to propose, but since nothing came of it, I had forgotten about it until just now.

Julia broke the awkward silence by saying, "You are more her companion than her lady's maid then. As a gentleman's daughter you were far too … that was very kind of you."

"A motherless girl should not navigate such a world on her own," Miss Bolton said. She poured tea for Julia as if she were taking another little bird under her wing. The outer bell rang.

After a shuffling in the entryway, the door opened and the butler announced: "Lord Devon," and bowed to Edmund. The old gentleman hobbled in, tired from the exertion. We all bowed to him. He nodded back but looked at me expectantly.

"Hamlet," he said. "The players will not wait for us." I stared at him. "Come now, your aunt said you may come at dinner. She did not think to take it back after."

"I cannot focus just now," I said.

"Steeped in reason as you are, you must see your father will not be here for a fortnight, and you cannot deny yourself this pleasure you have been looking forward to in order to sit home and mope?"

"Perhaps she is under the weather," Edmund responded.

"I suppose my status is no shock to you?" I asked.

"Of course not. I never understood Henry's little lark, but I respected him enough to know he had his reasons for it." Lord Devon spoke as if it were a trifling detail.

"Upon reflection, I will go with you. I need to pose a few questions," I said. Miss Bolton watched me but did nothing to stop me from going. I left in search of my bonnet and gloves, and she followed me.

When we were alone, she said, "Lord Devon does not have all the information. He has his own biases. It would be best to pose your questions to your father."

"Well, I would, but he is not here. He sent me to London, forcing you to take on the role of a lady's maid so I would not be left completely vulnerable, Myra," I said.

"He did not ask me to come," she defended. "I insisted."

"Exactly, you risked your respectability to keep me safe. He did nothing." I kissed her cheek and walked away.

Chapter Eighteen

Once the carriage door closed, I did not draw breath. "How much of this did my father know?" I asked Lord Devon. "All. He went to school as Master Hull," he answered. "Why did he not admit as much to me at my grandfather's death?"

"I can only suppose he is trying to decide whether he wishes to be the scholarly Baronet or the all-important Marquess."

"Uncle wishes him to take the family seat?" I asked.

"Very much. The Marquess of Beverly went extinct, for being unclaimed."

"I wonder what he will decide. Stature has never been important to him before. I doubt it is something he desires now."

"This has nothing to do with stature. It is your very remark that contradicts it. The sons of earls do not go to war anymore, because they no longer amass armies. Now they represent the people. The Marquess of Dorset Shire governs the southern border. Henry was exceptionally good at taking care of the people, and the crown often depended on him to keep the Marchlands in order. Now it is your father's duty."

"I thought that the responsibility of his Baronetcy," I said.

"You may not have noticed, but the marquess is not constricted by county lines as an earl is. Henry could see a million different ways to resolve disputes. Landlords and their tenants from all over the south would end up appealing to your grandfather's good sense. Even now, there is much being said in Parliament dealing with the farmers. There will be outrage if Parliament opens up free trade for crops."

"There has been much grumbling among the farmers on that topic," I admitted.

"The Southern Counties must have representation. They cannot afford to lose another seat in The House of Lords," Lord Devon said. I nodded, but still felt unsure what to think. "Did...Did my mother know I was an experiment?"

"Ah, your mother was such a lovely woman. She was very happy for your mind to be improved, without the added burden of status. I believe she saw it as a responsible way to raise a daughter in these modern times," he said.

"She did not mind being so deceitful to Aunt?"

"Your aunt spent all her youthful days with a very mean sort of governess, while your mother was doted upon. I once heard her say she did not mind keeping the secret, because she could not tolerate seeing the look on her sister's face when she learned she again was put lower than her."

"And Grandfather... did... did he value me, other than as his finest scholarly quest?" I asked.

"Oh, dear girl! He gave up on the experiment long before he died. Your uncle began writing him after your sixteenth birthday asking for you to be presented. Your grandfather refused. He said his interests had moved in other directions, and he had other plans for you. He said you were his heir, and as capable as any male apprentice."

"I thought you stopped speaking to him," I said. "He wrote me many letters. I read them. Unfortunately, I did not respond to them," Lord Devon said, and his face crumpled in pain as he looked to the ground. I did not know what to say. Sadly, I was too distracted by my own quest for knowledge to respect his distress.

I said, "Grandfather did not just see me as an opening to the female mind?"

"Of course, he did. By your tenth year, he was fascinated by you. Could you imagine him not examining everything about you? It would be like asking him not to breathe, but that is no secret," he said.

"No, I suppose not," I said.

"He was grateful for the extra push into giving you the education you deserved."

I smiled. I didn't know if that was true, but I appreciated the sentiment. Emotional support did have a place among women, and I felt sorry for men like Uncle who only valued the support of his opinions. By the time we arrived at the theater I only had one question left, but I did not dare ask. I wanted to know when Duke Garrett learned about my title. Did he single me out because of it? It felt like an accusation to ask. I wasn't sure I possessed enough impertinence. I was silent helping Lord Devon up to the theater box, as before, but everything was different now. Duke Garrett slipped into the box after the curtain rose. He squatted in front of me instead of curling into his drape. "Are you...?" he examined me. I knew the hurt flashed in my eyes, but I could not pretend with him. When he looked at me what did he see? The future marchioness, or Eva?

"I do not know how to give it back," I said.

"Yes, I understand that,' he said taking my hand.

"I am... I have lost all sense, and am thrown into the grips of my emotion. Do you think me weak?" I asked. I felt humiliated as I took the handkerchief he offered to wipe a tear.

"No, I've never aspired to the idea that logic should banish emotion—it isn't sensible to me," he said.

"I will have to think on the idea that logic and sense are not the same things," I said.

"To be clear, I understand you categorize logic as the antipathy of emotion, and sense as ...."

"Simply understanding which is which, and when they are, each in their turn, necessary facets to the human experience, he said. "Even your Uncle Claremont Hull uses his emotions to form his ideas. He simply does not admit as much to himself."

"How do you know that?" I asked.

"He wished his friends, and especially Edmund, to know your identity. This became a matter of pride and frustration to him. Would it not have been more logical to have told his wife and daughter, even his son, about your title in private?"

"Yes, he exposed us all, even himself. That was not wise of him. It is all the Ton will be talking about today."

"He wished for the news of it to spread quickly," Duke Garrett said.

"Why?"

"I do not know, but I believe it has something to do with manipulating your father," Duke Garrett said.

"I have known him all his years," Lord Devon said. "Claremont has never been concerned with logic. Even when he was a little boy he would try to convince Henry he was looking at things logically, but he always skewed things to his advantage."

"Yes, exactly," Duke Garrett said. "Would it not be more logical to understand how your emotion is swaying you rather than pretending it does not exist?"

"Oh, your Grace! That sounded almost scholarly; do take care," I said. He looked up at me and smiled. I stared at the way the smile lit his face. It might light my darkest moments. Then I didn't care if he knew about my title when he singled me out. For the first time, my title was desirable as it brought me nearer Duke Garrett's rank. It was not at all inappropriate for the daughter of a marquess to be courted by a duke. A loud voice came crying from the stage below, and he nodded his head to me, then moved back into his curtain and I settled in to watch the play masterfully performed. I found I preferred it without the ornate costumes and extravagant scenery. Watching as human sorrow spoke to me from the stage, I thought about my father and my grandfather. I should have known something of the sort was afoot, considering all they valued, and what they did not. Not to mention how isolated they kept me. Moving only among those I must learn to protect instead of those who would overvalue me for no reason. Unless my wearing a pretty gown could, in fact, change their circumstance somehow.

When the ghost haunted the stage, I almost wished an apparition of my Grandfather would appear and give me answers. But Hamlet was not so calm about the prospect. At an interval, Lady Garrett came into the box.

"Mother," Duke Garrett exclaimed standing, "I did not know you meant to join us!"

"My afternoon cleared and I thought I might take in a play," she said, smiling at me and sitting down. I glanced at her. Did she come because I was suddenly the daughter of a marquess? The thought tasted metallic in my mouth.

"Son, Father, did you mean to get some refreshment?" she asked.

"Of course, mother, sorry, but I…" Duke Garrett said, realizing he would be seen.

"You've accompanied your mother to a play. This legitimizes your presence. I think you'll find your way through your admirers."

"My dear all you had to do is ask," her father said with a gleam in his eye. They left. The Lady turned to me, and I thought she was going to school me in the art of being a marchioness.

"I was always very good at my numbers," she said.

"Yes?" I asked.

"And I read and understood your grandfather's published works," Lady Garrett said.

"I have no doubt, my Lady," I said.

"My point being, you are not so special as the Arabians away from the Desert, or fishes breathing outside the confines of water."

"I also enjoyed Mr. Purchas' travelogues," I said smiling. She was comforting me.

"There are some men who do not recognize, nor appreciate what women do for them. Nor are they willing to accept that the mental acuity necessary to function does not belong exclusively to their sex."

"Clearly my uncle is of that set," I said.

"I think," Lady Garrett said, "you may have taught him a thing or two. He, masculine dominant as he is, could not deny your high learning capacity, and that your grandfather's efforts are quite a success."

"He did not admit as much," I said.

"Oh, he did, but veiled it in an insult to diminish the value of your success," she said.

"I am sorry if he insulted you along with me," I said.

Lady Garrett continued with her rant, seemingly needing to talk. "Yes, I admit to being affronted. I cannot say my father did not do the same thing to me as yours did to you. He often quizzed me along with my brothers and another sister to be sure we progressed in our studies. He never so formally, nor publicly admitted he experimented on my ability to learn; he just expected me to keep up on my schooling," she said.

"Yes. That is how I grew up as well," I said.

"I am grateful," continued Lady Garrett. "He ensured I had the best governess, and supplemented my education when her knowledge failed. And are you sorry?"

"No, I am very grateful to Miss Bolton, and my grandfather for teaching us both at times," I said. "I would not wish away my education."

"Do not suppress it. We are not the only ones concerned. More women of the upper classes are being educated than your uncle or many men will admit. Though we are only a handful now, that number can only increase."

"Miss Bolton's brother educates his daughters," I said.

"For them you must always speak when you have something to say. As a Marchioness in your own right, few will dare contradict you. You can make headway for women. There are many concerned with women's sufferage."

"My mother did vote. Aunt is so sure it should embarrass me, but I have always been proud of her for making a stand."

"Do not let your Uncle Claremont Hull degrade it out of you. There are many of our set who will value you for it," Lady Garrett said. "I cannot imagine my late husband examining me like a brand-new species because I am capable of intelligent thought."

"Your husband …."

"He was a kind man. His father and older brother were Dukes and talked down to everyone. It disgusted my husband. He worked very hard to find worth in the people he met, simply to undo the offenses his father and brother were sure to give. Sometimes neglect and example are better teachers than cruel men can be. I do not think he would… I do not know how he would feel knowing Jonah inherited their titles." I followed her gaze to the curtain where her son disappeared. Her mind seemed to have wandered. I recognized the look she'd worn since the first time I'd met her. I often thought her haughty or disdainful of the company she kept, but now I realized hers was a watchful concern for her son.

"He is very considerate; I suspect he will make it intact through this ordeal of being a Duke," I said.

"It will be a test of his character to be sure. Many want to use him for his position. One never knows who his real friends are," she said. "That will be your circumstance as well."

"I cannot be in as much danger as a Duke," I said. "You are heir to Grey Manor," she said.

"Yes, and Uncle assures me the title is mine unless my father remarries and produces a male heir," I said. "Is that likely?"

"No," I said.

"You recognize you are going to be sought after. Most especially by your cousin as your Uncle clearly means for you to be his wife."

"Edmund?"

"Yes dear. Sometimes a man feels he must put a woman down until she accepts what she is given."

"I am not sure I understand," I said.

"If you are a fish out water, then your cousin coming to your rescue is a gift. I have found it is the tactic some men use when they are married to a stubborn woman," Lady Garrett said.

"That is not kind of him," I said.

"No, but is it your Uncle's way," she said delicately. "Consider last night when your Aunt came to find Julia after she left her." I nodded. "To get her to go back to the card table, your Uncle told his wife she would not understand the discussion and would only humiliate him with her interference. His manipulation was very effective. She left, demoralized. His cruel statement was not correct. She clearly understood the extent to which she had been lied to for years. He humiliated her. Then he behaved as if her reaction to his betrayal was an annoying quirk in her personality instead of being legitimate. Her anger was justified."

I thought about this. My aunt pushed until she obtained whatever she sought, simply by making as much trouble as she could. It was the only way she could get

Uncle's attention. Uncle then responded by mistreating her until she walked some line only he could see.

"It is a sad sort of way to live," I said.

"Yes," Lady Garrett said. "Marriage is a partnership; each person affects the other. They could choose an amicable interaction or pure torture. Some seem to prefer the latter."

"It cannot be the type of partnership they desire," I said.

"No dear. They fight each other for every step they take forward. That would be exhausting, but as neither seems likely to yield, I do not think it will ever change," she said.

I agreed. Just then the men returned with a woman pushing a tea cart. I looked up and smiled. Lord Devon smiled back. Duke Garrett stopped and looked at me and then his mother. Satisfaction crossed his features. I questioned him with my eyes, but the orchestra indicated the play would begin. He seemed embarrassed and took his seat next to his mother. I sipped my tea while watching Hamlet's perfect angst to compliment my mood.

Chapter Nineteen

When the carriage dropped me off at Uncle's house, I went to my room to get ready for a supper party.

Julia came into my room and said: "You are not to join us this evening."

"Am I being punished?"

"No, my mother and father are pretending as if you never entered society. I suppose it is no coincidence that the date of the next drawing room is in four weeks. Your name has been submitted for presentation."

"But I've been to dinners, and a ball since arriving in London," I said.

"Yes, but we are all to pretend you haven't. Mother insists the Crown Prince will never know," Julia said.

"Uncle is agreeing with her?"

"He... He was not pleased when he found you were gone to the theater with Lord Devon," she said looking away.

"He seems to dislike him, does he not?"

"I do not know. He... he very much wants me to please Duke Garrett," she said flushing.

"Oh, yes," I said, "I suppose he always has."

"No, my mother has. But remember, he could not be bothered to meet him at first, and now he... I do not understand him at all."

"No," I agreed, swallowing hard. She watched me carefully as I closed my eyes to shut out the pain.

"Don't be downcast Eva, your father will come. He has a way of righting things," she said.

"That is true," I said with little enthusiasm. I did not find the idea of my father comforting, but rather frustrating.

"Until he comes you are at the mercy of my father who is arranging that you should be out in time for the Derby, but mother hopes your father will consider taking

152

you to Paris for new clothes before the Ascot. It is the first time they have gotten along in years."

"I do not think–"

"The French Dressmakers in London can be used in a pinch. It is simply required of you to know which shops are to be used."

I stared at her. My whole world was ash drifting through a blustery storm, and she spoke of dresses?

"I will consider that. Thank you, Julia."

"Evie," she said.

"Yes," I said, surprised at her using my childhood nickname.

"Did my father call me... a simpleton last evening?"

"No, dearest. He said that you have a different type of knowledge than I do. He even said your knowledge will serve you better as a woman in your station, than mine will."

"But he made me look lacking in front of Mr. Percival... oh, and Duke Garrett, whom he now insists I must marry," she said apologetically.

"I am sorry he exposed you like that. It was unkind of him," I said.

"Is that why you were so upset?"

"I played the fool," she said. "I do not think he... He ignored me my whole life, and now it is offensive to him I do not have his education."

"No, he firmly believes that educating a woman is a waste of time and resources."

"He always calls Edmund to him. He never showed any interest in me. How would I ever have learned what he expected of me without him—"

"None of this is your fault, Julia. The truth is you will make a perfect wife someday, and I wish you much happiness when you do," I said, telling myself I would be happy for her if she married Duke Garrett. It felt a tremendous order.

"Thank you, Eva," she said. A bell rang at the door, summoning her.

"Oh, yes. Father sent word you may have free rein of his library," she said looking down.

"Thank him for me," I said.

"He's never let me in there, but you are to have free rein."

"I am sorry, Julia," I said.

"It is of little concern," she said.

After the house settled into stillness indicating the family left, curiosity drove me to Uncle's library. It was a small room toward the back of the house and I had only been in there to write the letter to my father. Uncle kept the door shut and often spent all his time away from Parliament in there. I stepped in and examined the room more closely. A window on the far wall let in a little light. A desk was situated near it, to use the light. A stone fireplace in the corner smoldered to ashes, warming two leather chairs separated by a small wooden table with a book on it. The room could not accommodate any other furniture, and the other two walls were used to full advantage covered in bookshelves. I went to the desk – all straight lines and dark wood – and lit the gas lamp.

The only items out of place were a pen with a metal tip next to an inkwell with the lid off. I put the lid back on and wondered what Uncle had been writing and why he left in such haste. No letter, nor bits of parchment, were present, so he must have finished what he worked on. Any hasty instructions or letters sent were probably on my behalf.

This burned my heart and rose up into my throat with anger. His actions were odious. My father would be in town within a fortnight at the most. Certainly, any arrangements to be made should be made by him, or at the least with him. Yet, Uncle already confirmed my turn in Queen Victoria's drawing room? Julia was right about one thing. Uncle arranged my affairs with haste before my father could arrive and take back his role of my guardian. Having no library to inherit, Uncle's books were all his own purchase. I walked around curious what he chose and found his reading skewed so far into the political realm, I couldn't help thinking a book of poems would do him some good. I found a family bible. It looked too new to have many names it. I took it out, curious to see what heritage it contained. It only went back to the time our family had been awarded the earldom, and every name was written in the same decidedly feminine handwriting. This was odd, but the fact that it excluded my father and grandfather bordered on the offensive. I did not grow offended. Uncle and Edmund were not signed in their own handwriting, nor did it seem to be Aunt's overly large flourishes, either. I was familiar with all, and none was so delicate. I put the book back and lined it up perfectly so Uncle would not know I had seen it. Instead, I sat down on a worn leather chair in front of the fire and opened a periodical of sorts that had been left there. Surprised, I found Uncle used The Tamworth Manifesto, Mr. Peel's conservative ideals, as a bookmark. Uncle had underlined many statements and made notes in the border. It seemed he believed, as Mr. Peel stated, the reform bill irrevocable. He even wrote down the sentiment that it had to be worked through and not around. I found this interesting, considering his party voted the reform in place. The volume he examined was opened to a page about how to run for office as a Member of Parliament for the House of Commons. I thought that strange, as his seat in the House of Lords was fixed. Uncle Claremont Hull's idea of entertainment left much to be desired. I replaced the periodical, so Uncle could not tell I touched it. Without finding a single volume of Shakespeare I turned to leave the room. On a shelf, I saw a

155

cribbage set, which I figured I could use, so I picked it up. Then I took another quick stroll around the room to be sure it looked untouched before turning out the lamp. Vexed with Edmund, I thought I would mention his promise to get me a copy of *The Old Curiosity Shop* or write Duke Garrett to send his copy over. Instead of reading, I played cards with Miss Bolton, the quietest evening by far since coming to London.

Chapter Twenty

I spent the next two days idle, confined to the upper rooms of the house so as not to be seen by Aunt's constant visitors, all hoping for a glimpse of me. She cheered up considerably being in the center of a gossip storm. Daily she was sought out for information, everywhere she went. In the evenings when the family left, Aunt instructed me to practice the piano rigidly; I would eventually be called on to perform. On the third afternoon of my confinement, Miss Bolton woke me from where I dozed in our room over one of Uncle's books, to tell me that my father was in the sitting room.

"How is that possible? Uncle only sent my letter three days ago?"

"I do not know, but here he is," she said.

Unsure what I would say to him, I allowed her to fix my appearance. While she worked, Miss Bolton pleaded: "I know you think him wrong for not telling you, but dearest, everything he does is for you. You cannot know how blessed you are to have such a father. Look at Julia. She would give anything for just a touch of the affection you feel from your father."

"I... I will try," I said.

"At least be civil," she said.

"Very well," I said. I stood and walked out of the room. I went into the sitting room next to Julia's bedroom now set aside for both our use. My father stood at my entrance looking anxious, his hickory brown eyes contracted in concern, and his wavy dark hair streaked in grey at the temples was messy. The soft contours of his face covered in stubble made him look kind and agonizing at the same time.

"How is it possible you are here already?" I asked.

"I rode the train. I caught it in Winchester. It took me five hours to get here. I flew, darling, I really flew. I've never experienced anything so heady in my life. In a few years, after it has been thoroughly tested, I will take you. You will love it," Father said.

I glared at him. He promised to wait for me to ride the train for the first time. Oh, and he lied to me all my life. I crossed my arms.

"Come now, you did not think such an opportunity to explore the human mind would be lost on your grandfather, did you?"

"No, I suppose not, and yet you have made it to London in record time, braving those metal contraptions, indicating some kind of regret," I said.

"You know I am the emotional fool of the family," he said opening his arms to me. I walked to him and allowed him to hug me, but I could not return the embrace. After a brief closeness, I broke away and sat down.

Feeling me disconnect, he said: "Eva, by the time you were fourteen, your grandfather was so proud of you, he regretted he'd not given your grandmother some education of the kind. She lost so many children in infancy, he thought if women could be trained in medicine, they may be able to couple it with their natural intuition to save babies vulnerable to the environment."

"An interesting thought, but I will not be distracted. Uncle accosted me in front of a group of titled men, with information about myself that I did not know. You did not think to inform me of who I am before this turn in town?"

"I thought he would respect your grandfather's wishes. I supposed too much on his familial honor," Father said, disappointed, "I am sorry Eva."

"Are you sorry for not telling me, or sorry for what he did?"

"I am sorry he disrespected your grandfather."

"And you do not care he allowed your daughter to be publicly accosted?"

"Did Uncle really humiliate you?" He sounded disbelieving.

"He called me a fish out of the water. He said I would never marry and have a family of my own because who would want me, educated as I am?"

Father pursed his lips and looked away. I could see him fighting his anger. He answered, "We have taken the measure of that man."

"He has been agitated as of late. Let us not be too quick to decide his character," I said.

"It has long been your uncle's fondest wish for you to marry Edmund. He has always encouraged the lad to befriend you. I cannot imagine he wishes for you to end a spinster."

"Edmund is always being called away when I am at hand," I said.

"Yes, by his mother who lectured him, or I'd wager, threatened him, away from you. She would not see the Earl's son attached to her poor country relations," Father laughed.

"Edmund chose not to court me," I said, remembering the many times Edmund only permitted himself brief encounters with me, even when his mother was not around. Many times, he hinted at affection, but would not allow it.

"Only because he felt it irresponsible to court you in his position," Father said. He watched me work through it.

"If that were the case, then why did Uncle not tell Edmund my status, considering he values such things?"

"Your Grandfather said he would not bless your match with Edmund, unless the lad chose you as the daughter of a baronet," Father said. "I thought Uncle would respect that even in your Grandfather's death."

"He did not," I said.

159

"No," he agreed, "and what's more, he has made you a target. All the Ton must know who you are by now. It does not make sense. Edmund is young. I knew Uncle would eventually push the issue, but I am surprised he did so soon. Especially considering the very public way he announced your identity. One would think he would keep it quiet with the fortune hunters about."

"Edmund has been paying particular attention to Lady Alice, and Uncle is most upset about it. I believe he wished to put a stop to the thing before it becomes an official engagement," I said.

"Lady Alice?"

"A most respectable lady and the daughter of The Honorable Marquess of Stratford."

"Yes, that does shed some light on the situation," Father said.

"I think this is more about Uncle wanting you to come and take your place among the Lords. Lady Alice and I are equals, so I cannot be sure he even prefers me for Edmund," I said.

"He does," Father said. "I suspect this has something to do with Uncle's mother and her aspirations for her son since his birth. He may not be capable of turning away from trying to obtain your grandfather's titles, even after her death, though in it, he disrespected his revered older brother."

"That seems rather complicated."

"It is. Now as recompense for my bad behavior, I will stay with you and we will discern the truth of it by Uncle's behavior.

"There is no truth within society," he said. "They say one thing with their mouths but one must watch their faces to discern what they really mean." Father grinned and his eyes lit with enthusiasm.

"Oh dear," I said. "This turn in town will be a lark for you, will it not Father?"

"Human behavior is so precarious to witness at such a time as this," he said.

"I suppose I must allow it," I said, slowly conceding to Grandfather's experiment. "Your examination of them is the only way I will know what relationship I have with anyone now."

"Exactly why Grandfather ruffled feathers in his written word," Father said.

"Or perhaps why Grandfather lived as a baronet," I said.

"He quickly learned who valued him, and for what reason," Father said, "He made a name for himself without his title. It was his life's work."

"Father, how do I know what relationship to have with myself, since I've only just learned who it is, I am?" I asked bitterly.

"Eva, nothing has changed. A title, wealth – it is what it has always been. That was the whole point of the thing. Immersed in the Ton, you could never have learned who you are without conceit, or others continually lifting you up or setting you down for their own selfish purposes. You can have no clear picture of yourself if you allow someone else to paint it for you. No. You are simply Eva."

"And what about you? Will you take your title?" I asked. I felt everything had changed and I was Eva no longer.

"It may be necessary. People trust our family, and the southern counties are not quick to trust. I am struggling to keep order as it is. The older gentry see your grandfather's death as an opportunity for a coup. I am not sure I will ever be suited to the life of marquess. It is not something one can be inoculated against, but I must show myself to be supported by the Crown."

"I imagine Duke Garrett understands something of your apprehension," I said.

161

"Yes, I would imagine. Do you like him very much?" he asked.

"Yes. Do you know him?" I asked.

"Not well. Your grandfather did. Duke Garrett's father, a lower baron, had a small house of his own in the country. Duke Garrett lived with Lord Devon much of the time. Lord Devon meant to give him a living after he took orders so he would have an income and a home. Lord Devon brought him to town often, where he interacted with your grandfather. Grandfather took such a liking to the boy; he fancied a match between you two."

"Really!" I said, trying to slow my heart, but the blush on my face could not be mistaken. "Your grandfather spent much time when he came to town with the naturally happy lad. Duke Garrett did not go to school until he was eleven. Lord Devon preferred to educate him," Father said. "Grandfather took Duke Garrett and Lord Devon to the continent?" I asked.

"Yes, but long before that Uncle saw Grandfather's attachment to young master Garrett and out of fear wanted to arrange an understanding between you and Edmund. Your Grandfather refused, mostly because of Aunt Claremont Hull. He said Edmund could only marry you if he chose you ignorant of your titles."

"How did they keep Aunt in the dark for so long? Uncle said there was an estrangement between him and Grandfather, but they always seemed like friends to me," I said.

"Yes, Uncle could only visit once a year during his mother's life. He never said he was going to Grey Manor, but just a tour of the country. By the time Uncle married Aunt, the brothers were already growing apart. When Uncle bought his bride to meet his brother, they visited two houses first and never mentioned the name of the third. She never heard the name Grey Manor until her mother-in-law died. Not that Uncle's mother ever listened to anything your aunt said, anyway."

"That is sad," I said.

"Yes, but then I married your mom. That's when the estrangement eased. They never told Uncle's mother they went to visit grandfather, but Aunt would visit her sister in the country. It gave the brothers more of an opportunity to see each other. The estrangement ended entirely when Uncle's mother died, but your Aunt was still in the dark."

"It is hard for me to even fathom Uncle and Grandfather as brothers. Their temperaments are so different," I said.

"Yes, but they had very different mothers. Your grandfather's father, The Most Honorable Marquess of Dorset, The Earl of Somerset, The honorable Baron of Dorchester—"

"I understand," I said.

"You will not forget the Baronet," father said.

"Perhaps his first given name will suffice for your explanation," I said.

"William was his name," he said, "William loved and respected his first wife. She died when Grandfather was in his twentieth year. William remarried within a year to a young, ambitious woman."

"Uncle Claremont Hull's mother?"

"Yes. It was hard on Florence to always be compared to his first wife. She insisted her son be given a title, and wealth, despite being the second son. Grandfather loved his studies and the little scamp of a brother and did not object to giving him one of his titles. Florence insisted on calling Uncle Viscount Claremont Hull, a courtesy title while William lived."

"Grandfather went only by the title of Baronet?" I asked. "Why?"

"It wasn't a courtesy. He actually held the title after his mother died. My father grew so accustomed to the title of Baronet, few people in the country ever called him Lord Hull. By the time you were born, many of the younger generation never realized he held so many titles."

"Grandfather was very generous," I said.

"Yes, it was with his blessing William petitioned on your Uncle's behalf. He was granted the earldom, along with the unkempt house in Somerset, but the land was worked and very profitable. Upon his father, William's, death, both men inherited their titles, and your grandfather, seeing how much his brother enjoyed politics, bought him this respectable house in town upon his graduation."

"Uncle's mother must have been pleased by this," I said.

"No. Too much happened between Grandfather and Florence before this."

"What"? I asked.

"Florence was a young, ambitious woman and William aged quickly after their marriage. William was sick for many years before he died. Florence claimed her husband incapacitated, and your grandfather did not use the titles to advantage. So, she petitioned the crown to give her his titles."

"She claimed Grandfather neglected in his duties?"

"She did not understand all Grandfather did. Especially during the war, he and William, knowing the area so intimately and with great skill, helped organize the protection of the channel against invading ships. Grandfather settled many disputes over trade, not to mention the pursuit of smugglers. The crown rewarded our family many times over the years. Despite this, Florence only saw him wasting his social status among the Ton."

"That is brazen-faced," I said.

"Grandfather defended himself. Florence was set down in a very public showing by her peers in the House of

Lords. She hated Grandfather after that. Not to mention how sorely she embarrassed her husband."

"Did she stop in her pursuit of his titles after that?"

"She lived in a much quieter manner until William passed away. Grandfather bought Uncle this house in London. He delicately hinted Uncle needed to take responsibility for his mother after he graduated from Cambridge."

"There is no Dower house on any of Grandfather's properties?" I asked.

"It was a matter of the settlement. After William died, she only had access to the house in Somerset. Despite this, Grandfather would have sent her anywhere, but she insisted London was her true home. Florence always spent more than she had. They thought the best solution would be for Uncle Claremont Hull to … take care of her."

"Was it?" I asked.

"No. Grandfather regretted it after a time. Florence was angry. She kept Uncle in a state of never-ending dread. Uncle was not mature enough to disregard his own mother. She spoiled many of Uncle's relationships, and even ruined a few women's reputations. We thought Uncle Claremont Hull would never marry, but Aunt finally made it through Florence to marry him."

"And that is why Grandfather withdrew from the Ton?"

"Well, things happened that almost forced him to withdraw just before he married, but they have little to do with our present story, if we may continue on our current path," he said.

"Of course," I answered. "I am most concerned with the understanding between myself and Edmund."

"Grandfather realized after years in London with Florence, Uncle was without the grounded guidance his father had passed on to him. He felt Edmund lacked even more."

165

"Edmund could use a little guidance," I said.

"Grandfather thought so. He did not wish for you to marry Edmund unless he grew into the kind of man you deserved."

"Much less advantageous matches have been made," I said.

"Perhaps, but as you grew up, you looked more and more like your lovely mother. Grandfather loved her more than his brother or myself. There is something about daughters that can keep a man's heart young," he said kissing my cheek.

I had nothing left to give him. Every part of my emotions strained toward acceptance of the situation, emptying my reservoir of daughterly affection. I refocused him by asking: "He did not arrange my marriage to either gentleman then?" My heart beat up my throat. The vast affect the answer could have on my life and happiness twisted my stomach while my father thought about how to respond.

"He left it all very vague," replied Father, finally. I nodded and paced as Father said: "He felt if Edmund would choose you as the daughter of a baronet, he would bless the match. If Edmund could not, he would instead favor a match between you and the grandson of his oldest friend. He and Lord Devon grew up nearer brothers than friends. Uncle always resented Lord Devon for that."

"Uncle does not like Lord Devon," I agreed, now understanding the antipathy between them.

"Uncle was insulted Grandfather spent so much time with Lord Devon when he came to town. But while Florence lived, he could not invite Grandfather into his home," Father said.

"Grandfather was not supposed to associate with his friend because he could not associate with his brother?"

"Grandfather and Lord Devon met as lads in school. Uncle was born after Grandfather was grown. It cannot be compared, but Uncle could never understand why he could not have their relationship."

"Lord Devon has not come out to Grey Manor for many years."

"Lord Devon understood the situation in his own way. He has for many years withdrawn so that the family might be restored through a marriage between you and Edmund."

"Oh," I said, quietly feeling my heart drop. "Uncle must have appreciated that."

"Well, he accepted it. The son of an earl who is admitted into your society from a very young age, versus the son of a lower baron with nothing to recommend him, whom you did not know. Those were circumstances he could live with," Father said, nodding. "Why does Lord Devon not wish me to marry Duke Garrett?" I asked. I looked away so Father could not see my disappointment.

"He believes the family line should stay intact. Your marriage to Edmund would restore the line."

"He was more concerned about our family line than his own?"

"Well, that and he did not think it appropriate for you to marry Mr. Garrett. Lord Devon has two sons, with sons of their own to inherit his Earldom. His youngest daughter married a lower Baron. When you were born, Duke Garrett, a few years senior to Edmund, was to inherit his father's lower Barony with only a small country house attached."

"Like Mr. Percival," I said.

"Who?" Father asked, examining me. "A kind sort of man with whom I have been often paired because he is the lowest in rank at most of the functions we attended." My father looked at me apologetically.

"That is the real reason you did not tell me isn't it?" I said, the pressure in my chest expanding.

"Dearest, do you understand what it means to be an heiress in your own right?"

"Everything is mine," I said.

"It is not just wealth but the titles you will inherit," he admitted. "I am sorry, but in the next few weeks you will understand why this experience of coming to London with nothing was so important."

"Duke Garrett was attentive to me, even without a title," I said, "Unless … did he know?"

"I doubt it very seriously."

"Uncle does not like Duke Garrett's attention toward me," I said.

"No, I imagine your Uncle, being reassured by Lord Devon's sufficient heirs, did not bother to find out much about Garrett's family line. He did not realize they were related to the Duke of Surry, though the last name was obvious enough."

"Why did Uncle make Aunt invite me to town only to meet Edmund's rival?" I asked.

"Ah well, I must confess to a little…. I may have sounded reluctant to come to town in the many letters I returned to Uncle's insistence put on paper. It was a little manipulative on my part to let him believe he must bribe me with the fair play of our social experiment, but it was Grandfather's dearest wish that you would at least meet Duke Garrett and Edmund in the same venue."

"Because Lord Devon would not come to us, even after Grandfather grew sick," I said.

"Yes," Father said gritting his teeth, "but Edmund came and Uncle was satisfied the boy loves you. I allowed you to come to town on the understanding you were to be ignorant of my titles until I arrived."

"If Uncle had not manipulated the situation, when would that have been?" I asked.

"I was waiting for you to tire of society and ask me to come. I did hint in the letter I wrote you that I would come," he said.

"Yes, but I knew you hate London or I would have asked," I countered.

"That is fair," he said putting his shoulder next to mine when I sat. I crossed my arms and said: "I find it curious Uncle did not think Duke Garrett had a chance. I was being raised unaware of my own title which would have made me more suitable for the son of a lower Baron. All the while Edmund believed me to be beneath him, and therefore resisted me?"

"Yes. He never dreamt Lord Devon's favorite boy would one day be a duke outranking you instead of the other way around," Father said. "I believe that is why Uncle kept your titles a secret as long as he did, so he could put the gap between you and Duke Garrett in the other direction. Uncle must be beside himself." Father laughed to himself.

"Well, to add upon all this, Edmund has paid his regard to Lady Alice, and the Ton is watching that development with interest," I said.

"Which brings us full circle in explaining Uncle's desperation for Edmund to know who you really are," Father said.

"Edmund was very upset when he found out," I said.

"I can imagine. He would have started courting you at sixteen had he known," Father agreed.

"Are you certain Duke Garrett did not know about all I would inherit?" I asked.

"Lord Devon would never taint the experiment. Who would the intelligent woman prefer? An extremely clever baron, or the heir to an earldom who never attended his studies because he had a story to

The Lark

tell. Edmund does have a delightful wit about him, does he not?"

"You seem to prefer Edmund," I said.

"I have loved the lad and see far more potential in him, and his adoration of you than Grandfather ever did."

"You do not know Duke Garrett," I said.

"Not well, and Lord Devon's unwillingness to bring the lad to Grey Manor because of his lowness in rank, I confess, rankled me. Is the son of an earl refusing to pay his regard to you because he is too high in station so different from a man refusing to give it a go because he feels he is too low in station?"

"In other words, he did not bring him and it interfered with your experiment. My very marriage was part of the experiment then?" I asked crossly, standing up.

"I doubt Uncle would mention that, especially in front of Edmund."

"Yet it is so?"

"Dearest, you are heiress to too much. You do not understand the length to which fortune hunters will go when you are presented. Your grandfather always felt your future would be more secure with one of the two men."

"Yet, they do not know that. Instead they are being manipulated into showing interest for me, as if all our lives are one big chess game, and we are only the pawns," I said folding my arms and trying not to cry.

"It seemed the perfect solution until just now when you put it like that," Father answered. His face creased in concern.

"Please encourage Uncle not to say anything. It is so humiliating."

"Eva, I assume your Aunt knows the extent of my titles?"

"Yes," I answered. "We are no longer in charge of this experiment. She will dote on you, knowing you should

170

always have been her daughter, simply to inherit Grey Manor," Father said dryly with a lift of his eyebrow.

"And Duke Garrett?" I asked.

"Lord Devon would never pollute his observations. He will not know," Father said.

"I like Duke Garrett's mother very much," I said.

"Yes, I've never met her, but Lord Devon doted on her, and your grandfather liked her as well," he said. I could think of nothing more to say that might endear Duke Garrett's relations to my father.

I asked: "My uncle is also your uncle. That is a strange family relationship, is it not?"

"Welcome to thick of it my dear. The only concern is everything remains in the family, no matter how ornately the family tree begins to twist."

I laughed bitterly. "I suppose I am meant to twist just as strangely."

"Ah, there is my girl! My goal from here to the end of the season is to get you home in one piece," he said. He put an arm around my reluctant shoulder. "You need not be married so young," he continued. "We will invite Edmund for Christmas, and Duke Garrett for Easter. Then we may see what we think in a quieter atmosphere."

"Or the other way around," I said feeling this perfect solution release the tension in my stomach. All the expectation Uncle placed on my shoulders disappeared. I did not have to marry so soon.

"I suppose," Father said rolling his eyes at me. We were quiet again. I felt the walls closing in on me. I did not want to be under Uncle Claremont Hull's roof. Then I remembered my grandfather had many holdings. I asked: "Did you not say Grandfather has a house in town we inherited?"

"A grand estate. Shall we have it put to rights so we can stop intruding on Uncle's generosity?"

171

"Yes, and shall we go to Paris where my dresses must be purchased? I would like to go to Paris, Father," I said relieved at the idea of leaving Uncle's protection.

"Perhaps after our race at the Ascot in June. We are to be held hostage for a time. You've been granted admission to the queen's drawing room. You haven't enough titles coming to you to neglect the Queen, dearest," Father said.

Chapter Twenty-One

We did not spend another night in Uncle's house. Father's London home stood tall in a fashionable neighborhood, and, as a free-standing structure, it gained even more distinction. A tower rounded one side of the house. Steep roofs and tall chimneys indicated the Tudor style of home Sir William preferred, but the loveliest large windows, and ornate veranda indicated Grandfather did much to improve this house, despite that it was much newer than Grey Manor. It was kept in perfect working order by a full-time staff, simply due to Grandfather's unwillingness to allow those in his employ to want simply because he chose not to live in London.

My father gave me first choice of the rooms, and I choose a large chamber with a private sitting room attached to a room for Miss Bolton. I suspected this was the space reserved for the Lord and Lady of the house. Father seemed quite content to have us, his ladies, so comfortably established and took a slightly smaller chamber for himself. The staff had been retained for years, and the housekeeper, a woman we called Hetty, with no other title for some reason, appeared thrilled to have more than the old man's visits to look forward to. Trim and prim with excessive height for a woman, Hetty had been caring for the house in every role possible for many of her forty and some odd years. Her youthful energy made her presence felt in a room, and I could see how my grandfather would have liked her. Hetty redid my room in a matter of days, having all the furniture recovered until I floated on fluffs of white clouds. My huge bed was hung in lace then covered in flounces and pillows that could hardly be slept in for fear of one disappearing. The pillow on the window seat slowly sucked the unsuspecting into its deep recesses if one chanced to sit too long. The walls were papered in white patterns that swirled with gold. Miss Bolton was re-situated in blues after she indicated a preference for them. The light blue walls were accented in airy silks that swayed with little provocation. Her bed hangings were dark navy satin and the whole room moved when the door opened. To tie the rooms together, Hetty had the sitting room papered and carpeted in varying shades of light blue. The frames that held pictures of the countryside, trim work, and furniture were all white with gold accents. The room felt like the puffy mists in a summer sky tinted by the gold of the setting sun. Then if one went into Miss Bolton's room, the blue-sky shown clear, but in the other direction the world floated on my cloud. This garnered my father's devotion to the housekeeper, and he gave her a raise in salary.

When Hetty learned she would present a ball for me after my presentation, her enthusiasm overflowed. I was not offended when she did not stop and pretend to want my opinion on anything from the table settings to the menu. She even convinced Aunt Claremont Hull on points of decorum and the latest fashionable foods that must be served. She would not hear of the fruit being ordered locally when only exotics would do for her master's young lady. She often talked about Grandfather in that way, like he didn't pass away, he just left town. Sometimes I believed her, especially when I went into his study and could smell his books. My father, when unoccupied, followed Hetty around just to see what she would do and say as a guide to effective time management. He spent his first few afternoons watching her have our rooms redone until Miss Bolton gently reminded Father that the woman was a person and not an oddity growing in a vase. After this Father was careful not to let Miss Bolton see him when he trailed Hetty. Hetty liked the attention, so I said nothing. The next four weeks were full of lessons, fittings, and practicing duets with Julia. Now we might perform together since I was no longer a lower relation putting myself forward. During this time, my father presented his coat of arms to Lord Chamberlin, and easily took his seat in the House of Lords. He was welcomed enthusiastically into all the best circles; circles in which even Uncle was not privy. Many young men sought him out to indicate their excitement at meeting his daughter, while their mothers plagued Aunt's drawing room. I did mention to Father I had been in the same room with some of them when my dance card could not be filled. Aunt Claremont Hull used the situation to her full advantage and appointed herself our unofficial liaison to the quality. She assured us every day at Tea that any one worth knowing spoke of nothing but Father and me. She was sure to keep us in the spotlight, claiming my ball would be exclusive, but grand, unlike anything the quality had witnessed in years.

Under the strictest guidelines of edict, she ensured I did not see Duke Garrett the entire four weeks before my presentation. My Aunt kept me under her watchful care, coming into my father's home after her morning callers and never leaving until she was required to attend Julia in the evenings. At first, I worried Duke Garrett would find some other woman to make him laugh while I was forced into confinement. Julia, in a quiet moment, confided he left London on business for his grandfather. He asked Julia to send his regard to me and assured he would be back in time for my ball. Then I wondered what his business was, and if Lord Devon were well. Edmund was permitted into my father's house for family dinners, and at hand far more often than he had been before. He seemed withdrawn and even miserable at times. I could coax him out of his despondency for a time, but this eventually wrenched him down even further. The effort grew tiring, and I found ways to avoid him when he was not finding ways to follow me. When we were alone, Aunt happened to mention Edmund waited impatiently for the day he could dance with

175

me. I thought this odd but quickly learned not to encourage, nor discourage Aunt's fancies. She could grow offended with too much or too little support for her ideas.

Lady Garrett came to see me the day before my presentation. Fortunately, only Julia sat with me and therefore the visit was allowed as an old friend of our families. She carried a note to me from Duke Garrett, asking for the dinner dance at my ball. I wrote back with as much familiarity as I dared to accept him with pleasure. I regretted Lady Garrett leaving before my father could come back and see what a fine woman she was. My isolated days took forever to pass, but then, all too soon, my moment arrived.

My presentation was long and brief in the same experience. As the daughter of a marquess, my carriage stood in front of a long row of carriages filled with debutantes, who would greet the queen, then be marriageable. Aunt and I waited, and waited in the dark carriage. Drawn windows kept the increasingly foul air bottled up with no concept of how much time passed. Aunt, to stem my impatience, said: "I heard the new Palace of Westminster will have a clock tower that will be heard all over London." "Is that so?" I said. I had heard the exact same thing from Uncle the night before because neither of our society varied as of late. Each time the tallest of the Ostrich feathers I wore grazed the roof of the carriage she inhaled to indicate she feared I would break it, and lamented we had not left it in the hat box until our term inside our people box ended.

I slouched so she did not have to watch it so closely, but three servants had helped tie my corset, and I could not breathe in a slumped position. I soon forgot why I turned blue and sat up straighter. Then we started the process over again. I made a vow I would take every item I owned out of hat boxes for an airing when I arrived home.

A hollow knock echoed foreboding on the carriage door. The door was opened by a servant clad in Queen Victoria's livery. Fresh air swept into the box, and the red brick facade of St. James Palace could be seen.

"Your wrap," Aunt hissed. I reluctantly slipped out of the shawl and left it on my seat. Then I allowed the man to help me from the stuffy carriage. Straps of white satin cut across the bottom of my shoulders in place of sleeves and the dipping neckline amply exposed my chest. The exposure of so much of my body was foreign to me, and caused a shiver on my neck, though the fresh spring air did not bother me. My heavy hair twisted ornately and dipped in ringlets, Miss Bolton's most magnificent creation, bounced down my bare neck. A heavy lace veil trailed nine feet behind me with the train of my white dress. I stepped out of the carriage, and the servant picked up the excess of my dress and veil, draping them over my left arm. He led us to where we would again stop and wait. I stood for a quarter of an hour in a drafty gallery listening to dim music played by stringed instruments from the drawing room. This time I quavered, but no matter how I reprimanded myself, I could not make my stomach feel less queasy. I did not envy the hours it would take for the many young women who lined up behind me to make it into the drawing room. I was ushered to the door first.

Aunt hissed: "Stay in your bow as long as possible. Do not to be presumptuous, do not offer your hand, or look to be reaching for hers. Make sure she makes the first move. Queen Victoria is trying just as hard to earn her title as you are, so you will, I am certain, receive a kiss. Pause, oh child, pause and see if she will kiss you instead of shaking hands. I do believe she will accept your father's efforts in the past weeks to secure his place so that you might not be slighted."

After this encouragement, she took my heavy train and veil from my aching arm. I was ushered into the drawing room. Fear presented itself in the form tears at the back of my throat that had to be swallowed two or three times. Lords-in-waiting pulled my dress out behind me, tugging on my sore neck to be sure the veil was seen to full advantage. I handed my card over to the speaker at the door. I moved slowly, dragging myself and the bulk of my dress like I walked through a stiff wind, toward the queen while all my father's titles were announced loudly over the music. Queen Victoria's crown looked like a dainty fan filled with diamonds upon her dark head, though I did not think her hair as dark as mine. She wore an extravagant cream dress of silk and lace draped in a blue sash. Her blue eyes watched me, and I tried to stand up even taller, worthy of her appraisal. When I reached her, I curtsied low holding the whole weight of my body and heavy dress within inches of the floor. I paused. My body shook holding the pose. I held my breath. I am not certain anyone breathed. I was not offered her hand so I rose. The very young queen leaned forward and kissed my forehead. She seemed to offer me a slight smile. My eyes brightened as they connected with hers and I felt something of a camaraderie toward her. I bowed carefully to the other members of the court. I offered my final bow to the queen. Then, an attendant handed me my train and I hung it over my left arm again so I might back out of the room without turning my back on the monarch. A servant took small steps to help me see which direction I needed to go, guiding me out of the room in this way. The weight of the dress kept me from moving with ease. I stumbled. Horrified, I worked to regain my footing quickly, against the bulk of my skirt. My face, I am sure turned bright red, but I kept moving backward, my only goal to leave the room. Once out of the queen's presence, I turned. My aunt swatted at the train in my arm meaning for me to drop it so she could re-situate it to keep it from creasing. I did not; I only wished to relieve my neck of the heavy veil.

"Well done Eva. I did not think you capable, but you did almost as well as Julia," she said, clearly meaning to praise me.

"Thank you, Aunt," I said, "Thank you for the hours you spent teaching me to bow, and all the trouble you went through with my gown."

"Of course, Eva. You are my dear sister's child. Of course. It was my duty to present you at court."

"Thank you," I said again, though I did not mention she neglected the duty when I was only the daughter of an insignificant Baronet and would have been nearer the end of the line of carriages instead of at the beginning.

"Now, my dear Eva, you are eligible for all the delights of London, and I assure you the invitations have poured in. Let us take tea at my home, and we will discuss your schedule for the next few weeks. Starting this evening, we will celebrate at your ball."

"Will my father be at your home?" I asked.

"Of course. He will be anxious to see how you did. And aside from your slight tumble picking up your train, you will, I think, have nothing to blush over," she said.

"May I change before tea?" I asked.

"Of course, and I will have the bodice of your dress redone. It will do as your wedding dress, I am sure."

I said nothing. I did find it amusing only a month ago my aunt lamented I'd reached my twentieth year with no prospects and could only hope for an early death. Now I felt certain if she had her way, my veil would trail all the way through the church in Somerset Parrish before autumn came.

179

Father met me in the hall and helped me off with my bonnet while Aunt called for tea.

"How did you do?" he asked quietly.

"You mean was I able to transcend the pomp of the queen's drawing room?"

"Were you?" he asked with half a smile.

"No, I was so terrified. I stumbled," I said. "It turns out no matter how much one studies, one can never become immune to the human experience."

"I did notice you turned quite pale when Julia mentioned seeing Duke Garrett at tea last evening," he said.

"You suppose my show of jealousy already gave my illness away?" I asked.

"You were very kind to Julia after," he said, "perhaps transcending is just a show of kindness when lashing out would be easier?"

"Grandfather did try to cure me," I said.

"It was worth a try," he said with a little laugh as we walked into the drawing room. He announced to Julia, Edmund and Aunt: "My girl is a woman because she looked upon the queen who is only one year her senior."

"At least I did not wobble on my bow, though my legs are sore from the exertion," I teased. For effect, I leaned against the burnt orange settee as if exhausted.

"Yes, well if you'd spent longer at practice …." Said Aunt.

"Mother, she did well, and I have no doubt, enchanted them all," Edmund said as he took my hand and kissed it. I studied him. He never tried any measure of friendliness with me except our usual banter.

"Eva, did she kiss you?" Julia asked, giving me the opportunity to turn from her brother.

"Yes, and I think she even smiled at me," I said, pulling away and moving toward Julia.

"No dear, that was her serene expression," Aunt said trying to kindly rebuff me.

"No. Look, like this," I said demonstrating for Julia.

"That does perhaps look a little like a smile," she said, but I could see she was only placating me. I went to the gold-plated looking glass Aunt hung between the windows so she could see what her face looked like to passersby. I made the face. I looked like Miss Bolton when she found something amusing, but decorum, that insistent mistress, kept her from smiling.

"Eva, would you stop making that face and come away from the window," Aunt chided. We all stopped. She had, up to this point, fought her instinct to outright scold me since I became titled.

Father lifted an eye to me. He promised me her act would eventually crumble, but I did not join his amusement. I saw something more in Aunt's eyes. Something broken, her ancient pain, and it had something to do with not being listened to. I moved away from the window and vowed to be patient and a little more obedient to my Aunt's constant instruction. I did prefer our relationship from before when she never gave me any more attention than she would an out-of-fashion rack to hold her coat, but I would try. I would not purposely put that look of hopelessness in her eyes again.

"Eva, would you do me the honor of the first set tonight?" Edmund asked, breaking the tense silence, "Now that you are out, I shall have the pleasure of dancing with you for the first time, again."

"I would like that. Thank you, Edmund," I said with a bow. I handed him my card to keep him at arm's length. "Perhaps you should claim the dinner as well, since she will not know where to sit," Aunt said.

I blushed. Edmund turned white.

"Her dinner is already taken," he said. Confused, Aunt looked like she would question who got through her defenses, but Father quickly said: "It is for the best. Otherwise we may start a tabby party. We do not want to imply there has been an inappropriate connection before she was presented."

"No, of course not," Aunt said, reapplying her persona of unwillingness to argue with my father now that he was a marquess. If she were entirely open, she could have comforted him, that she, among the harshest of the tabbys, would say nothing.

I smiled at Edmund and he grinned back. It relieved me he did not want people to suppose something existed between us that did not. I took my card back.

I only had two of my sets filled because of my isolation. Unlike the last time I found my dance card bare, it filled quickly. Greeting all of my guests as they entered my father's house, Uncle performed the necessary introductions. Every unmarried man, even some who possibly left their first wives in the grave and did not look fit for exertion, asked for a dance. Lord Harley and his enormous son came early in the evening. The ease in Lord Harley's manners were entirely absent in his sons. Viscount Harley, whom had no interest in me at Lord Holland's ball, could not be more attentive to me at my own, but his attentions were tinged with so much conceit it made him boorish. He took my small hand in his enormous one and shook it with my dance card still between them after writing his name in it. When I only had one set left, Mr. Percival came down the line. I bowed to him and he glanced at Julia who pretended not to have much of an acquaintance with him. His usual jovial manners failed him. I handed over my card. "Oh, Miss, or rather Lady Grey or Hull?"

"I think you must say Lady Eva Grey Hull," I said.

"Well, I do not think you need to...." He glanced at the line queuing up behind him, many of whom would no doubt expect to dance with me.

"Dance with my friend," I asked.

"Are we friends"? he asked.

"I only see two or possibly three others I've been through a riot with," I said. "How is one to know who can pummel three men at once if they've not seen it? This ball promises to get rowdy." He smiled at me. "Besides, though I have gone through much backache to meet the queen, I do not think myself so weak as to require only an Earl or above to hold me up," I whispered, "especially when one considers some of the more dilapidated earls."

Mr. Percival smiled his gorgeous smile at me. Julia, who stood next to my father, flinched. "Eva," Aunt hissed, and I realized I was holding up the receiving line. Mr. Percival quickly put his name down on my final dance.

"Thank you," he said handing it back and bowing.

"No, thank you," I said bowing. After he left, I happened to look down the line and my heart leapt. Duke Garrett watched me. I let go of the breath I held since I had seen him last and everything righted within me. The smile he brought to my face was the first natural and effortless of the evening. Caught up in the act of examining his face, I could not even be civil to the man I declined for a dance. I watched eagerly as Father renewed his acquaintance with Duke Garrett. I hoped for any sign of pleasure. Duke Garrett tried to be warm, but Father acted aloof with barely a handshake and a slight bow then he moved on quickly to the next in line.

"Where are Lord Devon and your mother?" I asked when he reached me.

"My grandfather is ill but sends his warmest regard. My mother sends her excuses, she chose to spend the evening with him," he said.

"Of course," I said. We were silent.

He examined me and said, "You look...."

"All grown up," I supplied, looking down at the layers of my soft peach ball gown.

"Lovely," he said watching me for signs of something. His examination brought the blush to my face without my permission. He smiled as if he found what he looked for.

"Is it serious?" I asked.

"Excuse me?" he asked.

"Your grandfather. Is his illness serious?"

"Oh, pardon. He says it is not," Duke Garrett said. He could not look at me.

I took his hand and said: "He is a very dutiful man and so you must assure him it is his duty to get better. They have finally moved on to Romeo and Juliet. Now that I exist again, we must go," I said. "May I call on him tomorrow?" "Of course, Miss ur... My lady."

I grinned at his misstep and he relaxed.

"Eva darling girl, you are holding up the line," Aunt said glancing at the Lady in front of her with an indulgent smile. Beyond her I noticed Uncle and Father watch me interact with Duke Garrett, and I wished to be invisible again.

Chapter Twenty-Three

The ballroom shone gloriously, every corner lit, every pillar draped in garlands of flowers. Hetty must have been bored for some time. Even Aunt Claremont Hull could find nothing lacking in the arrangements. Miss Bolton, now my companion instead of my Abigail, accompanied me into the ball. She saved my seat and looked out for my every comfort while she enjoyed the music. We spoke to each other as friends in public as we always had in private, and the arrangement suited both of us better.

Aunt openly resented Miss Bolton for taking the place she meant to have as chaperone until a little circumstance happened. After which she said nothing derogatory to her again. At the beginning of the ball, my father introduced Miss Bolton to Lord Pennington.

"Ah, Bolton. That is a promising name. Are you a relation to Baron Bolton?" Lord Pennington asked. "He is my uncle," she said.

"Really," Aunt Claremont Hull said with tight lips. I hoped she remembered sending Miss Bolton down to the servants to take her dinner.

"Yes," Father said, "her brother was at school with me, a great friend of mine. I have trusted her with much, giving her the charge of Eva's upbringing since my wife passed on."

"Didn't one of your cousins reject Baron Adley's marriage proposal?" Lady Pennington asked with a memory that gave her half a laugh. Miss Bolton blushed scarlet, her mouth opened, but nothing came out.

"What is this?" I asked her.

"Were you engaged to a Baron?" my father asked.

"No, never engaged," Miss Bolton said.

"I would never have let any of my relations near him, rich as a sultan as he was," Lady Pennington said kindly. "The man had no conscience. It must have been your brother who stopped the thing after your father died, did he not?"

"Yes," she said. Aunt Claremont Hull was ashen white and looked to be fighting to swallow. She must never have heard of a woman turning down a title and wealth before. Sadly, Edmund picked me up for the first set, pulling me away from the discussion I found immensely interesting. While we danced, Lady Alice watched us, not minding her steps, nor her partner. Edmund usually showed her the attention of dancing the first with her, and then a second time for the waltz. Aunt arranged for the waltz to be among the first set of dances to deprive Lady Alice of both. This left Lady Alice to Mr. Percival, because she held back the first dance for so long, assuming Edmund would eventually ask her.

I felt sure she would have me skewered if she could. Edmund, for his part, curled me into his arm and gazed at me with soft eyes denoting admiration. He said little, no doubt trying to build a tension between us with simply his stare. The whole thing turned a touch awkward after the first few chords. As children we danced the waltz together when it was still scandalous, before the embrace was loosed, the beat quickened, and the dance found favor with the queen. It felt more intimate back then, with only an echo of that memory to give this turn about the room any spark. When only one set loomed before me and my dance with Duke Garrett, Viscount Harley came to claim his dance. He took my arm in a possessive way and escorted me to our place on the floor. His rounded arm muscles smashed my hand uncomfortably as he escorted me to the head of the line.

"I understand this is your first trip to London," he said.

"Yes," I replied.

"My father is very fond of you," he said.

"And I him. Your younger brother is a charming fellow," I said.

"Charles," he laughed with condescension. "Surely you jest." He spoke to me largely of his little brother's deficiencies as we danced. I said little to defend him as I spent all my energy trying not to be crushed. I took three steps to his one. As we danced, I had to leap to keep up with his turns. His hands, the size of earth spades, were covered in enormous grey gloves. He sweated profusely and the dye on his gloves bled into my bright white ones. After he no longer used all his mental acuity to dance, he kept my hand smashed in his arm while he mentioned his many holdings to me instead of leading me back to Miss Bolton. I almost cried with relief when our dance ended.

I barely bowed as Duke Garett took my hand and he was forced to relinquish me. I discreetly showed Duke Garrett my gloves as we danced the first of our set.

"He ruined them. I do hope my aunt does not notice," I said.

"Did you at least tromp on his toes?" Duke Garrett asked.

"No. I feared retaliation. He may have crippled me," I said. I looked at him slyly.

"Well, at least you considered it. Now that you are the daughter of a marquess, I did wonder if you'd still consider it an honor to tromp on my toes this evening," he said, moving me forward so we could bow to another couple.

"I am forgiven everything these days, and, as it would not cause a scandal, it has lost its draw," I said. We moved away from them. "I see you are settling into this rise in stature with some disappointment, then," he said, but his face held a faint smile. I glanced at the Viscount Harley, who nodded, and smiled at me, but not his partner. She looked in fear of her life as he hopped clumsily into her space. "I do not know how you adapted," I said.

"I tromp on the toes of those who outrank me. It is satisfying, if not scandalous."

"I think you are trying to tempt me onto your toes, sir," I said focusing back on him entirely.

"I am," he said, looking too serious, pulling me in closer to his side where our hands were connected.

"Well then, I will warn you, I have ample opportunity. Hetty insisted the Polka is going to be the most popular dance within the year, and would only do for our last dance before supper," I said.

"I would prefer the Waltz, but your cousin had that honor. The Polka will do," he said.

I blushed and he grinned as the music stopped. I turned to face him in preparation of the Polka. Duke Garrett kept my eyes to him as he slid one hand up my side and rested it on the back of my rib cage, clasping his other to my hand. He pulled me just a touch closer than necessary and I wished he would have brought me in the rest of the way, closing the gap between us. We waited in this intimate stance and everything that was or would be existed in the circle of our arms. Nothing could exist, if not enclosed between us, and I was alive for the first time ever. The music struck and we began. Duke Garrett picked me up and swung me around the room. The slow intimacy Edmund tried to force with me was nothing to the way I flew with Duke Garrett. The room turned in a whirl. Duke Garrett tethered me to the earth, supporting me in a way that kept my feet from hitting the ground with too much of a jolt before he pushed me back up into the air. The movements hinted at what the rest of my time upon earth should be and the music heightened my hope. Encouraged by my growing enthusiasm, Duke Garrett moved me higher on our steps. The layers on my dress never expressed themselves so joyously, and the flounces on my sleeves refused to be outdone. The song ended before I was ready to land.

"Thank you," I said, my soul still flying outside my body.

"That was my pleasure," Duke Garrett said, squeezing me before he let go of his embrace. I took the arm he offered, and we walked together to dinner.

Hetty removed the furniture from the large drawing room. She had many small tables set up around the dining room and drawing room to accommodate all sixty-two of my father's guests a place to sit. Father escorted a dowager in. She sat to his right. Many dignitaries came to honor him in his first attempt at hosting. Being engulfed by them, he was unable to fill a plate for her. I sat at a table with our younger guests. Duke Garrett, with considerate attention, helped me to my seat. To my astonishment, Edmund set a plate of food before me and sat to my right without being invited. Duke Garrett and I looked uncertainly at each other. It was an informal occasion; I hoped it did not matter. Duke Garrett filled a plate for Lady Alice and her sister since they had not been tended to, and they filled in the seats around me. I could see the looks of dismay on the faces of the Tabbys, and couldn't be sure what to do. My concern deepened when Julia was set even lower when Viscount Harley joined us, and she was forced onto a separate table altogether. She did not seem to mind; Mr. Percival claimed the seat next to her and was attentive. She looked content, while I had to curl in my legs not to meet the gigantic feet under the table. I was called upon from my father's table to describe the young queen's gown and appearance, her yet being something of a novelty. Aunt Claremont Hull felt I did not describe the lace to great enough detail and took up the conversation while I ate. I tried not to notice my father, who found too much amusement in the proceedings. Eventually, Viscount Harley spoke to me over Aunt's descriptions of

The Lark

finery. "You have an estate in Dorset Shire, do you not?" he asked, his huge hand spooning the soup to his mouth. He did not take off his gloves.

He must have noticed the coloring did not stay on his gloves. I did take my gloves off, and the grey on my fingers could not be mistaken. I did everything in my power to display the coloring, but he did not notice.

"Yes, it is a beautiful place," I said.

"I meant to inquire after the acreage. My own manor is fourteen hundred acres," Viscount Harley said.

"I think my father would be better acquainted with those details, though it is a ... sprawling estate," I said. I glanced at Duke Garrett who cleared his throat then with a smirk, said: "I myself like to measure my estates in how long it takes to ride from one end of the property to the other. My lady, how long would it take you to ride such a distance?"

"Would you have me walk or trot, Your Grace?" I asked.

"Then you cannot gallop the distance?" he asked, and he must have felt the Viscount stretching out under the table because he extended his legs. The large Viscount flinched. The whole table moved. Even Lady Alice stopped looking peeved to be startled.

"It would be hard on the animal. It is rocky in places, and there are steep inclines. I do not think galloping would be a reliable measurement. I must slow my horse in places," I said as if I did not notice.

"I suppose we cannot have a reliable measurement then," Duke Garrett said.

"It is sixty-four hundred acres," Edmund said, glaring at Duke Garrett.

"And how do you know that so exactly, sir?" Lady Alice asked.

"I spent every summer there as a boy," Edmund said. "That is a significant sized property, and you stand to

190

inherit more than one property, I understand," Viscount Harley said. Soup dribbled down his chin.

"Yes," I said looking down, my stomach rolling.

"You are heir to it all, I understand," he said. We all stared at him. I nodded and tried to focus entirely on the lovely apricots in cream in front of me. That did not stop him from questioning me about my holdings, and which of my father's titles my children would inherit. I was not sorry to get a reprieve from all the attention when, after dinner, Miss Bolton assured me I needed to refresh my hair, so I could replace my soiled gloves. I slipped away, but instead of moving to the dressing room, she followed me quietly to the back of the house where we slipped up some hidden steps to my chamber. I rested for a quarter of an hour in a chair near the open window while she fixed my hair. I used a cloth to scrub the gray dye from my fingers. After the repose, I pulled on new gloves and we slipped back down the hidden stairs but halted before the empty hallway when we heard voices.

We were about to make ourselves known when the feminine voice said: "You have spoken to my father, Edmund. You have engaged yourself to me, and that cannot be undone, no matter how many of your cousins turn out to be marchioness."

"I am honoring my obligation to you, Alice, I am. But you have to understand, she has been my ideal since–"

"I do not care. You offered to me, and I expect you to honor that. I have saved you the next dance, certain you meant to single me out with a second set as you have at every other ball this season."

"I would rather–"

"I did not ask you your rather sir, but what is expected. Le bon ton has seen you singling me out. I acquiesced to your whim at waiting to announce until you spoke to your father, but as you well know, I have already discouraged every other marriageable suitor available to me. I will not be set aside and humiliated for an ill-mannered, countrified upstart," she said as they walked away.

"Actually, the line extends back to …." Edmund answered. We could hear no more as they left our range. I looked at Miss Bolton for her opinion.

"I did not think everything settled between them," Miss Bolton said, examining me.

"Nor I," I said.

"Are you injured?" she asked.

"No, but rather relieved. I thought myself taking on the pomp of town, but as Lady Alice sees me as countrified, I suppose I can still look myself in the glass."

"Eva," she snapped.

"I confess, I am also relieved my cousin is honor-bound elsewhere," I said.

"You and Edmund have always gotten on well together, not to mention the way you looked during your waltz—"

"That was him, not me," I said.

"Eva, you are not hiding disappointment?"

"No, I am not. Edmund holds something of himself back. I cannot see past the role he plays. There is a part of him I cannot know, no matter how I try for intimacy. I do not trust that," I said. "I do not regret him being out of my reach."

"Then perhaps the handsome Duke Garrett ought to pay you the courtesy of honoring you with two sets this evening," she teased.

"My card is full, but that I do regret," I lamented.

My father met us at the door to the ballroom to escort me back in. I danced until the early hours of the morning. Finally, our guests began leaving. Even Edmund's intended could hold out no longer and allowed her father to take her home. Duke Garrett gave me his arm and supported my weight as he and the last few guests waited for their carriages to be brought around.

Uncle staggered into the entrance hall. He watched me chatting with Duke Garrett and growled: "Are you still here then, Sir?"

The late hour and champagne must have gotten to Uncle because he came toward us and put a hand out to claim me, but didn't quite make it close enough to reach me. I looked at my father who glanced at us while speaking to the last of his guests.

"Uncle," I warned in a low voice, wishing him to be civil in my father's home.

"She is intended for Edmund," he snarled. "They have been intended since her birth. I went along with this rather ridiculous scheme, leaving her out of the limelight as my brother wished, but that is over now. It is time for her to grow up and take on her responsibilities."

"What responsibility, pray tell, have you thrust upon her – as if you had any right – has she not hoisted upon her shoulders?" Father asked. He stepped toward us, heated.

"She and Edmund should marry before this goes any further," said Uncle. "Duke Garrett, you are a man of honor, a man who understands familial obligations. You must understand what it means for my father's two households to eventually be one again."

"He never wished for that. He felt it fair to spread the wealth around, not amass it in ridiculous quantities," Father said.

"It was your mother's fondest dream for the two houses to be joined again."

Father goaded Uncle in this most unguarded moment. "Your mother always meant for you to rise to your brother's title."

"She should not have; it was always out of my reach," he said. His ears turned bright red in embarrassment. "But not out of Edmund's. She doted on him as a child."

"The title would not be his, but their child's," Uncle snapped.

Father seemed to find this answer interesting, but my face burned. I closed my eyes. Is this how the rest of my season in London would progress?

"Father, I…" Edmund started.

My eyes snapped open. Was Edmund going to announce his betrothal? Would he put an end to Uncle's mistake, freeing us both from the exposure this outburst was causing?

"Edmund, can you say you do not wish Eva to be your wife?" Uncle asked.

Edmund stuttered, looking at me intensely. I looked down unable to bear the connection, especially to a man who was promised to another woman.

"Father, can we speak of this later?" Edmund asked. "Eva looks very tired."

Duke Garrett looked down at me. I clung tightly to his arm. "Are you quite all right, my lady?" he asked. I smiled up at him. He was just saying my title, but I liked the way I felt claimed by him.

"I confess I am tired, mostly of this scene. If my Uncle will consent to halt this discussion until he is in better possession of his faculties, I will be fine."

"Perhaps Miss Bolton should …." said Father.

"Please Sir," Uncle said interrupting my father to address Duke Garrett in his slurred voice. "Let their intended union stand. On your honor, you must see it is right." Duke Garrett looked at Uncle. I could see him considering.

Father put a hand on Uncle's arm pulling him and encouraging him to go home before he exposed us all. Uncle pulled away. He pushed around my father. He pierced Duke Garrett with his desperation. "I must do right by my family name. I must bring the honor back to the house of Hull."

Duke Garrett looked at me. I shook my head at him to ignore Uncle in his drunken state. I clung to him tighter, begging him with my very posture to stay with me.

"Sir, upon your honor, you must see what is right," Uncle said. Duke Garrett looked miserable, and I saw something relinquish in his eyes. He moved, pulling enough to detach me from his arm. I stood shocked with my mouth open. Duke Garrett chose my Uncle's drunken ranting over me? I looked at Edmund, waiting for him to say something, anything, to clear up this confusion. Edmund smiled at me. He moved toward me as if to claim me as his father intended. Duke Garrett moved away. I backed up toward Miss Bolton uncertain I could trust anything I saw in this moment. I looked to my father, desperate for someone to keep Duke Garrett in the entryway. Why did no one expose Edmund's commitment to Lady Alice? My father looked back at me sadly. Could he see my heart breaking? "I think it is time for Eva to turn in," Father said, nodding to Miss Bolton who put an arm around me to support my weight since Duke Garrett was no longer willing.

"Duke Garrett, may I still visit your grandfather tomorrow?" I asked.

He turned back, but would not look at me. "I believe my mother is expecting you to return her visit," he said looking up at the chandelier.

"Please have her send word if tomorrow is inconvenient for her," I said, piercing him with my eyes, trying through intensity to get him to look back at me, while also trying not to cry. He did not. He said nothing, but bowed to my father and took his leave.

I turned, furious with Uncle. What right did he have to such liberties with my future? And Father, why didn't he stop him? I opened my mouth ready to voice my fury, but Miss Bolton quickly turned me to the staircase before I could say anything.

"It is late. Do not join this ruckus tonight. Wait for the morrow, or you will expose yourself, as they are," Miss Bolton whispered. I bowed to the last of our guests, who were very pleased they managed to endure the whole ball that they might be on hand to witness what would, no doubt, be talked over in their drawing rooms in the morning.

I allowed Miss Bolton to lead me away. We were halfway up the stairs when I asked: "Why did Edmund not confess?"

"Eva, he does not need to. Everyone has seen Edmund's attentions toward Lady Alice. They all know, especially your uncle, that Edmund has obligated himself to her. The servants have even mentioned the likelihood of a fall wedding."

"And yet, Uncle goes so far as to frighten off my suitor when Edmund is taken?"

"He is hoping to claim an attachment from your very birth which would prove a prior claim and void his heir's attachment to Lady Alice," she said.

"That seems very dishonorable," I said. "Could he accomplish his scheme?" I

"If there was anything put into writing, even a mention in a letter between the brothers, Lady Alice would indeed have to relinquish her hold. Edmund never asked for his father's blessing. Lady Alice sounded more concerned about playing the fool in front of the Ton than pain or any overwhelming affection for Edmund. She might be grateful for such a letter. Your uncle would be blamed for not noticing his heir's attachment, and be expected to pay a settlement amounting to the cost of Lady Alice's season, as it was spent on Edmund."

"Is there a chance Grandfather put something like that into writing?" I asked.

"I doubt it, or your uncle would have produced it by now. It is more likely your uncle will have put something of the sort in writing and sent it to your grandfather. He can claim the existence of such, and propose a search of Grey Manor.

"I would not be startled if your uncle proposed a short outing to the country soon, using his right as closest relation aside from your father to pursue your grandfather's papers."

"And if he did write my grandfather, I would then be obligated to marry Edmund?" I asked.

"Eva, could he not write a letter this very night, absolving himself of all wrongdoing? He could promise in such a letter not to mention the betrothal until after you were presented."

"It would hardly be worth anything," I said.

"Unless he back dates it and plants it in your grandfather's papers," she said. She sighed at my naivete.

"So, if we go to the country?" I asked.

"Something like that will be found, and then publicized. Edmund will be absolved of his attention to Lady Alice on the grounds of ignorance to a pre-existing claim. He will escape all blame. Hopefully, she will recover somehow, and you, as your grandfather's heir, will be obligated to fulfill his wishes."

"I...I can't think about this now. I need to sleep," I said.

"That is wise, though may I caution, showing a preference to another man through this process may be unwise. Especially if it serves to intertwine your heart with his. It may very well lead to heartbreak."

"I understand," I said, but my heart didn't, squeezing painfully until exerting its will over my eyes. A few tears dropped.

Chapter Twenty-Four

The next day, responsible or not, I called on Lady Garrett. Instead of just leaving my card, I was shown into her old-fashioned drawing room, where every surface was covered in lace doilies.

"Dear Lady–" she said, standing to greet me after I was announced.

"Please, call me Eva," I said.

"Of course, dear," she said.

"How does Lord Devon?" I asked.

"Much better this morning, thank you. I have sent word you are here and believe we will see him before long. Won't you tell me how your presentation went?"

"I am sure the Queen gave me a little smile," I said.

"Oh, yes, well," Lady Garrett looked confused so I did not imitate the face for her and instead said: "My head is full of something else. Can we speak plainly as two women of sense?"

"Of course," she said.

"You were right. Uncle wishes me to marry my cousin," I said.

"Yes, my father explained as much to me before I came to visit you."

"My uncle is trying to find proof that Edmund and I are engaged, even though Edmund is promised to another," I said.

"I suspect he will do whatever it takes to find proof," she said looking at me, her eyes sad.

"Then my uncle will be able to force the union?" I asked.

"It will depend very much on your father. We have not been introduced, but living for years as the son of a baronet, instead of the heir of a marquess, implies he is not bound by certain proprieties. I cannot imagine such a man is to be bullied into marrying off his daughter by his uncle. Have you spoken to him of this?"

"There has been a barrier of sorts between us since I learned of my title."

"I can imagine, but you must confide in him. It is harder to be a parent than you think. We are more apt to make mistakes than our children wish to believe."

"I will try," I said.

"Eva, what do you want?" she asked, eyeing me.

I glanced at her embarrassed. Instead, I said: "Did you…um did you know my grandfather and your father, they…"

"Intended a possible union between you and Jonah?" she asked.

"Yes," I said, feeling the heat rising in my face. She nodded. "Does he know?" I asked.

"No, but he would be… I believe Jonah would be honored to oblige," she said.

"If I…. Would he interfere on my behalf, trying to prove his claim more recently arranged between my Grandfather and his if my uncle forges a document implying an arrangement exists between myself and my cousin?" I asked.

"I think your father would have to do that," she said apologetically.

"Yes. Miss Bolton thinks so too, but I was hoping she was wrong," I said. I wanted Duke Garrett to fight for me. He relinquished me so easily. Even now if his only inclination would be to accept me if he must, why would I put him in the position I fought to get out of?

"You seem to get along well with your cousin. Would you be so unhappy to marry him?" she asked, tilting down to look at me curiously.

"I … I," I closed my eyes so I did not have to see the words I was saying, "I will try my best to fulfill every duty of wife if it comes to it. I could find myself in a worse situation." I folded in on myself. Having said the words out loud, I knew I did not want to marry Edmund simply because I adored Duke Garrett.

"Then I'm sure you will find joy in your future no matter which one awaits you," she said. I sagged and tried to hold back my tears. She looked at me with pity, but to my disappointment, she gave me no more encouragement toward her son than that. I waited longer than propriety dictated hoping for a glimpse of the son but wasn't even graced with a sight of the grandfather. When decorum and my pride could no longer be ignored, I left, rejected. With every intention of going to my father's house to pout, I climbed back up into his lovely dark Phaeton.

The hood was pulled entirely down, as it was such a pleasant day. I nodded to the footman. He bent down to get his whip and movement from the house caught my eye.

Framed in the drawing-room window, Duke Garrett looked at me. Confusion colored my face as I remembered clinging to him, clinging to him past what was appropriate, and he pulled away.

Tears started in my eye, and I must have looked pathetic because his whole face took on an indescribable sorrow. The carriage tore me away from him as it jerked to a start. Not only did he pry me away when I would cling to him, now he made the effort to prove he avoided me. It could not have been clearer; he chose his duty to my Uncle and his sense of propriety, over me. He did not even bother understanding the situation. He just retreated. For some reason, I was reminded of my Grandfather, wishing his old friend would come to visit him before he died. Lord Devon never came, and now, it seemed, neither would his grandson.

Chapter Twenty-Five

"How was your visit?" Miss Bolton asked as I walked into our personal sitting room and sat hard upon the white recliner with gilded trim where she was sewing.

"Fine," I said.

She put down her sewing and turned to me. "What is it?" she asked.

"Myra, can you please send Julia a note asking her to take a ride with me?"

"Of course," she said, perplexed by my stoic expression.

"Thank you," I said, standing and moving to my room. My new lady had me in a riding habit before Miss Bolton returned with Julia's acceptance of my invitation. I walked down the stairs and a groom waited for me. I couldn't believe how quickly any slight whim I had was accomplished. I picked up Julia. My footmen helped her mount and we rode.

"Shall we go to the park? We have an hour yet before the row must give way to the people of fashion," she said.

"Yes, please," I said.

"Are you unwell?" she asked.

"I don't know," I said. Fighting back the stinging in my eyes I asked: "Do you ever feel like the direction of your life can be changed at the whim of everyone around you except yourself?"

"Yes," she said pulling her reins in too tightly, and her horse reared back.

"Why is it what I want does not matter?" I asked.

"What do you want?" she asked. Duke Garrett – the name echoed through my head before I could stop it. Instead, I said: "I want some measure of control over

my own course. I want time to get used to this new
position I've been thrown into."

"Eva, that is unrealistic," she said. "Nobody lives in
that manner."

"I did. My whole life I was raised in ideas. My
daily existence was an examination into what I would do,
with free rein over my life. Now after twenty years, I am
told it is over. I must bow until my legs ache with the
effort, and when I am sure I will fall, I must back out of the
room without turning, while being nudged on in what
direction I do not even know," I stammered.

"Is life not a series of finding your footing without
looking? But that does not mean you cannot eventually
find your way," Julia responded.

I looked at her. "That was wise, Julia."

"Oh no, I just emitted a series of metaphors like you
do, as if stringing them together gives them sense," she
said. I laughed without mirth. Julia was right. Just because
I was being shuffled backward, didn't mean I couldn't find
a way to control my direction. I was still in charge of my
legs.

"After we ride, let us go spend a great deal more
money than we ought," she said. "That is how my mother
takes back control of her life."

I laughed again.

"Come, Eva, there is a pair of silk slippers that I
must have for the musical in a fortnight, or I am sure I will
not be confident enough to play."

"Well then, after we ride, we will spend more
money than we ought. I may need some kind of fortitude
to get me through the evening as well," I said.

"When you sing, the world will pause to hear, just
as it always does," Julia said. "My friends' praise will not
be sufficient to bolster my confidence when the privileged
ears of London have heard masters," I said.

"You sing well …no, you read well, almost as if you could break into song. You sing magnificently."

"I have not been asked to sing since I came to London." "Our duet is well practiced … and perhaps we will purchase you a new pair of slippers as well," she said.

"It is worth a try," I said feeling lighter.

"Edmund loves to hear you sing. It will bring him great pleasure," she said. She glanced at me coyly.

"Yes Julia, perhaps I should try to please Edmund by singing my heart out in the home of the woman he is honor bound to marry," I said.

"Oh, we were not sure you understood this as you have so little experience in social rituals," Julia acknowledged.

"He is honor bound to her, and I will not interfere," I said.

"What will you do?" she asked.

"I will end a spinster and hope to die young," I said.

Julia laughed, and, as we'd reached rotten row, she gave her horse its head and we galloped hard. I threw caution to the wind, refusing to be bridled, and almost beat Julia, but even after everything, Julia still seemed to recklessly search for freedom. Even more than I. The footman following us stayed behind the wooden fence to watch. Our horses worked into a steady pace until Avon galloped, but Pegasus flew. After our ride, the groom drove us in my father's Phaeton to a shop Julia swore by. We had our feet measured and Julia spouted instructions to the Madame.

We went to other shops, shops her mother had not taken me to. I bought ribbons and a few pairs of gloves since I couldn't manage to keep mine clean. Julia insisted the trick was to get them so tight they literally became part of one's flesh. I was measured for a new dress to perform in. Julia and the woman helped me fashion a look that would not drown me out. We went back to my father's home exhausted, only to prepare for a Tea, and then an evening party.

"Why did you stop interacting with me like this?" Julia asked.

"What?"

"We were great friends like this growing up. Why did you stop talking to me like… like I was a person instead of the daughter of an earl?"

"I did not withdraw. You did," I said, "when I became too belligerent."

"My mother said that, not me. I certainly never thought of you as belligerent. After a time, you would talk openly to Edmund, but never me. It… it hurt my feelings."

"I didn't realize I was the one who stopped the connection," I said, thinking back to when Julia had become so refined, and I felt we could no longer be friends. I felt insecure, but never realized it.

"I did do that," I said finally, "I was intimidated. I felt diminished around you because you'd become such a fine lady and I was still so backward."

"I am glad you outrank me. Belligerence is always forgiven in the titled, and now we might be friends again," Julia grinned. She handed me a simple headdress that could be woven into my hair for the evening dinner party.

"I am sorry it had come to that, Julia. I never realized what I was doing," I said.

"I'll forget it all if you let me pick out your dress for tonight," she said, working her way through my dresses.

"Think of me as your paper doll," I said sitting at my dressing table. It didn't matter anyway, the man I preferred avoided me when I called on his mother. What else mattered after that?

Chapter Twenty-Six

Nothing of consequence happened over the next fortnight. Duke Garrett was absent everywhere I went. After I petitioned Lady Garrett for his interference, I could not bring myself to go anywhere near Drury Lane and missed *Romeo and Juliet* altogether. Uncle made sure my father received invitations to all his functions, and Aunt made sure I attended.

Lord Harley's heir made a nuisance of himself. His lazy eyes always in the act of opening or closing made him look bored. Though he stood by me often, I could never think of anything to say to him. I much preferred his younger brother. Mr. Harley talked to me often but looked even more twig-like next to his brother, who cast his shadow over us both, dulling our discussions with his interruptions.

Aunt carefully planned our days to avoid being in the same room with Lady Alice and Edmund. She used me to exponentially widen her circles. Julia stayed wherever Miss Bolton and I were, and the three of us managed to weather the storm of visits, rides, teas, parties, and even four balls in the same week.

Miss Bolton kept a close watch on me. No mother could do more, especially, as Viscount Harley, and a few others, thought to force their affection on me as if it would automatically give them access to my titles and wealth. Edmund did little to court Lady Alice, which did nothing to dispel the rumors that he had changed his preference to me. Finally, the night of the private concert arrived. Lord Holland held the annual concert every season to showcase his daughters along with up and coming professionals. His concerts held such repute that several cabinet members had confirmed, and two dukes aside from Duke Garrett were to be there. Julia and I had been

included on the list of performers as she was already known
to be an accomplished flutist. My gown arrived from the
maker the day previous and Julia came over to dress for the
evening at my father's house so she might be sure the frock
appropriate for my musical debut. Julia and Miss Bolton
scrutinized me from every angle, taking in the striking
white of the gown against my dark hair. The gown pointed
tightly at my waist and the gossamer skirt trimmed with red
ribbon flowers floated. Miss Bolton pinned miniature red
roses that contrasted lovely with my chestnut hair. I looked
extremely grown up, no trace of the girl I once was.

Strangely, I looked like a young version of Aunt, a
reputed beauty.

"I think I am pretty," I finally said.

"Yes, I think every man of your acquaintance has
already come to that conclusion," Julia agreed, laughing at
my naivete as Miss Bolton did her hair. I thought maybe
I'd rather be a little less pretty, and not so much a copy of
my aunt.

"I wonder why Aunt did not flatter my appearance,
even after learning of my titles," I said.

"I do not think she wished you to be as pretty as she
once was. It is hard for her to see her beauty fade," Julia
said. Julia wore a light pink dress with miniature pink
roses in her hair. Miss Bolton made her ringlets appear
thicker by putting some of the hair from her brush inside
them. When we were just finishing our ministrations, a
knock came to the door.

"Your uncle waits for you in the morning room," a
maid said.

"Thank you," I said. We walked out of my
bedchamber, and Miss Bolton gave me a sardonic smile
and moved ahead of us in the direction of my father's
library. We went to the morning room as instructed and
Uncle paced there.

"Father," Julia said lightly bowing.

"Ah Julia, good, I must ask the two of you to send your regrets to Lord Holland for their musical evening."

"I have so been looking forward to finally doing my flute duet with Eva," Julia objected. "We have practiced these six weeks."

"Yes, there is a complication... it isn't wise just now for," he glanced at me, "for the two of you to go."

"Because you cannot find a way just yet to disconnect Edmund from Lady Alice?" I asked. Uncle scrutinized me. He looked to Julia like she'd betrayed him, but she looked so shocked at me, likely because I spoke so bluntly. He absolved her and turned back to me. As he did, Father entered the room. "Ah, Miss Bolton said you were in here," he said. He looked between Uncle and me. He stopped, feeling something in the air between us.

"Edmund will not marry Lady Alice," Uncle assured.

"He is honor bound to her, and I will do nothing to push him to break his honor."

"That is noble, Eva, and in that same strain, it would be best for you to stay home tonight."

"Actually, I saw the Marquess and his daughter this afternoon, and confirmed us for this evening," Father said, feigning innocence. "They seemed rather anxious to have my firm acceptance."

"I wish you had not done that," Uncle said.

"Is there some particular reason you did not wish our young ladies to perform?" he asked.

"The rumors are... Lord Holland is..." he looked at me, "is insisting on seeing Edmund's financials."

"Oh, then it is progressing rather swiftly, is it not?" my father asked. He searched me as he had so many times before. I gave him a half smile.

"It must be slowed. The entire family showing up tonight, Eva being at the party, it is as if she concedes to the engagement. It would rather confirm we have accepted this… this ridiculous claim for what it is."

"I wish you had said something sooner. Coming to us in the hour we are to leave after we have given a rather hard acceptance of the invitation seems careless," Father said.

"I was with my solicitor and a barrister all day. Holland is attempting to entrap us, and I for one will not have it."

"Perhaps Eva and I shall show up then, and you and your family may stay away. That would have the desired effect, would it not?"

"Edmund must go, for the sake of appearances. It is a legal issue. Just until…."

We all waited. Would Uncle have Edmund court the poor girl along until he could forge a document proving a prior claim existed? Then what? Feign surprise that such a document surfaced? Did he think he could undo through means of contrivance what had been done? What is one Marquess's daughter for another, really? Especially when the other Marquess clearly meant to see Edmund secured to his daughter, or drive both their family names through the mud. I watched him, none of us speaking.

Finally, my father said: "From what I see, it would be best for all of us to go tonight and pretend nothing is amiss. It seems Edmund's honor would require it."

"Then perhaps," Uncle looked to be fighting himself, "perhaps in the next week we could slow things down. Perhaps we could take an excursion to the country for a time."

My father looked at Uncle, the disappointment clearly written on his face. "Let us speak of it tomorrow," he said. "Tonight, I will enjoy listening to my daughter serenade me." Uncle stared hard at me.

"Eva, Duke Garrett will most likely be there tonight. Please, please do not encourage him," he said.

"She is not obligated by any entanglement to reject suitors as your son is otherwise engaged," Father said.

"Have you raised your child only to satisfy yourself, with no thought to preserve her title or family name?"

The men glared at each other. "You need not worry Uncle," I said.

"I would not put him in the same compromised position Lady Alice has Edmund. I respect him far too well to do anything of the sort. Nor would I strive to create feelings in him, which I would have to then destroy if Edmund is found to be my intended."

"There is hope for your sex after all," Uncle snorted.

"I suppose then we can only wonder after the demise of yours," I snapped back. Uncle looked taken back. I was so sick of all them. Uncle ready to drag his family name through the legal process to break an engagement, for what I could not even tell anymore. He stared at me trying to understand this opinion. Was there anything so great in his mind as a titled male in the House of Lords?

"Take care Eva, the weakness of your feminine sympathies is not meant for proceedings like these."

"Femininity, as in compassion, and the consideration of Edmund's honor and wishing to stand back from Lady Alice's prior claim, is legitimate. You know it is. I did not know acting with decency is solely a feminine trait that ought to be brushed aside as weakness when it is tiresome."

My uncle said nothing. Everything I held bottled up burst forth at him:

"I am grateful for my sex and these decencies that I am, in your estimation, bullied by. I would not wish them away for anything. Being kind does not denote an unsound mind, but even if it did, I would take my feminine sympathies over your sense any day, Uncle."

"What of Lady Alice's femininity, entrapping Edmund before his father could even consider the match to approve it? Is that a feminine trait you may not be so proud of?"

"There are many men, titled men, who would find a way to entrap me if they could. It is not exclusively a feminine trait."

"More women than men—"

"Uncle, my whole point is you ought not assign gender to these proceedings. Clearly, Lady Alice will take whatever steps necessary to secure Edmund, but he is as much to blame as she. He openly courted her without your permission. I do not attribute this behavior to the feminine nor the masculine, but rather the act of self-preservation. Lady Alice knows he prefers me, but will not let him go. This is her right, but perhaps not right of her."

"Your sex has a tendency toward this selfishness," he said.

"That is neither fair nor true, but simply the observations of your limited vantage," I said. "If you took the time to know your own daughter, you would find a most sympathetic heart and a woman with an entirely selfless nature." He said nothing but glanced at Julia in doubt. I could see it was simply to end the argument, not because he found value in my gender beyond the beauty that satisfied his eyes and the ability to birth the son that satisfied his generational pride and sense of immortality.

Unsatisfied with his withdrawal I said: "There is beauty in femininity. I am not speaking of outer beauty but a charity that resides within a woman that blooms into humanity, benefitting everyone for the better."

"Which leads them to weakness," Uncle said. "Preserving their homes and their children out of an unfailing duty to them? Tenderness for their families, the poor, those in need of compassion, leading them to sacrifice their own well-being for the well-being of those around them? This you would call weakness? I have seen women stand up for what is right, even after their husbands' crumble. Is not endurance the greatest power a person can possess? The greatest loss our society could ever face is the demise of these traits. If women stop sacrificing, who will be left to do it?"

"That in itself is a very emotional sentiment," Uncle said.

"Kindness and hope when nothing is left to hope for have kept mankind in existence," I said.

"I suppose, but it is the emotion that leads to these sacrifices," he said.

"I would not trade my sense for your emotional blindness."

"Which is to be expected, as long as it does not lead to that most devastating pride that makes you believe you have the right to put yourself above those around you—especially women," I said.

"You sound exactly like your grandfather," Uncle said.

Well then, I suppose, even as a woman, I am his next generation, his true heir, living on after he has gone," I said. "And in the future, you will be so kind as to remember you are not my father, nor my grandfather, and therefore have no right to tell me what action to take." I glared at him then said, "Father, I would appreciate a word when you have a moment." I bowed to Uncle, then to Julia. I excused myself from the room not waiting for his reply.

Chapter Twenty-Seven

I paced my sitting room, unsure what to do next. Uncle suggesting our country trip made my stomach churn. Father's tentative knock finally sounded at the door.

"I am here," I said. Father, smiling at me, walked in. I paused in my pacing, curious to understand why.

"Oh Eva, my Eva! I knew you would resurface eventually."

"Excuse me?"

"Since arriving I have waited for your perfect spice to resurface," he said.

"Very well Father. Would you like a little spice to come in your direction now?"

"No, but I do most assuredly deserve it," he said.

"What are we going to do?" I asked. "Well, perhaps you will now consider acting like Eva, and not a marchioness. Eva does not follow after her aunt as if she must do everything she instructs her to do," he said.

"I … I don't understand," I said.

"You, Eva, are kind, considerate, yet, firm in what you know is right. Do you feel that assessment is fair?" he asked.

"I hope so," I said.

"Then what are we going to do?" he asked.

"I am…you are asking me?" I said.

"It is your life, Eva; I've never forced you in any direction before have I?"

"No," I admitted.

"I did warn you the Ton would tell you who to be, did I not?" he said.

"Several times, including in a letter you sent before I even reached London," I said rolling my eyes at him.

"Then my dear? What are we going to do?" he asked. I looked at him. He wasn't allowing Uncle to take over; he was waiting for me to tell him what I wanted.

"I … I need your help," I said.

"Yes, you do, and all you have to do is ask," he said.

"How did I get so mixed up in this?"

"It is the nature of the beast, my dear," he said, sitting on the sofa.

"Could we just go home?" I said sitting next to him.

"Yes, and Uncle would follow us, come back and your presence wouldn't even be necessary for your wedding arrangements. I haven't the pull he has, dear. If he gets some supposed document into the hands of his solicitor, we will have no legal recourse."

"All right," I said. "Do we have some document proving I am not obligated to marry my cousin?"

"Eva, I am confused. I always had the impression you were fond of Edmund. At your ball, you danced with his as if you liked him. Is it merely Uncle's heavy-handed involvement you do not care for?"

"I… there is something about Edmund I do not trust," I said. "Did he do something?" he asked, growing serious. "Not that I can give reliable testimony to … it has rolled around in my head, but I dared not confess it to anyone. Will you hear and not think poorly of me for judging with no real basis?" I asked.

"I wish to hear anything you have contemplated," he said.

"Aunt mentioned when I first came that I should not expect marriage prospects. She told me that my greatest hope in being a spinster would be a short life so that I might not run out of income," I said.

"It is a wonder the woman was even your mother's sister," he said. He let out a frustrated breath.

"I found it amusing, knowing I had been well provided for," I said.

"But Edmund came to my aid. He turned so only I could see his expression and promised me that he would always support me, and I should never have anything to worry about."

"That was kind of him," Father said.

"Yes, except the way he looked at me then, and ever since then, I wondered what I would have to do to garner his support."

"Eva, the Ton has raised him. He does not know such a thing is immoral," he said more to convince himself than me of Edmund's innocence. "Perhaps you are right, but after the conversation, I could not get the image out of my head. Even as Edmund courted another lady, he would discourage Duke Garrett as a suitor toward me, not that the Duke meant to ... clearly, he was never ... but if Edmund meant to marry Lady Alice, what role does that leave me to play for him?" I asked.

"Things have changed," he said.

"You were the one who said I needed to know how people treated me without a title. Well, Edmund would not court me. Duke Garrett seemed more inclined to me before I had a title. Now he has deserted me," I said.

"I do not believe that is the case. If it comes down to it, I believe Duke Garrett can be called upon for assistance in this matter."

"No, his mother made it clear he would not get involved," I said looking away.

"You petitioned for his assistance, before mine?" Father asked.

"I did not mean to offend, I ...."

"I am not offended dear, just sad. It is hard on a father when his little girl appeals to the gallantry of the man she prefers before her father."

"It was all for naught," I said. "He did not even come to the room though I am certain he knew I was there. He cannot be depended on to come to my aid."

"Uncle peeled him harshly. Edmund's prior claim would keep any man of honor at bay," Father said.

214

"If all these claims materialize, how am I supposed to let Edmund into my heart when it is already occupied?" I asked quietly.

"Edmund has much potential. He could be molded into greatness by the right woman," Father said.

"Duke Garrett is already great, no molding required," I said. I felt so tired of this manipulating.

"Edmund could not love me when I was not a Marchioness, and now all he can do is love me."

"I suppose that is why your grandfather told Uncle he would never approve the match unless Edmund chose you without the title. I never thought his distrust of the lad fair, but perhaps it had foundation after all."

"I do not wish to speculate on Edmund's honor. I just do not wish to marry him," I said.

"Do you know why your grandfather left society?" Father asked. "He chose his studies," I said.

"No, not really."

"Then why?" "

He was invited into society as a very young heir. He was let into the best circles, even invited to plays and parties hosted by the Prince Regent; King George being mad, his son was for all intents and purposes the monarchy."

"I have been attentive to my lessons, Father," I said. "Well, there is much Miss Bolton would not include in your education," he said.

"Very well," I said. "Enlighten me."

"It is not enlightening, which is why it was excluded in the first place," he said. "The Prince Regent was not a chaste man. Inspired only by the latest fashions and remodeling any place he was expected to reside in, he ran up debts he could not pay. His wife Caroline had a daughter who died, and after this, she and George did not get along. Grandfather met her at a country party in

Windsor Palace. She took such a liking to your grandfather she invited him to her rooms."

"Oh, grandfather!"

"Yes. What was his duty?"

"I...."

"A marriage of the monarchy sanctified before God in St. James chapel? Grandfather's lovely young intended waiting for him in London? A seat in Parliament to direct the country with an opportunity toward immoral behavior at every country party he was expected to attend? His lovely young bride expected to arrange trysts when the party was at Grey Manor?"

"Grandfather would never lose his honor," I said.

"He politely rebuffed the advances of the Princess of Wales. Disillusioned, he pulled away from the Ton, throwing himself into the duties of his territory. Soon after the princess left the country with another. Your grandfather spent his life publishing philosophical research that would be widely read and I believe it has helped shape the moral behavior of a nation. Queen Victoria is certainly insistent on moral behavior."

"Every man I have met seems to have read his works," I said.

"Queen Victoria, before she was crowned, even wrote him a letter to clarify a point she found confusing."

"I think she did smile at me when I was presented," I said.

My father smiled.

"I cannot imagine grandfather's Sire, William you called him, who held so many titles, approved his withdrawal?" I asked.

"He thought your grandfather's work so important he went to the great effort to separate his titles and confer the Earldom on his young son from his second wife, so your grandpa was free to follow his conscience."

"Uncle did not fall into the same folly upon entering society?"

"By Uncle's ascension, Caroline had died and George was failing. Uncle was given a certain level by his father, but never the same grandeur Grandfather gained. As the heir to an Earldom and younger brother to the Marquess, who by then was considered a recluse, he was never admitted into the same circles. Considering Edmund's lack of direction and moral integrity, I do not think Uncle escaped entirely."

"Why does he not check Edmund?"

"He has never worried about it one way or the other," Father said. "Politically minded as he is, Uncle is sure to wish Edmund Prime Minister one day, even before a marquess," I said.

"Very good, Eva," Father said. "That is what I have conjectured over the last fortnight."

"Yes, but politically speaking, Edmund is already engaged to the daughter of a marquess. I cannot see why I am being leveraged. What can I give that she cannot?"

"I do not think, nor can Uncle believe, that the office of Prime Minister can be achieved simply by marrying above one's self into the correct connections, as it could have been years ago. Parliament is being restructured," he said. "Then what?"

"The key is young Mr. Harley, the brother to the Viscount, who is often asking you for dances."

"It is assault. You ought to intervene," I said.

"Would you like me to?" he grinned like he'd love nothing better.

"Please, and I know who you mean. Mr. Harley is a Member of Parliament in the House of Commons, which must play into this."

"There are one hundred and forty-four seats in the Southern Counties. The influence of the House of Commons will soon outweigh the House of Lords."

"The Whigs still control both," I said. "No dear, they lost the last budget reform in the House of Commons to the group called the conservatives, which is, of course, the new way of saying Tories, to attract the factory owners."

"I know that, but Prime Minister Melbourne did not step down."

"Not yet. But with another loss, he will."

"Will he?" I asked.

"Yes, those old Tory gentry are refusing to support any more Whig acts and are therefore supporting the Conservative movement. The nobles are scrambling to take over smaller Boroughs that still have two MP votes despite their size, which the Gentry lost due to the reform act."

"Most of them are still in the hands of the Tory party," I said. "I do not understand how this concerns me."

"It is an ancient war between the titled nobility and the untitled gentlemen who have the right to suffrage. You happen to be stuck in the middle of it."

"How? I cannot vote!"

"You, my dear, own a majority of the land in a borough along the southern edge of Dorset Shire County that controls two MP votes. You have not yet inherited a title."

"Eligible as I may be, it is illegal for me to vote in the House of Commons," I said again. "But not your husband, who would not ever inherit your title, you being the heir, nor would he inherit a seat in the House of Lords until his father dies. However, he would, upon your marriage, own your land. Therefore, making him eligible to run for a Member of Parliament in the House of Commons," he said.

"So if the conservatives take over, after Edmund married me, he would own my land, and as a landed gentry, he'd be able to raise himself up through the House of Commons, instead of the House of Lords, to be Prime Minister," I said.

"It would seem so."

"And if the conservatives do not take over?"

"That is very unlikely since Mr. Peel is organized, registering as many voters as possible while the noble Whigs are still meeting at parties to talk about the possibility of another election, and what should be done if it occurs. I have spoken to many cabinet members. Most have accepted they will be dissolved. If the Whigs did, by some miracle, retain control of Parliament, Uncle is close to a cabinet seat, which would put him in line for prime minister," he said. \

"I see," I said.

"In Grandfather's life, the nobles ran Parliament, and he ran from them. On the other hand, Uncle worked his whole life politically climbing. Can you imagine Uncle's frustration at his party losing power just as he is positioned for a seat?"

"It almost makes one feel sorry for him," I said.

"Until you remember how ill he has used you. Then it is only tragically diverting. His older brother who ignored the Whigs for years, positioned his heir better in the new government than he did?"

"Even if Edmund marries me, can Uncle ensure his son will comply? He is more prone to Aunt's need for stature then Uncle's politics."

"But dearest, Uncle is depending on the love Edmund feels for you to mold his potential."

"Is that possible?" I asked. "King William turned his life around before he took the throne, and it is often credited to his wife, Adelaide."

"I can never make Edmund into what Duke Garrett already is."

"No dear, even if you can encourage him to turn his great energy to his duty and his family, he will always be Edmund. It would be unfair to ask him to be anything else."

"He is much more charming and capable of leadership than Uncle's awkwardness makes him," I said.

"As a boy, when Edmund organized that day of games, you asked him to include all the children in the Parrish, and he did. It went off without a hitch, proving at his core, he is more likely to work with even the radicals who will only gain ground from here on out."

"I have witnessed the anger of the lower classes," I said thinking of the theater.

"Yes, it is in the streets," Father said. "I predict one day the Whigs and Tories will find they should have worked together, considering they have more in common than they think. Especially after the poverty-stricken learn they outnumber the wealthy a million to one, and should have a say. Edmund could do great things if you choose him."

"Which brings us full circle. It does not seem I have a choice. If Uncle pushes the point, I will marry Edmund and we will live—here in London?"

"Or if you choose, I will save you from the marriage, but you may be shunned by society."

"Then I could come home and live with you?"

"Yes," he said, and held his arms out. I wrapped myself in them. "What is your solution dear?" he asked.

"I do not know."

"What do you want?" he asked.

"I… Duke Garrett is not…he will not help. He is the one I … I had hoped… I do not wish Edmund to break his honor to Lady Alice."

"We cannot control Uncle. He will make his choice," Father said.

"I would prefer Edmund marry Lady Alice. But, if Uncle carries his point, and we end up married, could we come live with you for a time until the house on my property can be brought up? I cannot ever live with Aunt and Uncle again," I said. "I would have you both," Father said. "If I'm to accept Edmund, I'd at least like my heart to stop yearning for Duke Garrett," I said.

"I'm afraid only time can do that," he said.

"Can we find the time?" I asked.

"I cannot be sure. All your old papa can offer is an invitation to attend a scientific demonstration tomorrow while you think it through."

"Yes, please," I said, "and I suppose we must be on the hunt for many other reasons not to leave London just now. Our priority ought to be Lady Alice and Edmund's honor. Her reputation may never recover from the scandal Uncle proposes."

"I suppose we shall," he said, "besides Hetty is a wonder and I cannot very well leave when she is having all the guest rooms aired out in hopes that you might find someone to invite."

"Julia would come. Apparently, Uncle blames Aunt for Edmund's engagement and they are not getting on well in private," I said.

"Poor Julia. She did look forlorn when she went with her father. Let us invite her to stay with us at this evening's musical," he said.

"Oh dear, we are growing more than fashionably late. Lady Alice will think she frightened me away," I said moving to Miss Bolton who had come in with my cloak to remind me of the hour.

Chapter Twenty-Eight

Within minutes of entering the extravagant ballroom transformed into a music room, I regretted not taking Uncle's advice to stay away. Lady Alice was so far from civil to me; she exposed both of us to a few astonished stares when she refused to greet me.

Duke Garrett was already situated when I arrived. He sat between two extremely fashionable women who doted on his every move and kept him from having to acknowledge me. Chairs had been set up in rows to accommodate several dozen people. I sat next to Julia, who looked extremely glad to see me. "Are you nervous?" Julia asked. She sat up straight, pretending nothing was amiss. "No, I am metaphorically bleeding from the daggers being stared at me from Edmund's intended."

"We shall mop you up and put you at the pianoforte, then she will regret not being more gracious," she said. I leaned into her, wondering if Duke Garrett would speak through my performance. The two ladies would not be put off, even when he stood up to get refreshments. When we were all seated, the host stood. "We will have three amateur performances before we move into our performances by Mademoiselle Peirce and her chamber ensemble. To start off the evening, my own two daughters will perform. Then we will hear from Lord Peter Marshal and his sister Lady Harriet Marshal, after which Lady Julia Claremont Hull and her cousin, Lady Eva Grey Hull, will perform for us."

"I did not think we would go last among the amateurs," Julia whispered.

"It is for my sake, I am sure. No doubt they think me incapable of the complicated trills necessary to keep up with your flute. It is only to show my deficiency they put us just before the professional chamber ensemble."

Edmund came over and wished me luck. I nodded my "thank you," trying not to look overly friendly. His intended, who had been distracted by her music, quickly came over as well. "Edmund, you will sit at attention through my performance, will you not?" she asked.

"Of course," he said, and the look on his face was smug. He glanced around to be sure his friends saw two women fighting over him. I folded my arms and leaned over to speak to Julia about our piece, ignoring the couple until they left. Lady Alice looked very superior at me like she won this round of our competition. The haughtiness on her face did not dim as she performed with her sister a simplified aria to perfection.

The next singers were even better, and their song far more complicated than the first. The crowd politely listened with one ear to the performers and allowed the other to the small groups that formed before the performances began. When Julia and I stood to do our number, I wished we had chosen something simpler.

I sat at the pianoforte. I stroked the keys finding my finger's placement while looking to Julia who stood in the piano's bent with her flute. She nodded and I began. My fingers ran across the keys comfortable enough in the first half of the piece, as I simply accompanied her complicated flute solo that she performed flawlessly. All too soon I forced air into my lungs and started into my vocal: "Lo hear the gentle Lark," my voice rang out a little too shaky at first, but soon my love for the Bard's words came through just as Sir Henry Bishop's did in the flute solo he arranged.[4]

I hit every note in every trill, keeping my voice steady until the end, giving just enough vibrato to be artistic, but not show off. Julia's flute joined the effort and chased my singing until she caught up. Pausing I started in and she began chasing my voice again. Then my hands stood still on the piano, her flute quieted, and I went up into

an intricate vocal solo. The flute joined in, our duet
moving into my most complicated notes in the piece. I hit
every note with precision, ending with vibrato in my
highest note. Then in unison, we finished the piece. I stared
at the music I didn't need. Nerves made my performance
stiffer than usual, but it wasn't horrible.

I slid off the piano bench and looked up. The
applause wasn't just the polite smattering of the other two
performances. Unable to keep my eyes from him I looked
to Duke Garrett for his approval. He clapped, and his eyes
held such a longing as they connected to mine. I blushed
and looked away. I noticed Lady Alice watching me in
disbelief, and I could not look at her, either. Julia did an
extravagant bow outlasting mine, which I could not have
matched even for the queen. I bobbed my head again and
helped her up, with an urgent pull to sit down. I collected
our gloves and shoved Julia's at her, then replaced my
own.

A footman collected my music and packaged up
Julia's flute. The host announced a brief interlude for
Mademoiselle Peirce to set up.

"I need some punch," Julia said.

"I will join you," I said terrified of being left alone
in this crowd. We walked only a few feet when we were
followed by three men, all giving us their
congratulations. Viscount Harley singled me out, taking
my hand and slathering such profuse praise on me I felt
sure it was leaving a grimy residue on my skin. He even
drew my hand up as if he would kiss it proving to the group
my favor of him. I pulled my hand away.

"Cousin, you performed so well," Edmund said. He
took my hand midair and shook it with a warm caress. I
stepped back cautiously.

"Here, here," Viscount Harley said, and he looked
at me as if I were a prize he'd already won. Edmund's
intended came up and took his arm, effectively pulling my

hand out of his while looking at me for disappointment, but I smiled at Julia who took my other arm defensively. The glare Lady Alice had been throwing me softened.

"Edmund," she said, then feigned embarrassment and said, "I mean Lord Claremont Hull, of course, can you give my mother your opinion on these lyrics our Mademoiselle will be performing?"

"Of course," he said throwing me an apologetic look that was not near genuine, but rather full of conceit allowing himself to be led away. I watched the back of him, astonished. He could very well ruin Lady Alice and me with his attentions toward both of us. He only found amusement in the situation. Where was my cousin's honor?

Perhaps I would prefer being a spinster. Father watched Edmund with a look of sorrow that told me the nephew's behavior was too marked for him not to have seen. I curtsied and moved around the group to the refreshment table leaving Julia to deal with the throngs of our admirers.

"You sing very well," a hesitant voice said from behind me. I turned to find Duke Garrett. His eyes held mine and my breathing increased as he moved in a little closer like he couldn't help himself.

"I am sure Shakespeare's words lent me their charm," I said with a curtsy. I looked down, feeling shy.

"Come now," he said taking my hand. "That excuse is tired and must be worn out. Your performance was astounding, capped off by... you look... your gown is –" I turned my eyes to his. He could not finish his sentence. I searched him intently trying to find the affection I knew he felt for me.

"Eva," Uncle said coming up behind me, "You were marvelous. I haven't heard you sing since you were a girl." He took my hand from Duke Garrett, "You have come a long way. Won't you join your–"

"Your Grace," my father said, stopping Duke Garrett from backing away. Father took my hand from Uncle and kissed it. He said, "my own Lark was marvelous, was she not?"

"Yes sir," he said bowing.

"How is your grandfather?"

"He is better. I think in the next few days he will be well enough for society."

"I am so relieved," I said, taking my father's arm to avoid being led away by Uncle.

"Excuse me, my mother is warm and requires a drink," Lady Alice said moving through our group. She looked at me, but her look was curious this time, with no hint of anger. I looked back confused and she glanced at Duke Garrett. I gave half smile and looked down, certain my adoration of the man showed clearly on my face.

"Lady Grey Hull, your performance was charming," she said. I curtsied and said, "as was yours. I have always loved Italian Arias."

"I meant to ask you to join us in two days for Tea," Lady Alice said pouring a cup of punch. "We will be eating al fresco, young people only. Lady Julia and her brother will be there, along with a few others who will be known to you. Here she glanced at Duke Garrett indicating he would be there but said nothing as she glanced at Uncle.

"I'm sure Eva is needed …" Uncle started.

"We have no plans, and the fresh air would do her good," Father said. "She rarely has the opportunity to interact with young people in her own station. I insist." Then he pulled out a card. He held it out and said, "Duke Garrett, I would like to call on your grandfather as soon as he is well. I have inquiries to make that I think only he can answer."

Here my father looked at Uncle, and Uncle blanched for some reason. "Of course, sir. I will relay your message," Duke Garrett said. He looked confused.

"Duke Garrett, Lady Grey Hull, won't you join us? I'm sure my father expects your father to join him," Lady Alice said nodding to the place where the older set and all the important guests congregated. I glanced at Duke Garrett unsure what to say. Would he avoid me as he had been? Julia, who approached only to hear this last, took my arm and said innocently:

"Eva, I do wish to speak with Edmund, and Miss Bolton is occupied by Lord Pennington." Father jerked his head over to my companion. Everyone knew Lord Pennington had a son from his first wife who was shy and did not come into society. He rarely associated with a woman who would be of age and social standing to marry him. Miss Bolton was just the sort of nourishing lady who would do for such a man, and Father did not like Lord Pennington's attention toward her.

Julia took my arm and we walked to where Lady Alice's sister and a friend sat with Edmund. I held my breath listening to hear if Duke Garrett would follow us. He caught up to us, and though he walked at my side he did not get close to me. Lady Alice's group looked up, surprised to see us. Julia pretended not to notice and sat next to her brother. Lady Alice sat on Edmund's other side, so I sat next to Julia. Duke Garrett could have sat next to Lady Alice's friend, but instead sat next to me. I glanced up at him. I caught him looking at me. I blushed and he moved closer to me until his shoulder grazed mine. We sat silently through the first song. When the professional paused between songs, Duke Garrett leaned over and said: "The production of Romeo and Juliet was very good. I am sorry you missed it."

"As am I," I agreed, "it contains some of Shakespeare's most beautiful passages."

"It is easy to wax poetic when the subject matter is love," he said glancing at me and then looking away. "It is not a picture of very mature love. Romeo starts in love

227

with Rosaline and ends only a short time later dying with Juliet."

"Perhaps he did not truly know love until he met Juliet. Juliet became his sun, then being with her was the only way he could stay warm," Duke Garrett said. He smiled down at me in a way that made me feel shy again. We stayed silent over the next song out of respect to the performer, but his shoulder rested against mine and I felt more an extension of him than belonging to myself. I could not marry Edmund. The only thought that entered my head was to meet Uncle's scheming with my own, so I might remain free to be a part of Duke Garrett. Lady Alice smiled during the rest of the performance, especially when Duke Garrett inclined down to say something to me every time the music stopped. I couldn't help but think her lovely after all.

Chapter Twenty-Nine

The next afternoon Father and I attended a demonstration of electricity in a music hall converted to a laboratory for the exhibition. Father was particularly impressed by a portable steam engine, and he could not stop describing his ride on the train. He even started to feel our English engineers could be trusted, and said perhaps when we went home, we'd take the train.

Unable to stay in the heat of the steam, I wandered away from him. I found a chemical powered bell, though small and unassuming, the more curious object. I could not, nor could anyone else, explain with satisfaction how the metal clapper was moving between two brass bells.

"What is this?" asked Edmund, escorted by his father and Julia.

"A most curious movement created with, if I understand correctly, zinc sulfate, and manganese dioxide between layers of tin. Yet, no one is able to explain to me exactly why it works, aside from a chemical reaction," I said. Edmund smiled at me, and I could see such things did not interest him. "Shall we go find my father?" I asked realizing how vulnerable I was without Miss Bolton, who stayed back to visit with one of her sisters who came to town. Edmund moved to offer me his arm. I smiled at Julia as if I did not notice his action and instead took her arm.

Father, immersed in a discussion of the steam engine, nodded to us, and we came in range to hear the conclusion of his enthusiastic questioning. I let go of Julia's arm and moved to hear what was being said. Edmund moved forward, taking my elbow to keep me from being jostled by the crowd. Father came over quickly and offered me his arm. Edmund held fast to my arm saying: "I would have my cousin's company."

"Not with the gossip mongers about. I will not have her reputation marred by the attentions of an engaged man. Even one I like so well as you, Edmund," my father said, holding his arm to me.

"I am sorry, Edmund," I said because he looked sad, but I broke free and took my father's arm. After exploring the exhibit and seeing all the demonstrations on electricity, we walked to the public rooms and had tea on the veranda.

"The London air grows thick with smog this last week," Uncle said. "I thought the days extremely pleasant for April," Father answered.

"I anticipate perfect weather for our outdoor tea tomorrow," I said. I looked at Edmund and Julia. "Yes, I would have enjoyed it myself, but my father requires me in Parliament," Edmund said. He looked disappointed. I was again reminded of the previous evening, and how much he enjoyed being fought over by the daughters of rank.

Uncle said, "The shooting must be in high season down at your estate."

"Yes, I suppose, but I have been invited into the royal box at the Ascot races," replied father. "I do not mean to go down until mid-June so I might spend a few days in Windsor observing them. I have heard the new grandstand alone is worth witnessing."

"Or if we went tomorrow, we could go to Windsor on the way back," Uncle said.

"I do not mean to come back once I am home, until next season," Father answered, nodding to an acquaintance that paused next to me.

"Lord Grey Hull, I heard your daughter was recently presented. Will you do me the honor?"

"Of course, sir," he said standing, which forced Uncle and Edmund to stand.

"Lady Eva Grey Hull, His Grace The Honorable Duke of Chandos Richard Camble Grenville Lord of the Treasury." I stood and bowed.

"May I be so bold to introduce my uncle, The Earl of Somerset Sir Peter Claremont Hull and his heir Viscount of Somerset, Sir Edmund Claremont Hull, and his daughter Lady Julia Claremont Hull?"

The duke bowed and said all that was proper. After the introduction, the man asked: "Lady Grey Hull will you take a turn about the garden with me. I have heard you are uncommonly clever and with such a pretty face we will draw the envy of every man in London."

"Of course, Your Grace. May I invite my cousin to walk with us? She and her pretty face, though diminishing mine, can only enhance the envy you seek."

"Perhaps you will not be able to amuse me, feeling inferior to your cousin."

"Or rather it will give me a reprieve, only having to be clever without the pressure of also being beautiful."

"I am not disappointed in the wit," he nodded, holding his arm out to us. Julia took his other arm. Uncle looked annoyed, but he could not speak to this seasoned Duke the way he had his younger counterpart. I happened to glance at my father. He looked concerned. I was on the brink of having a place in the palace, moving up to the company of royal dukes.

Chapter Thirty

Julia and I went to Lady Alice's Tea Alfresco without Edmund. Though small and confined when compared to a country garden, the Holland estate boasted one of the few private gardens in London. The mansion was on a corner lot, and even after the carriage houses and stables, it left a quiet oasis set apart from the fast pace of the city. Fenced in by a high brick wall, the garden was surrounded by oak trees and taken over by ivy. The quiet space unnerved me. Birds made their music in the small sanctuary. The breeze rustled through bushes manicured to look like spheres. We were shown down a gravel path and left at the white marble steps of a pavilion. The sweetness of the roses that climbed the columns mixed with the spice of the tea and hit me just as Duke Garrett stood at our entrance.

Julia had to shove me from behind to keep me moving forward. Lady Alice indicated I should sit next to Duke Garrett and Julia was placed by Mr. Percival. Because of Edmund's absence, Mr. Percival and Duke Garrett were sorely outnumbered. The former questioned Julia about all she saw at the demonstration the day before, which left Duke Garrett to Lady Alice, her younger sister and myself. Her younger sister showed herself to be in aggressive pursuit of a husband and Duke Garrett often looked to me to assist when she became overbearing. After Tea, Lady Alice asked me if I would like to walk the garden with her. I hated to leave Duke Garrett to her younger sister but felt she and I needed to ally if I had any chance of outwitting Uncle in a world he clearly dominated. The gravel path led us to a corner of the garden immersed in shrubs about the height of our chests. Once we were inside the maze of shrubs Lady Alice said: "Did you know this is my fourth season?"

"I did not," I said.

"Cynthia is twenty and just having her first season," she said nodding to her sister. "I have two other sisters, one is eighteen and the other almost seventeen. If I cannot make a match, my parents will not burden themselves to allow me out into society, though we have no country estate to escape to."

"You have made a match, and Edmund has great potential."

"I am no fool. He has changed his mind."

"I think he may like the attention of two ladies fighting for him," I said. I watched to see if this would offend her. She simply nodded in agreement as if it were to be expected. Duke Garrett followed us into the shrubs. He looked over his shoulder a trifle frightened.

"May I join you ladies?" he asked.

"Please," Lady Alice said.

"What we are discussing may be of interest to you. Can we count on your discretion?"

"Of course," he said with a tilt of his head.

"Edmund's father has made it known he wishes his son be released from our engagement."

"Yes, he wishes the family's titles to be reunited," he said.

"No, not really," I said.

"Then what is it? You and I are of the same rank, socially speaking," Lady Alice said.

"My Uncle's political influence is at an end," I explained. "He has spent his life with the Whig party in the assumption that they could never lose power. The commoners are living impoverished, as Mr. Dickens has written so poignantly about, which makes them ripe for revolt. The country is in disarray and whoever comes out of this turmoil on top may very well shape the future of the British Government. The nobles are scurrying to get their sons a place in the House of Commons. I own land in the southern counties. My grandfather willed it to me because he apprenticed me in all that must be done for the tenant farmers. They are successful, and in my Grandfather's borough everyone is making enough money to survive."

"I am not sure what this has to do with your marrying Edmund," Lady Alice said.

"Edmund has not yet inherited his father's title," Duke Garrett said, annoyed. "He is called Viscount as a courtesy. He does not actually possess it. If he married Lady Grey Hull, her land would then be his. He would be able to vote, and even run for a seat in the House of Commons."

"Can't his father give him land?" she asked. "It is entailed, so he will eventually have it, but with it, he will gain the title of Earl and no longer be eligible for a seat in the House of Commons," I said.

"This is about politics," she said, frustrated. "Yes," I said. We all walked in silence.

"Lord Harley is doing this same political maneuvering to great success," Duke Garrett said. He let out a deep, frustrated sigh. "I do not think my father has any land not entailed to my brother that Edmund might buy."

"It is very rare for worked land to come about in this manner. Not to mention, it is the placement of the land as much as anything. It is not popular to say but the swing of the vote is with the old Tory families in the South."

"Then I will be ruined over a piece of land," she said.

"No, that is the whole point," I said. "Edmund is honor bound to you. We just have to figure out a way to get him to do the right thing."

"You are...?" Duke Garrett questioned me. "What?"

"I...thought you liked your cousin very much," he said.

"I do. I like him as my cousin. I do not wish him to be anything more," I said looking away.

"When you met with my mother, you did not indicate as much. She thought you undecided in your…."

"I have never desired my cousin's hand. I believe I said I would make the best if I have no other choice," I said.

"But you have always …."

"Even jealous and ready to strike, I could see she favored you over him," Lady Alice said under her breath.

Duke Garrett stopped and turned to me. "Truly?" he asked. I nodded while Lady Alice eyed him narrowly.

"None of our preferences will matter if her uncle, who is a shrewd man with many more of the necessary connections than her father, pushes the point," Lady Alice said.

"Uncle is trying to take a trip to our country estate. My father believes he will forge a document that he may find it among my grandfather's papers which betroths me to Edmund."

"He lectured me about honor," Duke Garrett said. He swiped at the bush in frustration but walked much closer to me than before.

"Yes, my father and I thought that very rich of him, and very effective on you," I said. I sounded catty and very much like Aunt Claremont Hull. I wished I had not said anything.

"I did not understand his nature," Duke Garrett said patiently, not responding with the haughty indifference of Uncle.

"He is complicated, and has manipulated me many times," I comforted, touching Duke Garrett's arm kindly. He smiled down at me, standing so close our shoulders connected.

"What can we do?" Lady Alice asked. "What kind of a landlord do you think you would be?" I asked her. "Excuse me?"

"If I sold you my land, Uncle would have no reason to prefer me over you," I said. It was the only thing I could think to do, despite the years Grandfather trained me to take care of his tenants.

"I...I would not even charge them to use the land. Edmund and I do not need the income," she said.

"You can't do that. The other landlords will run you out. You must be fair. Not over easy, so your tenants must fend for themselves, but not overly burdensome that they cannot have hope for a good life if they work hard. The steward is getting on in years, but completely trustworthy. I was going to have him start training his replacement, securing what is best for your tenants."

"There has to be another way. You should not have to give up your inheritance over this," Duke Garrett said.

"I do not see it," I said. "Is there a house on the property?" she asked.

"Yes," I replied, "my grandfather bought it, so an aging gentleman did not have to go through the public humiliation of putting it up for auction. We took over management of the property to make it profitable, but the gentleman lived in the house maintaining it until his death four years ago. My Grandfather kept the house up, and we would stay there when we had business in the area. It is old-fashioned, but structurally sound and could be improved with new furnishings."

"I have thought to live with..." Lady Alice stammered, "Edmund has no home of his own. From what I understand, the Earl's country home is near as small as his townhouse, without a separate dower house." She looked at me. "Yes, rendered even smaller by the whims of Edmund's mother, who is still very young."

"If you sold us the house, we could live in the country part of the time," she said.

"Yes," I said. "Would you like to live in the country?"

"The pace of London during the season always leaves me exhausted and in low spirits. We are invited to the country in the fall and I relish every moment."

"I can believe that," I said. I felt exhausted much of the time.

"I would pay a fair price for the land, I have... my father would invest in such a thing."

"Let me speak to my father and see what is to be done," I said.

"Thank you," Lady Alice said, with gratitude in her eyes. "May I tell my sister? She is very upset over the whole thing."

"Yes, but we best keep it quiet. If my uncle finds out he will undoubtedly do something to interfere," I said.

Lady Alice bowed and ran off to tell her sister.

Relinquishing my land would sting, but the way Duke Garrett stayed by my side, pushing his shoulder into mine as we walked, soothed the sting. "You are very kind Miss Eva," he said quietly into my ear. I looked up at him and could only say: "It is not entirely unselfish disinterest that pushes me to clear myself of my cousin."

"I am sorry I cowed to your uncle."

Duke Garrett was too kind-hearted for my spice. Perhaps in time, I would be able to engage his sharp mind and tease him, but first, he needed to know my intentions were never unkind. Instead of teasing him, I said: "He knows how to push a man, and I think perhaps I like you better for your sense of honor." He smiled a little and he took up my gloved hand under the cover of the shrubs. "My duty from now on will be to you. Being without you is the consequence I can never endure again." He covertly glanced at our group who did not

237

notice us and then placed a kiss upon my gloved
hand. Perhaps Duke Garrett would come to my aid after
all.

Chapter Thirty-One

Though heartbroken about the whole thing, Father agreed Lady Alice in her final season had to be considered. Early the next morning we went to Grandfather's solicitor to transfer the title of my land to Lady Alice. Father encouraged me to gift the land to her, rather than her using her father's money to pay for it. It left no room for argument as to who the land belonged to after the marriage took place. After a long and tiring meeting, the job was done.

As we finished with Grandfather's solicitor, he received a note with a stack of bound papers. We left so as not to be in his way as he conducted his business. It had grown too warm for more than a light shawl, and I was pulling it over my shoulders when the solicitor's clerk stopped us. We were drawn back into his office.

"I have just received a most distressing missive," he said.

"What?" "

The Earl of Somerset has claimed to find a letter he wrote to his brother many years ago. This letter is of him assenting to the betrothal of his son Earl of Somerset to you, Lady Grey Hull. He has sent a marriage settlement over for you to sign, my Lord."

"Where would he have…"

"Hush Eva," Father snapped and I looked at him. He startled me with his abrupt censure.

"What action shall I take my Lord?" the solicitor asked.

"Has this settlement gone through the trustees of my father's land?"

"Just yesterday," he nodded. "Does it undo what we've done here today?"

"No, your signature is required for the document to be binding. Though I see here her property is to go directly to her husband once the marriage has taken place. He has been generous in her jointure. Should her husband die she would have half the property to use for income until her demise."

"He gave her back half of all she would have if she did not marry," Father said under his breath. The man looked confused.

"Let me speak to my uncle and I will return here this afternoon," Father said. The man bowed and gave me a look most commiserating. I could not get my land back if I tried. The title had already been expressed to Lord Holland's solicitor a quarter of an hour earlier. Father walked swiftly back to our waiting carriage. He handed me up. Seething, I sat hard into my cold leather seat. "We cannot openly accuse Uncle of forging the document. The shame of it will haunt you if you end up married to your cousin after all this," he said.

"If? Is it not a case of when?" I asked suppressing a sob.

"We will yet see my dear. The two of us together are quite cunning."

"I … Duke Garrett renewed his interest in me. I thought we would…."

"I know my dear. Uncle should not be so quick to perjure himself. Honor and truth do have a place, it would seem, even in modern society. For now, he has lost the land for his son if this marriage settlement is valid."

"And in doing so he picked me up in his gale force wind," I said. I slammed back into my seat again. We drove home so Father could consult a few of my grandfather's papers. Then we drove to Uncle's house. He and Edmund sat in the drawing room as if waiting for us. Julia rested in a chair removed, working her pillow and trying to look small. The red haze of anger in my eyes made the entire burnt orange room appear in flames. Uncle sat in front of a window, the bright sun gleamed off the glass which made the chair glow like he was in the center of the heat. Edmund looked quiet and reserved, engulfed in the settee. The smug smile on Uncle's face would not last.

"What have you done?" Father asked sharply.

"I have insured the future of this family," Uncle said.

"Very noble indeed," Father said, "I suppose your triumph will not wain when I tell you Eva gifted her land to Lady Alice this morning. It was meant as a wedding gift."

"You did what?" Uncle shouted, standing and coming toward me in a rage.

"I tried to save you from doing anything that would compromise your moral integrity, and Edmund's honor."

"You should have consulted me first," Uncle shouted.

"You are not her father, you have no right to assume that role, sir," Father said, having placed himself between me and Uncle.

"I have no right? Do you know what she has done?"

"Given a fine lady a chance, now that she is all but ruined by Edmund. At least she will not be entirely lost. I would assume there will be many of your set pushing their second sons toward her now," I said.

Edmund flinched and grew even more sullen. Uncle's eyes bulged and the veins on his neck stood out.

"You do not understand the ramifications this could have," Uncle said.

"I did nothing wrong," I said. "I gave land that was legally mine to give. I did not perjure myself to God and country, turning my back on all that is right and decent.

"You do not understand what is necessary to save this country from itself," Uncle spat.

The Lark

"We tried to give you what you wanted," Father said. "Eva sacrificed all she had to save Edmund from disgrace. You have thoroughly disgraced yourself and our family name, though every effort to save you from it was made."

"Thank you for your effort, Eva," Edmund said looking at me. His face in grief contradicted sharply with his father's self-righteous anger. I saw his potential, and I tried very hard to believe if we ended up married, we would find some measure of joy – after I ripped my heart out and flung it from me, with the love I felt for Duke Garrett attached.

"The settlement has gone through the trustees. If you do not sign it, not only Eva's reputation will be tarnished, you will be a most unbefitting heir," Uncle said more reluctant than before.

"It seems we have nothing more to say to each other. I do not know if we will ever speak again, Uncle," Father said, pulling on my arm and moving to the door just as it opened. "Lord Holland, Lady Alice Holland, and Mr. Price of the firm Price and Price," the butler announced. We all bowed as they walked into the flames. Lady Alice had been crying. Edmund stood, but could not go to her, because his father put himself in the way and glared at him. I moved over to link arms with hers.

"It has been an interesting morning, has it not?" Lord Holland said. "Most certainly," Uncle gritted out through clenched teeth.

"I receive a most distressing note from my solicitor only an hour ago. Then he came in person a half hour ago to tell me of a much more advantageous communication, both regarding my daughter." Edmund quietly moved from behind his father and crossed the room cautiously. He saw the distress on Lady Alice's face and moved toward her, slower this time. He stopped in the next moment when

Lord Holland said: "We accept your terms of ending the engagement between my daughter and your son."

"I did not…" Edmund started, looking at his father surprised. He must not have known his father took the legal steps necessary to break off the engagement. Had the man not even been consulted before any such action was taken? No wonder he sat, a lump of unmolded clay no one had ever bothered to give his potential shape.

Lord Holland said: "Your father has given proof of a prior engagement and the only honorable thing to do is accept the unpleasantness and move on."

"I am sorry for the pain this must cause you," Edmund said, taking Lady Alice's hand. This started her tears afresh and I could not help but think they would have found love in a very short time if given the chance. Edmund handed her his handkerchief and put a consoling hand on her arm.

"Now that I see the couple is so distressed …" Uncle started.

"Do not concern yourself. A great friend of our family has long been looking to court Lady Alice. She will not be lacking in admirers."

"Yes, I'm certain her new-found land will bring all the younger sons out of hiding, to be accepted with open arms," Uncle said. "Mr. Percival is a very decent man, and will treat his tenant farmers with the greatest respect." As he said this, he bowed to me. All I saw was Julia, who sat in her corner, contract in pain at his words. She truly preferred Mr. Percival. Now my land would effectively strip Julia of her lover as well. I wanted to scream.

"And as the man will do whatever you wish, and never inherit a seat in the House of Lords, he is the ideal candidate," Uncle said.

"I am so glad this all worked out to everyone's satisfaction," Lord Holland said. Bowing to me again he said, "Thank you for your generous gift to my daughter." I felt sick. I did not like this man any more than I liked Uncle, him getting everything he wanted. He meant to leave in triumph but now Julia, and Lady Alice were in tears.

"So much heartache," I observed out loud, "over a piece of land – land that you, Lady Alice, own free of any interference, no matter how close a family relation."

Lady Alice looked up at me. "I could live on the land, unmarried, even?" she asked.

"You could. The steward is a very reliable man and the living is ample if managed correctly."

"I…" she turned to her father, "You were to set me aside if I did not marry at least the heir to an Earldom."

"You will not be so hard to marry off anymore, and it turns out a man of distinction does not always come with a title these days."

"I do not have to marry," she said looking to me. I gave her a slight nod. "I own land, and with it comes a living. I do not need you or Edmund," she said turning to me again for confirmation.

"You would be comfortable, not extravagantly so, but with some measure of industry you would be very comfortable," I said.

"I… I would like for you to take me out there, Eva. Would you be willing?" she asked.

"Of course," I said. "Perhaps we can stay there together for a time until I am schooled in the management of such a place," she said.

"What would it matter?" her father snapped. "You cannot even vote!"

"Is that all you care about?" she asked. "An hour ago, I lost Edmund and was disowned, then a half hour ago I was your dearest daughter because I own land. I will not be a pawn in this any longer. You go about your business as if you disowned me, Father, and I will go about mine."

"Alice, we will discuss this later," he said.

"No, I have received an invitation to stay with my good friend Eva for a time. Considering the generous gift she gave me, I simply cannot refuse. I will be gone for some time until we can make a trip to visit my new holdings."

"Alice," I said, though the name sounded foreign on my lips, "I am so glad you can come." I took her hand pretending some sort of agreement did exist. Edmund smiled at me, but for the first time, the affection was for taking care of Lady Alice and had nothing to do with his juvenile fondness for me.

Uncle's rigid face looked fierce.

"Julia," I said, "we also desire your company as I do not wish for you to feel our established companionship would be slighted by this new friendship I am forming."

"I would not start planning your trip just yet," Uncle said. "The marriage settlement was approved before Eva took such an outlandish step. A step only comprehensible when considering her addled female brain. Apparently, there is an insanity that comes about when a female mind is so educated."

Only Lord Holland answered. He had the deed in his safe. The two men raged at each other.

"Do you have room for me as well, Uncle?" Edmund asked aside to my father. Uncle had insisted he move back into his old room as soon as I vacated the house. Edmund's flat had cost him a lot of trouble.

"It would not be appropriate. I am sorry to leave you to this, sir," Father said.

"Am I still a sir, then?" he asked, glancing at Lady Alice.

"Patience my dear boy. Do not let your tongue waggle at the club for a few days. All may be set to right. Especially when Uncle learns he will have to prove my insanity, as well as Eva's, to overturn the gifted land," Father said. Lady Alice patted Edmund's arm in condolence, and he looked at the beginning of understanding at what he lost in her. I was not the comforting sort. He had been in the slumps so often, I could do nothing but encourage him to make the best of his situation. Julia asked the footman to have her lady pack her a trunk, and send it to my father's house. Aunt then came in, with packages as if she'd been out shopping. Looking about, she asked: "What is happening in here?"

"I have been asked to stay with Eva," Julia said. "I was not consulted," Aunt Claremont Hull said.

"Mother, when a Marquess asks, one does not argue," Julia said in a loud whisper.

"Of course, dear," Aunt said. Uncle rolled his eyes, then went on discussing my mental instability with Lord Holland. My father shuffled us out before we had to hear Aunt's vantage point on what I'd done. Though she was more likely to resent the shame Edmund would face when she learned his engagement to Lady Alice was legally broken. She hinted many times that Lady Alice would simply go away if we all ignored the situation long enough. When we reached the entryway, we heard her shrill screams join the deeper bellows of Uncle and Lord Holland's.

Chapter Thirty-Two

We were quiet on the drive, listening to the horse's steady hooves compete with Julia and her melancholy shudders and Lady Alice fighting her sniffles to appear she was not crying. Once home, I led them into the drawing room at my father's house. The large room, papered in tones of peaches, complimented cream furniture. The tall windows looked out on the street and sunlight streamed into this room. It was normally a warm, inviting place to sit. Sadly Julia, Alice and I destroyed the peace there.

We spent a half hour in tirade against Uncle and Lord Holland until Father announced: "You sound very much like old hens and would do better to come up with a new scheme."

"I think you are enjoying this," I accused.

"That would be inappropriate as all your futures depend on a peaceable outcome of the situation," he said. He sat in an ornate chair trimmed in gold. "However, in a disconnected perspective, one must admit this morning did stir things up a bit. Uncle Claremont Hull blatantly forged a document that could have no origin.

Then he went to the trustees without both parties of the agreement in attendance. He is not even the head of our family, but he orders us all about as if he is. It is a bit of a Lark," Father said.

"Could his forgery not be declared a forgery?" Lady Alice asked. "Edmund would share in the shame of it. Would you accept that?" Father asked curiously.

"No, we must spare Edmund. He is a tender soul who would not bear the shame well," she said.

"No one would listen anyway," Julia said. "In private, Father boasts no one dares cross him. Even his solicitor is afraid to look him in the eyes."

"He is an Earl," Lady Alice agreed. "Then we will have to be clever in our resolves," Father said.

"What cunning is left, Father?" I asked.

"You ask and answer in the same breath," he said.

"You are left? I am not sure I follow," I said.

"He is your legal guardian," Julia said, piecing it together.

"He would have to sign any official marriage settlement," Alice said.

"Very good," he said.

"You did mention this to Uncle," I remembered.

"And he was correct. It will harm your name. Your reputation in town will be darkened. You could not expect to marry above yourself in station," he said.

I felt confused, as social standing wasn't my first language.

"Duke Garrett should, by honor, be out of your reach," Julia translated. "Oh," I said, discouraged again.

"Secondly, Uncle has more pull with the magistrates, and if he chooses to push the issue, he could carry his point without my signature. You could never live with Edmund and you would be legally bound to him."

While I poured us all tea, I said, "The very jovial tone in your voice denotes you have found a way around this, or at least doubt Uncle will push the issue, but rather look for a way to reconnect Lady Alice and Edmund."

"It certainly would do for the man to make an effort in that direction. With hope, he will wait and not push either issue until I can repair some of his damage," Father said.

"Well, I would expect an apology from the man before he even bothers forging another marriage settlement with me," Lady Alice said.

"I suspect Uncle Claremont Hull will soon discover I signed as a witness to the gifting of Eva's land," Father said bowing to Lady Alice. "Upon learning that he would have to prove my mental instability to get it back, things will change. Hopefully, he will start to show contrition and repair the relationship between his family and yours. That he could not do soon enough."

"I do not mean to reconcile with my father, though he would have to sign any settlement," Alice said.

"Can it be so bad?" Father asked.

"He was cruel to me when his solicitor sent news of the document, disconnecting me from Edmund," she said. "I could not be more of a disappointment. Then when the solicitor himself came, to follow up with a notice of gifted land, he did not apologize. He forced me to go to Edmund and gloat over my new situation while accepting our engagement dissolved."

"What will you do?" Father asked.

"I will go manage the land in a way beneficial to all involved as I promised Eva I would."

"What about Edmund?" I asked.

"He … he did not even fight his father to be with me. You are his ideal. Though I do wish you success in your desired marriage, Eva, I will not interfere in his happiness. If all works out, perhaps he can start over and find someone new to idolize."

"Did you see the way he looked at you in your distress? I am no longer his happiness," I assured.

"Do you think?" she asked, looking at Julia. "As of late, he has been thrown into indecision. I think he has not put a foot forward because he no longer knows which foot to use."

"Which will tip in your favor, because a man cannot love the same as a boy did," I said. "His grownup tastes are more refined than I can ever be."

"He would … he would accept me?" Lady Alice asked.

"I believe he would, with pleasure, if you can forgive him," Julia answered.

"I already have. He is so backward when it comes to his father I never blamed him in the first place," Lady Alice said.

"The beauty of femininity," Father said looking at me covertly.

"I would call that the strength of femininity," I said meeting his eye with a laugh. "If the time comes for Lady Alice to forgive Uncle Claremont Hull, do you think, Eva, that he will appropriately appreciate the trait or believe he has used his superior manhood to lord over her femininity?" Father asked, still teasing.

"I suppose whether he is using her or appreciating her, it will not change her strength in the situation," I said.

"Well, I hope he appreciates her, so that my gender may be redeemed in your eyes," he said.

"I was trying to carry my point with Uncle, not insult you," I said.

"I do not mean to end a conversation where I am being placed in such an advantageous light," Alice said, "but what can be done now? I cannot – "

"You are in the power position. You own what everyone wants," I said.

"I leverage the land?" she asked.

"I do not see any other way," I said. My father nodded.

"In the eyes of the law, Edmund is to be your husband, Eva," she said.

"No, Uncle used the letter to start a marriage settlement between Edmund and myself. As my father pointed out, he has not signed it, and therefore we have some room to manipulate the situation further without tarnishing any of us."

"How?" Julia asked.

"I do not know," I said looking to my father.

"We must find a letter, dated later than Uncles, refuting the first," Father said.

"You certainly would not perjure yourself," I said, knowing the answer.

"No, of course not. But I do remember such a letter being written by Grandfather with my permission, not many years hence."

"To Lord Devon?" I asked, catching on, "which is why you asked to see him two days ago before all of this even occurred. How did you know it would be needed?"

"I always knew how to arrange matters. I was just waiting for you to ask. I promised I would always give you your agency, and did not wish to act until you decided on the best course. It is how I give you my love and respect."

"Even down to watching me give my land away?" I asked.

"That sacrifice is perhaps the proudest moment yet in my role as your father. I am a parent before I am a marquess. To witness your unselfish action for your cousin's honor, your friend's salvation and even in the interest of your own heart is, I pray, a testament of your upbringing free of the quality. I am truly humbled to see the human being you are turning out to be," he said.

"I am a byproduct of the opportunities you have given me and I love you for them," I said. I buried my head in his chest. We all stopped at a knock on the door.

"Enter," Father called keeping an arm around me. Miss Bolton peered around the door and said, "Lady Alice was sent a trunk, with a letter from her father," handing a sealed envelope over. Alice opened it and the surprise showed clearly on her face.

"What does he write?" Father asked.

"My father is sorry we quarreled. If it is my intention to go to my new property, he would very much like to accompany me, to protect me along the drive."

"Ah, a return to civility," Father said. "I'll wager Uncle will write me soon to suggest that until this legal situation is resolved, we ought not pursue the marriage settlement lest the honor of all involved is diminished. Discretion must be shown at all costs."

"I suppose we can be silent on the matter," I said.

"Yes, because each of us wanted to run out and publish the ridiculous shame of the situation to anyone willing to listen," Alice said. I laughed, taken by surprise. Julia nodded in agreement.

"How have you so accurately predicted the behavior of each person involved?" I asked.

"I am no diviner, I assure you," Father said, "Uncle is somewhat stunted. He does not understand sacrifice. His mother taught him to take whatever advantage comes, creating one if needs be with complete disregard for ethical behavior. Always serving one's self first is very predictable."

"It is exhausting to be around such a person," I said. I walked to the window to look out on the street. Viscount Harley stood across the street. He scanned the area for something, and his eyes started back to the window in which I stood. I quickly backed away before he could see me. Was he waiting for me to leave the house? My father saw this and moved to the window. He crossed his arms and scowled, in a manner that looked practiced. I realized he often looked like that when he stood at the window of late and I wondered how often the viscount waited there.

Father turned back to us and said: "I mean to visit Lord Devon. I will be back before Tea. I will instruct the staff we are not at home, so you ladies are not disturbed. I think you might enjoy the calmness of an afternoon in peaceful reflection."

"Thank you, Father," I said, but stopped short of hugging him again. Lady Alice started sobbing. Father moved to her and said: "I am sorry for your pain, but I think all will right itself."

"It is not…" she gasped for air and could not speak. I thought she might choke trying to gain control over herself. Finally, she calmed down enough to say, "my father has never shown such a consideration to me, even when I could not keep myself from feeling down after a late-night ball. Without an hour's sleep, he would expect me out on morning visits and at the row by the fashionable hour. I am so tired."

"Perhaps Miss Bolton will take you to your room and let you rest. We have no expectation on you, and if you cannot come down for family dinner tonight, we will understand."

"Thank you," she said through her tears. Miss Bolton put an arm around her and took her away, another little bird to the protection of her nest. Father left right behind them. Julia sidled up to me. I watched her in anticipation. It was clear she wanted something but seemed to be fighting herself.

"Julia, what is it? You can trust me," I said.

After stammering and a trickle of sweat beading down the side of her face, and her swiping at a few tears, she finally said so quietly that I had to lean in to hear:

"If we are contriving situations, do you think you and your father could make one for myself and Mr. Percival?" I looked at her red face. Her eyes shimmered with more tears. This may have been the first time in her life Julia asked for what she wanted. Perhaps the first time Julia even examined herself to know what she wanted. After some thought I said: "I will see what can be done. Lord Holland showed Mr. Percival in such a light, we may find a way for him to be necessary simply for his not having a seat in the House of Lords."

"I would like that very much," she said looking at the ground and swiping at her tears. I smiled at her, feeling tired myself. What I could do for any of us? I took Julia to Hetty, who showed her to another vacant room. I went to my own room and paced. What could be done for Julia?

Chapter Thirty-Three

When Father returned, he sent word for me to join him in his study. The study was one of my favorite places in the house. The two-story room of rosewood shelves smelled like the Moroccan leather of book bindings. Ladders climbed into balconies of books. The only place the walls did not crawl with books brought in light through tall crystal windows or flames licking the stone fireplace. My grandfather's collection, on every topic, was complete, until that is, I started ferrying books to my room. To my surprise, Lord Devon was there in the library.

"Ah, you are like a child coming for a treat," he laughed at my buoyant entrance.

"Good day to you, sir," I said moving to him. "And you," he replied, "it seems you have found yourself an intended, without intending to do so."

"I am glad to see you have not lost your faculties in your illness," I said kissing his cheek and studying his face that was grey in pallor and thinner then when I last saw him.

"You may not be," he said.

"Why is that?" I asked. "I cannot get you out of the runaway carriage, but I can switch out the horses."

"What does that mean?"

"I have a letter written in your Grandfather's hand expressing his wishes regarding you," he said. He handed me a yellowing parchment. It read: *"My Dear Fellow: Condolences on the loss of the Baron, your Theresa was so attached to him I have no doubt her sorrow is great. His son must still be in mourning, but the situation has grown more desperate. My brother and his family have been here for two weeks. My brother grows more obvious in his attempts at connecting Edmund to Eva. I cannot wish for an alliance between the two after my last turn in town. I found Edmund in such behavior I must insist he not be the protector of my Eva. Though I believe Edmund loves Eva, he is not what I would wish for her, anymore. His intimacy with high society leads me to believe his interest in Eva is not wholesome. He believes her to be beneath him, and he has no thought to marry her. I fear he would satisfy his love for her in an immoral way. It is this willingness to ruin the one person he truly loves that scares me the most. He is not being taught morality among the Ton and is not being taught at all by his father. I would much rather your grandson for her. I know we have debated the matter at such length that you refuse to come to visit these last few years, but I must beg you to come. I must beg you to reconsider your position. I cannot rest at ease; I cannot meet my maker knowing I have left my darling girl so unprotected. You fear Mr. Garrett is too far below her in station, that he has nothing for them to live off. I have remedied this by giving her land, which, for all intents and purpose will go to Mr. Garrett, though Eva can be trusted to manage it. They can live on this until she inherits, and then they will be well taken care of. Your qualms about his not bringing enough fortune to the match are outlandish. The lady in question knows nothing of her fortune, and her family does not object to the match. Please reconsider coming for Christmas. I assure you the two will get along well. If they marry before they realize their fortune is established, what a treat it will be upon my death that they have so much? Do write back and give your assurances that you will come with your lovely daughter and grandson despite their period of mourning will not yet be complete. Yours, HG*

I looked at Father, my cheeks aflame. "How could you possibly know he would have this?" I asked. Father looked down. "I have many of these," Lord Devon said, "after he grew sick, he sent them once a week." "But you

256

never came," Father accused. Lord Devon did not answer. "This is why you did not come to Grey Manor?" I asked, remembering how sorely my grandfather wished his old friend would come to see him one last time.

"I did not think it appropriate for a lower baron to address a marchioness in her own right."

"I see," I said, understanding why my father always appeared so disappointed in Lord Devon. He could not get Grandfather the one thing he wanted most before he died.

"Grandfather predicted the two of you would get along well," Father said.

"I do like him very much," I said. Father turned on Lord Devon. "In the end, he begged you to come, and you would not."

"You could have come alone," I said trying to soften my father's accusation.

"I could not see his vision. I could not face him, so steeped in the concerns of this world," Lord Devon said. "If I had anything to give the lad aside from a living, anything… it felt so unfair Henry died before Jonah gained so many titles."

"We would have given him everything," Father said.

"I have known for many months I was wrong," said Lord Devon. "The closer I am to the grave, the more I see what is important. There is such a similarity between you and Jonah, intelligence and honor; I cannot deny you should marry him, even if he never inherited…."

"He would still be the finest man of my acquaintance," I said. I swallowed hard. My poor Grandfather tried so hard for me, even to the last days of his life.

"Yes, and you and Duke Garrett would have been great friends in a much easier, happier atmosphere than this," Father said. He glowered at the old man.

"It is the greatest regret of my life that I did not see my friend, nay my brother's, vision, sooner. I live with his disappointed face scarred into my memory. I made a mistake."

"I always felt Eva was too young to marry, anyway," Father said, kinder, "and it might all be for the best now. With this letter as evidence, we can all move forward."

"Of course, Henry. I shall not linger in my mistake, but on the duty I have to fix it," Lord Devon said smiling.

My father and I looked at each other. "Can this be used as evidence?" I asked Father quietly, sitting next to Lord Devon and taking his hand. "It may get you out of marrying Edmund, but only in favor of Duke Garrett," Father said.

"I do not wish to entrap him," I said. "He would not see it that way," his grandfather smiled. He looked back to me, like he hadn't just drifted away from us. "Would you ask him," I said, "just ask him without any pressure to comply? Or no, it must not be tempted; I will not entrap him."

"It may not be necessary," Father said. "And I am not ready to lose you just yet, anyway."

"What do you mean?"

"We can cover all of the letter except some of the first and second paragraphs. The parts showing your grandfather's change of heart toward Edmund. We can claim the rest is Lord Devon's private business that has nothing to do with the proceedings."

Father went to his desk and cut scraps of heavy linen paper to cover all but the message we wanted to convey.

"My grandson is honorable. He would, upon reading the letter, marry you, I am sure," Lord Devon said.

"No. Please don't show him then," I said.

"He is a good man. He would make you a fine husband. Don't punish him for my mistake," he said, betraying hurt feelings.

"No, you misunderstand. I would – nay, rather I am – devoted to him," I said feeling my heart rush.

"Then…." Lord Devon looked at me confused.

"She wishes for him to choose her," Father teased. "It is a romantic fancy of the feminine persuasion." I shrugged, blushing scarlet. Lord Devon laughed at me, then said: "Take care, dear girl, for there are many ladies who happen to be walking by his door when he leaves, wishing to be escorted somewhere. And many more who would put him in a compromising position in order that his sense of honor give way to marriage." The terror of this idea must have shown clearly on my face because the old man laughed again and said: "Do not worry, I will keep him occupied for the next few days in order to give you time to see your way out of this precarious situation. I will only show him the letter if some other lady happens to entrap him before you have the chance."

I smiled and kissed the man. I would find myself in his grandson's presence only after I was free to show my preference for him, and he was free to act upon it if he chose to. "How soon can this be rectified?" I impatiently asked Father. "Your Uncle has enough pull with the magistrates, if he throws his weight behind your grandfather's change of heart, I think he can simply read the part about Edmund not suiting and then mentioning to the trustees that if the betrothal can be severed, it ought to be. Edmund is honor bound to another. Therefore it is best that the marriage settlement is nullified for the honor of all involved. He has enough inducement to do so."

"How will you–"

There was a knock at the door. "Enter," Father called. The footman announced Uncle, and he walked in. I blanched, unprepared to meet him.

259

The Lark

"What is it you need?" Uncle asked. Father handed him the letter. He covered the most offensive parts, but Uncle Claremont Hull still had the audacity to act affronted and said: "I did not know my brother felt this way. If Edmund would not suit, then we best call the engagement off, considering Edmund is honor bound to another."

"I suppose so," Father said. "If I may take this to my solicitor," Uncle said.

"I will, of course, go with you. I would not wish my letter to be misinterpreted," Lord Devon said as Father helped him out of the chair. Lord Devon was not well enough to be out and about and I took his other arm.

"Thank you," I whispered. "No dearest, thank you, for being everything your grandfather said you would be. I could have no greater wish than for my grandson to marry you," he said. He kissed my temple.

"I suppose I shall come too, as I have a bet in this race," Father said, winking at me, but fully supporting Lord Devon.

"Shall I tell Lady Alice to expect Edmund for supper?" I asked Uncle. I did not even pretend he had any right to his indignation. "I believe he has such intentions," Uncle said bowing to me. As his head rose back up he glared at me with such venom I stepped backward. I had never received a man's unadulterated loathing in such a look before. It took my breath away, painfully contorting and compressing my heart. The men left the room, and I sat in an armchair trying not to feel wretched about Uncle's disdain. Weary as I felt, tears started to fall. I knew such vulnerability was decidedly feminine, but the anger Uncle used indicated his emotion, did it not? And was his betrayal of emotion more legitimate than mine? After all, weren't tears and anger were both emotions, a reaction to pain, or disappointment? I could not see the anger his sex spewed forth as superior to the sadness of mine for all my uncle's claim to the contrary.

260

Chapter Thirty-Four

Julia and Alice must have seen Uncle come. They sent Miss Bolton to the study with word they were in the drawing room having tea and requested I join them. Miss Bolton soothed me for a moment, as was the beauty of her nature. I felt selfish for indulging in it when I had such communications to make, but I could not help myself. I went to my room and washed away all traces of my tears. I would give Alice the good news without letting Uncle ruin her happiness. I entered the deliciously peach drawing room.

The anxious faces that greeted me indicated they hadn't slept. "Uncle has been here," I told Alice, "he says you are to expect Edmund for dinner."

"Truly?" she asked, standing with her hand over her heart. Tears of relief welled in her eyes.

"Truly," I said. Julia stood and hugged her. "Your father is a wonder," Alice said. She sniffled, wiping her tears as fast as they came. "Oh, cry dearest, you have earned it," I said. She started laughing letting her tears spill as they might. "I cannot tell you how nice it is to be one's self without reprimand," she said. She turned to sob into Julia's shoulder. Julia patted her back. I could not help thinking Alice and Edmund would get along well, being weepy together. After many hours, Father and Uncle returned from the magistrate and joined us for Tea, after seeing Lord Devon home to rest.

"The settlement has been dissolved. Edmund is honor bound to you if you choose to accept him," Uncle said bowing to Alice. She blanched at the menace in his face. Julia shrunk and took up her sewing. I glared back at Uncle. I tired of his disappointment justifying his bullying manners. Just then the butler came in, silver tray extended toward me with a nosegay and a letter upon it. I did not know if the flowers were for me, so first I took the letter that bore Duke Garrett's seal and I broke it to read: *My Dear Lady, I have been commissioned by my grandfather to some business that takes me out of town. I expect to be gone just over a fortnight but will be back in Parliament to debate on behalf of the Vaccination Act. The day after the vote is taken, I will wait on your father if it is convenient. Please keep the flowers near you so the fragrance is often upon you. Yours, JG*

I folded the note and put it in my lap smiling at the old gentleman's ingenuity. I took up the nosegay to smell the fragrant flowers. My face must have shown everything because Uncle glared and said: "You've chosen Garrett then? Over your family?" I looked to my father who gave me a reassuring nod that I could not decipher. Feeling the whole world should not bow down to Uncle because of his anger, I said: "Would you like me to marry Edmund?"

"Why did you give that land away? It would have been the greatest day, the rejoining of two ancient titles," he said.

"Is it really so important they be rejoined, or do you feel the guilt it was split in the first place?" I asked. He stopped and looked away. "My mother should never have…."

"I do not begrudge you the title, nor did your brother," Father said. "It shouldn't have been. It would have been set to right if… do you not understand the value of that? What it would have meant to my father?" He glared at me.

"From all that I have heard, I do not believe your father would wish to reclaim an Earldom over Edmund's honor," I said quietly.

"From my understanding," Father said, "my father took a hand in raising you. Would it not be very natural for him to sacrifice one of his titles to a boy he thought of as a surrogate son?" Uncle stopped raging and thought about this for a moment. His face softened into contemplation.

"A son is more to a man than a brother," Uncle said. "I do think Henry once said he saw giving me the Earldom as his inheritance to me."

"He said as much to me several times, especially when he thought I might regret not inheriting the Earldom. I never did regret it. You have fought for our country through politics in a way I could never have. I am proud of all the good you do," Father said.

"Thank you, Lawrence," Uncle said, looking lighter. "I suppose it must be, though I am sorry my father's titles won't be rejoined."

"Come now, let us make peace," Father said nodding at me again. I stopped before I could remind Uncle a dukedom was of higher standing than even a marquess. Father clearly wanted Uncle in a good mood.

"In fact, as a peace offering," Father said, "I will do everything in my power to set Julia forward if it will regenerate the feeling of brotherly love between us."

"Yes?" Uncle asked. He was ready to fight, having every right as her father to rule without mercy.

"It was something Lord Holland said, about Mr. Percival being a good man who would see to his duty. I know the lad a bit, and it seems he would be a natural politician for you to mold."

Uncle squinted suspiciously. "Yes, but if you mean for Edmund to give up his—"

"No. Not at all. I simply meant to give my niece her own piece of land upon her marriage. Mr. Percival has not a seat in the House of Lords, I understand."

"You would give Julia land?" Uncle asked.

"I have my own property that is not entailed, you know. It has a good living, and a pretty house on it," Father said.

"I did not know that. Why do you not give it to Eva?" Uncle asked quickly.

"For the sake of Edmund's honor, it will never belong to Eva. You must see that for what it is, Uncle," Father said sternly. "But I would be willing to give it Julia if you can arrange something of an understanding between her and Mr. Percival."

"Julia, do you know the man in question?" Uncle said.

"I have been in company with him at Lady Alice's estate," she said pointing to Alice.

"Do you think he could be prevailed upon to marry you?"

"I will write him at once inviting him to dinner if it is acceptable to my host," Alice said, showing herself to be a dutiful daughter to the man who would have ruined her.

"I would be delighted to receive him," Father said with a bow. "Julia, I expect…" he paused.

"I will do my best with him, sir," she said bowing her head in submission, her features trained in a somber expression.

"I expect this to go my way. I will not have any more disappointments," Uncle said. "I swear, Papa, I will not disappoint you," she said. "That is how a daughter should behave," he said looking pointedly from Father to me. His ridiculous blue eyes drilling into each of ours in turn so that we may know of his approval of his daughter and disappointment in me.

"Julia is a very good girl," Father said, betraying nothing. Uncle strode from the room with the look of conceit he needed, vital as his breath. Julia held her breath until she looked out the window and saw him mount his horse.

As she moved the curtain, I could see Viscount Harley outside the window again. I realized we had very few gentlemen callers since my ball, despite the number of flowers I'd received. This unnerved me. Duke Garrett could not get back from his business soon enough. Julia, as if she burst internally, ran to my father and threw her arms around him.

"Oh thank you, Uncle, thank you!"

"Of course, dear," he said.

"Thank you for interfering on my behalf, Eva," she cried turning to me. "I had not yet said a word to my father."

"Oh, come now, Julia, it was pretty obvious," Father said. "I suppose to one who bothered to look," she said glancing toward the window through which she watched her father leaving. "Then I will give you a little advice as sometimes is an uncle's prerogative and I hope you will not be offended," he said taking her hand in both of his. "Yes," she said looking frightened as her father's instruction must not have come calmly.

"Remember this day, and how much can be accomplished when men and women work together, instead of fighting each other at every step as your mother and father are wont to do," he said.

"Yes, uncle," she nodded.

"Mr. Percival is a good man whose station has made him amiable, and his love will set you up for happiness as long as you are willing to work together for it."

"Thank you, sir," she said bowing to him. "Father, would you be willing to part with the land by the ocean?" I interrupted, knowing he would talk for hours with such a captive audience, and Julia wasn't likely to fall into the pit he described.

"I may. Why do you ask?" he said. "Mr. Percival is very fond of sea bathing," I said. "Just how much land do the two of you have?" Alice asked. "I do not have any more," I said, "but my father has a few more." "Seven to be exact," he said. "Father was in a position to learn when landowners could not manage their properties. Landlords

265

that aren't willing to enclose or rotate their crops, are losing
their tenant farmers, who can't survive with the lost
profits. They are giving up and moving to factory-rich
cities. My father collected worked land as other nobles do
extravagances. But let us keep that to ourselves." "Of
course," Alice said. "And now I will leave you ladies to
discuss your good fortune, and I will tell Hetty the good
news – we will have more guests for dinner," he said.

"Leave that poor woman alone," Miss Bolton
insisted, following him, her serene smile firmly in place.

"I think first we must discuss Eva's flowers," Alice
said, and she and Julia moved in examining the flowers.

"It is a beautiful nosegay," I said, confused.

"Oh no, my dear naive friend," Alice said glancing
at the door to be sure the footman didn't hear. "It is a
tussie-mussie."

"Excuse me?"

"A talking bouquet," she said.

"The Forget-me-nots are pretty obvious," Julia said.

"As is the red rose to symbolize love," Alice said.

"The small white blooms, are saxifrage and must
only mean his devotion," Julia said. "And the herbs?" I
asked.

"The fragrance, he mentions in his note," Alice said
having wriggled it out of my lap to read it. "Let us put them
together and I believe he is saying not to forget the love
you share because he is devoted to you, and he will be back
before the fragrance dies," Julia said happily.

"A tussie-mussie?" I asked.

"Yes," Julia said. "Absolutely," Alice agreed.

"Very well," I said pulling the flowers to my face
that I might commit their smells of myrtle, basil, and
lavender to memory.

Chapter Thirty-Five

The next few hours before dinner, the bell rang thirteen times. Edmund sent Alice an obscene amount of tussie-mussies. The first being amaryllis and nuts which Julia and Alice deciphered as him being stupid in his pride. Then he was sorry with hyacinth, and the bluebells meant humbled. Next, a small bough of fir, dandelion and a holly leaf meant, it gave him great joy they would find domestic happiness. I did not understand how they got to this, but gradually, with flowers, Edmund came to beg Alice for another chance. By dinner, Alice was mush in Edmund's hands. Edmund showed his gratitude to my father for smoothing everything over. He barely noticed me anymore. Mr. Percival did not understand his good luck but quickly noticed Julia was no longer pretending to be indifferent to him. He basked in the glow of her affection and by the end of the evening he was reading to her and she sat closely to him.

At one point, she started to drift off, her head drooping to his shoulder. He did not wake her but sat very still, and we all tried not to notice when he turned his face into her golden curls presumably planting admiration there. The next day, a smitten Alice informed her father when he came to call, she would be marrying Edmund.

Begrudgingly, he agreed simply to have the whole ordeal behind them. The unfortunate situation had been noticed by the rest of society, so in hopes of repairing the damage, Edmund and Alice proved themselves attached publicly, by riding through Hyde Park together. Nothing of the trouble to keep them that way could be detected.

Mr. Percival came into my father's home as often as Edmund. After a week, he finally got up the nerve to ask Uncle for Julia's hand. An hour after Mr. Percival left to talk to Uncle, a visitor rang the bell in a way that felt insistent upon admittance. I hoped Duke Garrett concluded his business early. I looked anxiously toward the door to the morning room where we sat.

"Lady Claremont Hull," the butler announced, and my heart sunk. Aunt stormed into the room, tears upon her stricken face. "Julia, I will have a word," she said moving to her daughter who stood wide-eyed. Aunt grabbed her by the arm, jerking her to the door.

"Aunt please, won't you take time to calm down before you do injury to your daughter," I said.

"You will stay out of this," Aunt snarled, turning on me. Shaking Julia, she said, "How dare you? How dare you accept Mr. Percival? I did not raise you to marry a younger son. I did not give leave for that man to even look upon you, let alone marry you."

"Fa...Father insisted," Julia stammered.

"Oh yes, Father insisted. The foolish man doesn't, nay won't, believe he was hoodwinked by the lot of you," she squealed.

"It has become an advantageous match. My father is to give ...uh, Mr. Percival a property on the ocean near a place called Weymouth. A considerable effort is being made to build up a resort town there," I said. "You will love to visit Julia, especially in the Summer."

"Farmland? Of what use can farmland next to the ocean be?" Aunt demanded.

"Excursions to the beach are very popular these days, even being preferred by many to bath, My Lady," Alice said.

"The land may one day prove more valuable than Lady Alice's," I said.

"Nobody wants to live so far from society, along the ocean, always at risk from smugglers. Julia will come to ruin, and you are to blame. You've ruined everything just as your foolhardy mother did and I hate the lot of you," she yelled, charging me.

"My mother did nothing to you," I said. I defensively stepped behind a chair so she could not maneuver herself near me.

"Didn't she?" she asked in a harsh whisper. I did not answer, because I could see in her wild contorted face that apparently my mother had done something.

"Do you know what it is like following in the footsteps of a sister who is everything to your father, and an impertinent mess to society?"

"I do not have siblings, but it seems complicated," I said.

"My mother gave birth six times with no life before Anna lived. She was their greatest joy. Then four years later, after another stillbirth, I lived, and my mother died. I was my father's greatest sorrow," Aunt said bitterly.

"I do not think it fair to blame that on my mother, though I am sorry for you," I said. "It did not end there. I was always left behind with my horrid governess. Anna was never forgotten. It was my cross to bear. I thought it couldn't get worse for me. Then it did. Father fell to infection. If Father died, we had nowhere to go. He had no male heir, and the elderly cousin who was to inherit would do nothing for us. When Father grew too sick to function, we could not even wish death for him. We needed him to take every last breath because we were alone. Then my foolhardy sister carries our father's supposed vote to a proxy because she felt Father would have done anything to protect the forests in Gloucester, that bordered our holdings.

"She ruined herself in the eyes of every marriageable prospect to protect my almost dead father's holdings that would never be ours."

"That would be worrisome," I said.

She glared at me. "You are her," she said. "In looks, you are her exact copy, not to mention temperament and your mouth… oh, I cannot look at you."

269

"I do not mean to offend you, aunt, but I can hardly be blamed for looking exactly like my mother."

"Beauty is a curse. Without it, I would never have…oh how I wish some days I could not have attracted more than a country curate," she said gritting her teeth and a tear fell from her eye. I wondered if in fact there was a country curate somewhere whom she looked for in the faces of those she passed in the street.

"But no, after Anna's two seasons in London with no success, and a father struggling for breath, the burden to find a husband fell to me. None of you can imagine the sacrifice of going without, so a dowry sufficient to tempt a man can be procured. What decencies one can live without so that a season in London may be had for a sister who wastes her efforts and her beauty by speaking openly about whatever she may have in contemplation, scaring men away left and right," she said.

I could do nothing to ease Aunt's great distress. Bu she seemed to be calming down.

"Do you know how hard it was at seventeen to live down my sister's scandal and attract a marriageable husband?"

She required an answer.

"I do not suspect it was easy," I said.

"It was not. Most said Lord Claremont Hull would never marry, his mother terrifying every suitable young lady away, but I charmed her. I endeared myself to the woman, always allowing her the first place of affection in her son's heart. I was so well practiced at being set aside in favor of another I did it perfectly. All so I might have a home to invite my spinster sister into."

"But she married," I said, seeing the source of Aunt's resentment.

"I would never be first with my father nor my husband, my old cranky husband and his mother have been the very plague of my existence and it is all Anna's fault."

"I do not think she meant for you to——"

Aunt laughed a maniacal laugh, looking around at the absurd number of flowers in the room, flowers she would never receive.

"Anna ended up married to the head of my husband's family," said Aunt. Again she laughed while tears fell down her face, "a young dashing man. A kind man who doted on her every movement. A man who sorrowed with her when she inherited my mother's inability to have live children. My own husband hated me more with every failed attempt at giving him an heir. He only tolerated me after I succeeded in having Edmund."

"I am sorry," Julia said.

"The only gift of Anna's life is she didn't have a second daughter to ignore."

"You had a second child and did very well with her," I said tipping my head to Julia. "She is all I have had in this life. All I've ever had is my beautiful daughter, whom I trained at every turn to be a woman her father could be proud of. And he gives her to the second son of a baron," she raged, turning on Julia.

"Mama, please," Julia said. She moved to her mother when I would have run away.

"I will never accept your father's choice; as long as I live you will be my greatest disappointment because you were my only love," she said. She broke down as Julia held her.

"Perhaps after we marry you could stay with Mr. Percival and me, finding a way to escape Father's ... um, derision for a time," Julia said.

"In a house unfit to be inhabited by anyone but smugglers," she said sobbing.

"It is in fine condition," I contradicted. "I know my father would invite you to stay the rest of the summer at Grey Manor."

"Do you think he could be imposed upon to invite Lord and Lady Holland and their daughters?" Aunt seemed to be recovering her emotions.

"I am certain," I said.

"We owe them a country house party, but have never been in a position to invite them. Those of our acquaintance have noticed, and now that Edmund is engaged to their daughter, it is downright humiliating." She spoke in a whisper so Alice wouldn't hear, though the way she turned from the scene, I was certain she had.

"I am sure my father will accommodate," I said.

"Because my sister married an accommodating marquess and I married a horrid old earl," she said pouting, but she seemed better. She'd unburdened herself, and within her daughter's arms she was going to be all right.

Aunt stayed at our house for many hours that night after confessing Uncle could not be consoled and had become mean to her. Over the next few days, Julia and I kept up the pace Aunt had previously set. Not because we felt obligated to attend teas, dinner parties, and even a ball, but because we saw Aunt needed the hours she spent away from home to be all right.

Viscount Harley happened to be everywhere I went. He stayed near me and forced his presence on me. I started to fear he may just pick me up and run away with me like a charging bull. No one would be able to stop him.

Chapter Thirty-Six

My father quietly titled the land to Mr. Percival so Uncle, who began to see he may have been hoodwinked, couldn't back out on the engagement. Through some magnificent feat of conceit, Uncle believed he outmaneuvered us, but none of us could see through his glasses and therefore left the subject alone when he came around.

The marriage settlement ensured the land to be Julia's jointure upon her husband's death. Though not nearly as profitable as the piece I gave Alice, the land left both Uncle and Mr. Percival quite content. In return, Mr. Percival registered to vote and started to promote himself in the House of Commons.

Only then did Uncle publicly acknowledge his engagement to Julia. Mr. Percival turned his considerable charm and handsome face on Aunt Claremont Hull, and after a few days she thought her son-in-law to be could rival any duke in London. She claimed he'd be prime minister one day, and nobody could doubt her when they looked at him. Through nothing more than his gift of being amiable and very attractive, though Mr. Percival never spent time in any political venue, he was soon called an up and comer. Mr. Percival was invited to many political gatherings, some even thrown by the conservatives. Uncle began to take such a liking to the very moldable Mr. Percival; he soon held more hope for his political aspirations than for Edmund, who still showed no interest in politics.

Edmund's passion flared for arranging nosegays as Alice continued to receive several every day. The final week in April saw the two couples making ready for a double wedding by the end of June after the Ascot Races, because Father refused to give them up. Nobody involved thought a long engagement in the best interest; except Aunt who enjoyed parading her beautiful daughter and the beautiful Mr. Percival all over town. She was given little say in the matter. Mr. Percival, not capable of believing his good luck, trailed Uncle through Westminster all day, and Aunt to all her social events in the evening. He did not care what he did if he was within arm's length of Julia.

Alice and Julia were also inseparable purchasing their trousseau. Aunt's greatest pleasure in life was to shop, and since Alice's mother did not have a taste for it, she left the purchases up to the small group of three, who spent all their extra time at shops. Miss Bolton and I went back to sneaking out to see plays. Though with my father at the helm, I did confide my plans.

"Would you accompany me to the theater today?" I asked Father. "Lord Devon wrote and told me I could use his box," I said, holding up the ticket he sent.

Father sat at his desk in his study searching papers, looking for clues to resolve another sticky situation. "Parliament is hearing closing statements, then voting on the Vaccination Act. I wish to vote, if only for the children of the parish. I doubt any man of title will be on hand to accompany you, Eva. Parliament is being asked to fund it."

"I suppose you hint that though Duke Garrett came back two days ago, it is to be expected that I have not heard a word from him."

"The debate has gone on from morning until late into the night. He is not neglecting you, he is fighting for something he believes in. It is your duty to support him just now," Father said.

"Of course, papa. I did not suppose he would not be at the theater today," I said. "He will not miss the vote. Though he has been most attentive to me over the last two days," Father said winking at me.

"That is pleasing, but not as satisfying to me," I said. "Perhaps he will attend the evening party?"

"I suspect he will be there," Father said. "Uncle may not approve of him but would not be so vindictive as to snub such a crucial up-and-coming voice at a time like this."

"Then I will –"

"Give the gentleman a little encouragement. You may hint we will invite him for Christmas. He has been picked up and pushed aside many times through this ordeal."

"Julia insists a lady does not overdo her affection."

"Men are not always as confident as the fairer sex assumes."

"I will try," I said. I tasted my happiness and would not be so foolhardy as to pretend to reject it. Though, I wasn't sure what I could do to encourage Duke Garrett in a room full of political debaters.

"Perhaps I could still chance the theater with Myra this afternoon?"

"I do not see why not. Take my man with you," he said glancing out the window.

"I will don my plainest dress if I can find where Aunt hid it."

"Thank you, dear." I dressed down and we left with little fanfare as even Viscount Harley must have been busy in Parliament. The city seemed empty in our part of town, and I was thankful for the vote. Miss Bolton and I arrived at the theatre only moments after the curtain came up and easily slipped into the box. I stopped. Duke Garrett stood at my entrance.

"I... I did not know...," he stammered.

"Are you here to be seen?" I asked smirking.

"At this hour?" He grinned. "Or perhaps to entrap me?" He moved closer to me.

"Perhaps each of us could take a curtain and go unnoticed," he said.

"I would be seen with you. My lady is here," I said looking down and feeling the heat rising on my face. He stopped and looked at me. I forced myself to look back at him. What he saw written on my face moved him even closer. "I would have you for my wife, Eva. You know I would to keep you from any trouble."

"The trouble is resolved," I said. "What about Edmund–"

"Would you have me marry my cousin?"

"No, but to preserve your family."

"What family do I have but you? I have never loved anyone so well as to be tempted to leave my father's side before this," I said, my face glowing hot.

"Then will you do me the honor of being my wife?"

"Yes," I said, my eyes tearing up. "Yes, with the greatest of pleasure." He took my hand, and we sat in the very front center of the box. Miss Bolton, a little startled, placed herself to be seen.

"Why are you not at the vote?" I asked.

"I argued for the bill to include Scotland. Even if we cannot have physicians, we need to apprentice some of the distillers or apothecary so every county at the very least has access to trained individuals.

The opposition was so great; my grandfather said my absence would be the greatest form of protest for the Scots possible. The bill will pass with ease and does not require my vote."

I grinned, wondering if his grandfather knew the temptation to see Macbeth would be too great for me to pass up on such a quiet day. After the play ended, we strolled the public rooms together. Miss Bolton made her presence obvious, though neither Duke Garrett nor I cared. My father was appealed to before we went to Uncle's that night. He admitted he wished us to wait a year or two. Fortunately, Miss Bolton interfered on our behalf and argued for a fall wedding, pointing out the disadvantages of waiting, especially considering how many would scheme to come between us.

Chapter Thirty-Seven

Julia and Alice were each married before I could be. The settlement of my marriage turned out to be far more complicated, considering two ancient houses had to somehow be joined. Divvying out the land and wealth alone, were ridiculously complicated considering that neither could be used nor spent in a lifetime, anyway. Both of my cousins were invited to be wed at Grey Manor. After the Ascot Races, a few of us decided to catch the train in Farnborough instead of enduring the five-day carriage ride. The train station was a brightly painted wooden shack situated between the tracks. Miss Bolton and I waited on a bench while our tickets were purchased. Since my engagement she often took my arm when it was just the two of us, as if she felt me growing up in her very grasp.

"Ah, here is the train," she said in my ear. She and Father debated whether or not we would miss the day's train.

"I cannot wait to go for a ride," I said, my heart beating up through my chest. The thrust of hot steam filled the air. The shrill whistle cut through screeching brakes, beckoning me forward. The future and I were ready for each other. The train shrieked to a stop on the track. It would not pass me by.

"It turns out you were right. We didn't miss the train after all," Father said, coming toward us with tickets,

"How did you know, Myra?"

"My brother has been riding the trains with enthusiasm. At Christmas, he said I could count on them being at least an hour, if not two, late," she said.

We all laughed because Father looked bested over something so simple. He did not like to be wrong but admitted his defeat with grace. Duke Garrett took my arm and helped me climb up to the middle of what looked like three carriages stuck together on a set of wheels attached to the track. Six of us shared one first-class carriage. Edmund, Mr. Percival, and Duke Garrett sat backward. My father, Miss Bolton and I sat forward. The railway carriage lurched to a start, jerking us all wildly. Miss Bolton had my hand in a vice grip like she might pull me off the contraption if necessary. Finally, the jerking evened out and the ride became smoother. The windows were open, and we sped toward home, wind and steam rushing in our faces.

When we mounted a particularly steep hill with many lurches, Edmund said: "I may be sick. I will never ride a train again."

"I do not think I will ever travel by horse again," Duke Garrett answered. I agreed. My stomach swooped and dropped when the train carriage sped down the hill.

"I do not mind the experience if Lady Julia will ride the train with me," Mr. Percival said. The way he groaned for missing her over the five days it took his beloved to make it to Grey Manor, we all agreed he should stay with her, to keep the rest of us from having belly aches. Aunt invited as many people as the house with sixty guest rooms would hold, and required Hetty to arrange the party. Our housekeeper at Grey Manor, an aged lady named Mrs. Taylor, did not mind the assistance throwing the lavish parties. Hetty found the grandeur of the country estate close to that of the royal palace and a much more satisfying canvas for which to paint her enthusiasm. Mrs. Taylor had long been contemplating retirement. Grey Manor had not a refined staff, but the country sort whom the late master took pity on. Mrs. Taylor could not see how to accomplish such a thing without leaving her little miss, as she called me, sorely lacking. Now she started to openly discuss the possibility. Her relief with such an obvious replacement at hand was evident. Father, in turn, offered her a snug cottage on his grounds and reassured that she would not want in her retirement. He then offered Hetty more money to stay in the country. She accepted, but as his primary housekeeper, she would see to it he was not cheated by anyone. She reassured him the glorious estate would be brought into its full potential after a respectful duration passed to honor Mrs. Taylor. Only Miss Bolton found anything to cause concern in the naturally occurring progression.

Duke Garrett and I spent much of our engagement surrounded by our friends, and those of the enormous wedding party Lord Holland and his wife brought with them when they came. The heat was pacified by the proximity to the ocean, and fresh air welcomed them when compared with London. All who came declared the month-long country party the most entertaining and successful they ever attended. The proximity to the coast, ancient ruins, and other extravagant entertainments afforded the party many pleasant day trips. Aunt, of course, took credit for the success and even took seriously her friends' hints at coming back for Christmas.

After the dizzying pace, and exhausting task of marrying off Julia and Alice was accomplished, the whole party left. Lord Devon, Duke Garrett and Lady Garrett with her daughters were the only ones to stay behind at Grey Manor. Having the little makeshift family in my Grandfather's home could not have been more satisfying. We shared many quiet nights in laughter. Miss Bolton and Lady Garrett became great friends, simply because neither lady had as much enthusiasm for Shakespeare as the rest of us. During the coolness of the mornings, we often walked out into the gardens, and then to the shade of the forest on our grounds. The ivy clung to the ground and climbed the trees, making everything green and verdant. Duke Garrett took my hand whenever we were together. In return, I often forgot to wear my gloves, so that I might enjoy the way it felt when our hands clasped. Seeing us together, Father relented and gave permission for us to marry at the beginning of August.

Only a few days before our wedding Duke Garrett and I found ourselves wandering the forest, watching for fish in the stream so he could decide on his sport. He pulled me forward with eagerness until we came to the most beautiful spot in the rushing river where white frothy water tumbled over mossy rocks, and the trees shaded us from every direction except the path we trod. In our haste, we easily outstripped Miss Bolton and Father who argued about a plant species they found. I was very surprised to find myself alone with Duke Garrett for the first time in our acquaintance. He did not seem as surprised by the anomaly because he looked around to be sure we were truly alone for only a moment. He turned to me and without a word he touched his fingers lightly across my face. My face melted against his hand and he hesitated for a palpable moment searching my face. Then, with fervor, his mouth met mine. I pulled myself up his neck, meeting his passion with my own. He wrapped his greedy arms around me tightly, as I continued to pull my lips to his, consuming his mouth as if his breath was the only thing that could give me life. When I finally heard Father's voice teasing Miss Bolton, the only thing that reconciled my letting go of Duke Garrett was the knowledge I would kiss him for the rest of my days. He put his arm around my waist instead of taking my hand. I could not look directly at Father or Miss Bolton, but out of the corner of my eye, I saw them exchange knowing looks of amusement. As for myself, I no longer looked forward to my wedding day, as much as to my month-long wedding trip alone with my husband. The day I married Duke Garrett to become a Duchess was a calm, warm one. The breeze along the coast drew inland, and with its tang brought the perfect feeling of contented peace. I embraced this peace. I moved from my life as a child to that of a woman. We exchanged our vows in the same quiet chapel my mother and father had. Father gave a breakfast in the Hall for all those of our parish who wished to attend, and we were thronged by those I would be sworn to protect upon my father's death. During the wedding breakfast, Lord Devon, who had been growing thinner over the last few days, collapsed. He was carried to Grey Manor and the doctor called. We were told to make our final peace, as nothing could be done for him. "You did not expect me to live forever," Lord Devon said weakly looking up at my husband and me.

"I had hoped," I managed through my tears.

"Well, I have finally seen my boy married to Henry's lovely girl." He stopped to wheeze, then continued, "I have done right by my friend. There is nothing left for me to hang on for. I admit I am tired." He stopped to breathe and I sat on the bed next to him. He spoke again after a time, though now he seemed to be talking to someone unseen.

"I fixed the greatest folly of my life. I can now face my friend, nay, my brother, again."

"Grandfather!" Duke Garrett said, standing over me.

"Ah my boy, I have seen your joy. I do so wish to see my bride again, young and vibrant as God intended. Don't waste your time mourning me when you have your lovely bride to be with."

"Thank you for helping us," I said. "We were blessed … blessed by fairies the night you two met after all… or perhaps your grandfather helped things along," he said smiling behind me in the strangest way. He smacked his lips as if he could not get enough moisture.

"You said it would be so. I admit, I was wrong, Henry," he said to no one. I looked up at Duke Garrett and he shrugged. Lady Garrett came back into the room with fresh water for her father to drink so we moved out of the way. "Papa," Lady Garrett said trying to put the cup to his lips. He closed his eyes and rested. She took a cloth and wiped the spittle that came with the great effort his words took. A few hours later he left us. I had always supposed death, especially on such a day, would be a sad, dampening experience, but it was not. It was more proof that life, if lived in hope, would always right itself. Two years later when we had our first son, we named him Henry Devon Garrett, after the prodigious legacies of his great-grandfathers.

Made in the USA
Coppell, TX
04 June 2024

33107238R00173